WISH I DIDN'T WANT YOU BACK

MARCELLUS FALLS SERIES
BOOK ONE

S. JONES

Wish I Didn't Want You Back

Marcellus Falls Series

Copyright © 2025

S. Jones

All rights reserved.

Editor: Marla Selkow Esposito

Proofreader: Virginia Tesi Carey

Formatting: Leigh Stone @ Irish Ink

Illustrated Cover: Booksnmoods

Alternative Cover: Mel. D. Designs

CHAPTER ONE
HARLOW

Sweat dripped down my neck as the humid air turned my beach waves into frizz. My heels began to blister from running on the cracked sidewalks in my four-inch heels. People honked and waved, and some even offered me a ride.

I ended up in front of a local diner that looked like its best years were behind it, but my feet needed a break. I pushed through the doors and asked the hostess if I could use the bathroom. She blinked at me, and for a split second, I thought she might call the cops. I almost burst into tears when she pointed toward the restroom.

Today was supposed to be the happiest day of my life. Instead, I was hiding out in the bathroom of a rundown diner next to a 7-Eleven with someone in the stalls humming the lyrics to Lynyrd Skynyrd's "Free Bird."

The room smelled like smoke and grease. I was pretty sure something skittered across the floor behind the toilet. This was as far away from the cathedral and country club wedding reception as it got.

Baz Zimmerman wasn't the worst human being on earth. In fact, on paper, we were perfect for each other. But he was too much like my father—cold, polished, and had zero personality.

So, when the music started, and I saw his bored face at the end of the altar, looking like he was checking off a to-do list in his head, something inside me snapped, so I ran in the opposite direction, and just kept running.

I gripped the sink tighter and stared at my reflection in the mirror. When did my life stop becoming mine? How did I let things get so out of hand?

The toilet flushed, and the bathroom stall creaked open. Out stepped an older woman who was probably in her seventies, wearing a pair of glittery jeans and a black T-shirt with a taco on the front that said, "Nacho Average Old Lady." She looked like she could either knit you a blanket or hit you over the head with a baseball bat, depending on her mood. Her eyes nearly popped out of their socket when she spotted me. "Honey, I think you took a wrong turn off the highway."

I looked down at the ridiculously big dress and laughed, even though there was nothing remotely funny about my situation. "I wish it were that simple."

She grabbed a Marlboro Light from her purse and lit it with a match. "Are you a runaway bride or something?"

I tried to smooth out some of the wrinkles of my twenty-five-thousand-dollar Vera Wang dress that my father insisted I wear. "I guess you could say that."

She walked over and cracked open a small window above the top of my head to vent the smoke from her cigarette. I didn't know why she wouldn't just go outside, but something told me she didn't care if she got caught smoking in the bathroom or not.

"What did he do? Cheat? Push you around? Because you look worse than I did after my third divorce."

I shook my head, trying to decide the best way to respond. "He didn't do anything, really. I just panicked and ran when I realized I was making a mistake."

She tucked the cigarette in the corner of her mouth and played with the wild nest of yellow-blond hair on top of her head. I was ninety-nine percent sure it was a wig. "If you didn't love the poor sap, then why did you say yes?"

"Because my dad wanted me to marry him. The marriage was nothing more than a business arrangement."

Just two families being pushed together for the sake of power and convenience. The wedding bands were simply a formality. Love was never part of the equation. Neither was my happiness.

She squinted at me like I'd grown a second head. "Are you serious?"

I knew it was a bad idea to try to explain this to her. "It's complicated."

She set her giant purse on the vanity, held out a crumpled napkin, and shoved it into my hands. "You clearly need someone to talk to, but before you do, wipe those eyes. You look like a raccoon that got caught in a rainstorm." I scoffed as she continued. "Don't look at me like that. I went to beauty school when I was sixteen. Had to drop out when I found out I was pregnant with Junior."

I scrunched my nose up in disbelief at this woman. "I'm sorry, but you're telling me this, why?"

"Because in this day and age, there is no reason to look like that when they have waterproof mascara." Her lips pressed into a thin line as she eyed me up and down. "Judging by the shoes and dress, it appears you can afford the good stuff."

I blinked. "Are you always this blunt?"

"I'm too old to bite my tongue. I lost my filter before you were even born."

I let out a sad laugh. "I don't know if I should laugh or cry."

She leaned against the sink. "I've been told I'm a good therapist. So, tell me why you let your dad talk you into an arranged marriage like it's still the eighteenth century."

"My dad is a very powerful man and after my mom died, I spent my entire life trying to please him and do what was expected, but I have decided that stops today."

She puffed on her cigarette, and I watched as a tiny trail of smoke drifted out the window. "So, the old man was controlling. Good for you for running."

I gave her a tight-lipped smile. "My dad's probably furious. I have no idea where to go from here."

She wrinkled her nose. "Well, maybe it's time you start over. I've seen a lot in my seventy-five years on this planet, and what you did takes guts, sweetie. And take it from an old bat like me who has dumped three bad boys before. It's better to break things off now than years down the road when you're three kids in and turning to a bottle of Bombay Sapphire to keep you warm at night."

That sounded terrible.

"I have no idea where to start. I've spent my entire life doing what everyone else wanted. I forgot how to want something for myself."

"Why don't you start by calling a friend? If you don't have any, I can give you a ride somewhere."

Who the hell was I going to call? I didn't have any real friends. Not the kind that would drop everything to come get me. Every person in my life was tied to my dad.

Except for one.

My eyes snapped to hers. "I appreciate the offer for a ride, but do you have a cell phone I could use?"

My friend Molly had my phone, but she was likely still at the church.

The lady pulled out an old flip phone and passed it to me. "The battery is low, so make it quick," she said.

"Thank you." I blinked. "So, you've really been divorced three times?"

She parked a hand on her hip. "First one was a gambler, second was a hustler, and the third one liked my sister better than me, if you know what I mean."

"I'm sorry."

"Don't be. I heard they are both living in a nursing home. She just had her hips replaced, and he just lost all his teeth and can't afford dentures."

I bit back a laugh, but it slipped out anyway. "Wow."

"Yep." She leaned against the counter. Her mouth split into a grin. "I'm now on husband number four. Nice fella. Met him at a Jimmy Buffett concert. He's taking me on a three-day cruise to the Bahamas next month."

"That sounds like fun."

"That's exactly why I'm going. Gotta take advantage of the all-you-can-eat buffets."

I smiled, unable to help myself. This lady was something else. "You don't think I'm crazy for running?"

"I think you would have been crazy if you stayed."

I hadn't realized how far I'd fallen in life until I found myself in a dingy bathroom with a chain-smoking beauty school dropout who was on husband number four, giving me life advice.

"Thank you." I paused. "I'm Harlow, by the way."

"Blanche," she replied. "Now, are you going to call your friend, because I don't have all night? I need to get home and take my Omeprazole before my acid reflux kicks in."

I typed in the digits and was grateful when Molly picked up on the first ring.

"Hello," she whispered into the phone.

"Molly, it's me."

She gasped. "I can't believe you ran. Where the hell are you? Everyone is freaking out."

I inhaled a shaky breath and pushed my veil off my shoulder. "I'm at a diner not too far away called Stella's."

"Stay there. I'm on my way. Your dad is pissed, by the way."

I had no doubt that he was. What I did was unforgivable in his book. There was a good chance my dad would never speak to me again. But there was no going back now, even if I wanted to, which I didn't.

"I couldn't do it. I couldn't marry him."

I should have felt guilty. I knew I should, but I didn't. Instead, a strange sense of relief settled over me.

She sighed into the phone. "I'm glad to see you finally came to your senses. I'll be there in a few minutes. Stay out of sight until I get there."

I handed Blanche her phone. "Thank you. My friend is on her way."

She patted my shoulder. "Good luck to you, sweetie."

She was about to walk away when I stopped her. "Wait." I slid the enormous four-carat diamond ring off my finger and handed it to her. "Here, take this. Pawn it, keep it, buy a car with it, I don't care."

Her mouth pulled into a grin as she stared at the sparkling diamond. "I bet I could upgrade my interior cabin to a balcony suite if I sold this. Hell, maybe I could buy the whole damn boat."

I smiled. "You deserve it."

She frowned and looked up at me. "You sure you don't want to keep it?"

I folded her fingers around the ring, so it was tightly in her palm. "Positive, it's yours."

She pursed her lips before walking to the door. She glanced over her shoulder one last time. "Nice dress, by the way. It's a shame you had to waste it on that bozo."

Then she was gone.

I looked up at the ceiling. I just ran from my wedding. From my father. From the only life I'd ever known.

My throat felt tight, but I refused to cry, because I had finally made a decision that was entirely mine.

THE BATHROOM STALL WAS CRAMPED, leaving me with very little room to move around. The ridiculous, over-the-top wedding dress was bunched up around me as I tried to keep the heavy fabric off the dirty floor. I twisted awkwardly when I heard the bathroom door swing open, followed by the sound of heels clicking on the linoleum.

"Harlow," Molly's voice called softly.

I unlocked the stall door and peeked out to ensure she was alone.

"Molly." My voice cracked at the sight of her.

Her eyes were smiling. "You look like a runaway bride in need of a rescue."

I laughed and rubbed the tears underneath my eyes, probably smudging my mascara even more.

"That's one way to put it."

She stepped forward and wrapped her arm along my

shoulder. "Let's get you out of here. My car is in the parking lot."

We stepped out of the bathroom, ignoring the curious glances from a group of utility workers sitting in a booth. I could only imagine how out of place I looked. I scanned the room, looking for Blanche. She was perched on the stool at the counter, scratching off some lottery tickets while finishing up her food.

I gave her a wave as we reached the door.

"Hey," her raspy voice called out. "Make sure the next guy you plan to marry is worth ruining your mascara over, you hear? Life is too short to settle."

Molly and I both laughed. "Don't worry, Blanche, I've learned my lesson. Thanks again for all your help."

She held up her hand, displaying the ring I gave her. "Don't you worry about thanking me, honey. Remember, set higher standards for yourself. You deserve better, and if the next guy doesn't treat you right, you send him packing."

My face broke into a grin. "You got it. Have fun on your cruise."

Once outside, I slid into Molly's Rav-4 and was grateful she didn't say a word until we hit the highway.

"So." Molly glanced at me. "What's the plan?"

I snatched the veil off my head and tossed it in the back seat. "I want to go to the lake house."

She raised an eyebrow. "Do you have a key?"

Shit. "No. It's back at the apartment, along with my ID and credit cards."

She pulled up the map on her phone. "Do you want me to drive into the city so we can grab your things?"

I slumped into my seat, feeling drained. "It's too out of the way. I'll have someone overnight me what I need tomorrow. Right now, I just want to get off Long Island."

"Okay, it looks like you are staying with me tonight." She punched an address into her GPS.

My eyes flickered to hers. "Molly, you told me yesterday that Emma was sent home from preschool with a stomach bug, and let's not forget your husband hates me."

She adjusted her mirrors as we switched lanes. "Emma is feeling better and Finn doesn't hate you. He's not happy with how you handled things with Brooks."

I opened my mouth and closed it.

Molly's husband was best friends with the man I stupidly chose to walk away from years ago. I was young and scared and didn't know what to do, so I made a decision and I've lived with that regret every day.

"Finn is not going to want me crashing at your place."

She lifted a brow. "He'll get over it."

I almost laughed. Almost, because there was nothing funny about this.

Her husband wasn't the type to just get over it, but I didn't have any other options.

A tired puff of air escaped my lungs. Finn isn't the only one I was worried about.

Molly watched me closely as if she knew what I was thinking. "It's been years, Harlow. Maybe this is your chance to make amends."

It had been years. But years didn't erase the memories or the hurt I created.

I still remember the night we met. It was the summer before my senior year of college.

We were at a bonfire, and I spotted him first. When he caught me staring, he grinned and walked over. We hit it off that night, and that night turned into weeks of late-night swims, long drives in his truck with the windows down, kissing under the stars, and endless nights wrapped up in each other's arms.

I fell hard and fast.

But summer came to an end.

And so did we.

I had a life waiting for me back in the city.

I had a choice to make, and I didn't choose him.

I told myself that I was doing the right thing. I convinced myself that I would move on, but I never did.

And not a day has passed when I haven't wondered about what could have been.

I pressed my hand to my temples. "I don't think I'm ready to face him, Molly."

I wasn't sure if I'd ever be ready.

She studied me quietly. "You might not have a choice."

I sighed, leaning back in my seat. She was right. I knew she was right. She usually was.

Molly and I might have grown up together, but we lived completely different lives. She packed up after graduation, leaving the city behind, and never looked back. She chose love, real love.

As we drove along the highway, heading west, the irony wasn't lost on me. I just ran from my wedding and was now on my way back to a place I'd been avoiding for years.

But desperate times, right? Plus, it was the only place I could go to think. And with my life unraveling before my eyes, I needed to do some serious soul-searching. Just thinking about it brought me a strange sense of comfort.

"Do you think you could spot me a small loan until I get the rest of my things?"

She pursed her lips. "I have a better idea."

"What's that?"

"You'll see. Just trust me." She winked.

"You better not make me regret calling you."

She rolled her eyes. "Why don't you try to get some sleep. I'll wake you up when we get there."

I nodded and sank deep into the seat. My eyelids felt heavier with each passing second.

Molly's voice faded into the background as she talked to Finn. I rested my head against the window and allowed the exhaustion to take me under.

CHAPTER TWO
HARLOW

"Hey, sleepyhead. Time to wake up." Molly nudged my arm gently.

I blinked my eyes open and pressed a hand to the back of my neck. I had a slight ache from my head being positioned against the window for almost five hours.

"Where are we?" I asked, sitting up and squinting through the windshield.

"See for yourself." She pointed to the green and yellow sign: Welcome to Marcellus Falls.

An equal part of nerves and nostalgia hit me at once. The sign alone was enough to send a flood of memories rushing back. Summers spent soaking up the sun by the lake, bonfires at night, strolls down the main drive, and concerts in the park.

And of course, him. We would joke about how we never crossed paths until that summer. My mom's house was tucked away, on the other side of the lake, where it was quiet. We ran in different circles and led different lives until that night.

Marcellus Falls wasn't just a town to me; it was a piece

of my heart. It was also where I found my first love and experienced my first heartbreak. Every corner, street, and building held a memory of some sort. By the looks of it, this place hasn't changed much in five years.

As we cruised through the center of town, we passed by Clover's Diner, the place where my mom and I would spend Sunday mornings after church. It was our special spot. Now, it was closed and another reminder of all that I lost.

The feeling of nostalgia faded the second we turned off Lakeshore Road. Instead of turning right toward the lake, Molly took a left, heading up a hill. I sat up in my seat as we pulled into a curved driveway.

The structure in front of me was enormous. Long windows, oversized doors, beautiful stone accents, and a wrap-around porch with a wooden swing.

This rustic one-story home screamed Brooks Dawson. It was exactly the kind of house I pictured him living in.

My breathing became rapid. She wouldn't, would she?

"Where are we?"

"Before you kill me. This is the best option."

My fingers dug into my arms. "No."

"Hear me out."

I swung my gaze to hers. "I'm never trusting you again."

She sighed, rubbing her temples like she was the one who was emotionally drained. "You have no clothes, no necessities, and no money. This is only temporary until we can get you settled into the lake house."

"Are you out of your damn mind?"

There had to be an alternative place for me to stay. I picked up my phone and started scrolling, looking for options, but then I remembered that I couldn't book anything. Not without a damn credit card.

I looked through the windshield again. There was a

neatly stacked pile of firewood by the garage door. Maybe I could build a fire and rough it outdoors for the night. As I scanned the woods, all I saw was pitch black. I shivered because that was how people died in horror movies.

There were too many creatures with beady little eyes and sharp teeth that would view me as a snack. I wasn't a nature person; I wouldn't last five minutes.

I was still in my wedding dress and in need of a nice hot shower and a comfortable bed.

"Come on, I'll walk you in."

"Wait," I said as she stepped out of the car. "Is he okay with me staying here?"

Molly's hands froze on the door. She didn't move.

"Molly?" I asked sternly. "Does he know about this plan?"

"It will be fine. I promise."

"Oh, my God!" I slapped my hands against my thighs. "You didn't even ask him, did you?"

"I wouldn't do this if I had another choice."

I looked back at the woods again. "I think I'd rather get eaten by a fox."

She rolled her eyes. "You are so dramatic. Foxes don't eat people."

"You are the worst best friend," I muttered.

"Right now, I'm your only friend. Now let's get this little reunion over with."

I threw my head back against the seat and groaned. "This is a terrible idea."

She stepped out of the car and marched up to the front of the house, leaving me trailing behind her. I clutched the bottom of my dress, trying to match her speed, and prayed for divine intervention.

Molly knocked, and we stood under the dim light over

the door. My heart pounded as I glanced nervously at Molly. She tried to give me a reassuring smile, but it fell flat. So damn flat, I almost booked my butt back to the car.

Before I could get my feet to move, the door swung open.

I glanced up and swallowed hard. Jesus, why did he have to be so handsome?

Strong jaw.

Kissable lips.

Dark brown eyes that reminded me of the forest and were just as dangerous.

Even in the dark, it was clear he hadn't changed much. He looked exactly the same, but there was an edge to him that wasn't there before.

I always imagined what it would be like to see him again. And as I tipped my head back to stare up at him, I felt those familiar goose bumps break out along my skin.

Brooks Dawson would always be the boy who owned my heart and soul.

I wrung my hands in front of me, wondering how this would play out.

His eyes flicked from Molly to me, narrowing when they landed on my face. I could see him processing the absurdity of the situation.

"What the hell are you doing here?"

Oh, he was pissed.

Molly, bless her soul, stepped in front of me. "She needs a place to stay."

He looked me up and down with disdain in his eyes that he didn't even bother trying to hide. "This isn't a damn homeless shelter. This is my home."

"Seriously?" Molly parked her hands on her hips and

stared up at him. "As you can see, she's had a really rough day."

He crossed his arms, his eyes not leaving mine for a second. "Not my problem."

I wasn't sure what she thought would happen, but I could have predicted this. "Molly. It's fine. I'll just crash on your couch."

"Harlow. There is no reason for you to sleep on my couch. Emma is up at the butt crack of dawn and Brooks has bedrooms that never get used. You need to rest, and you won't have any peace and quiet if you stay with me."

While she had some valid points, I had a feeling that wasn't the driving force of her decision to bring me here. Of all places. To a man who hated me.

The muscle in his jaw ticked. "She isn't staying here."

Molly leaned forward, unfazed by his attitude. "I know you're mad that I just showed up like this..."

He threw his hands out and cut her off. "Mad? I'm not mad. I am furious. You honestly thought dropping her off on my doorstep like a stray dog without so much as a call or text to give me a heads-up would be a good idea?"

"I didn't know where else to bring her."

I finally reached my limit. "Would you both please stop talking about me like I'm not standing right here?"

He cocked his head to the side. "I don't like being blindsided. I thought you would remember that by now."

He was referring to when I told him that my dad had my future husband all picked out for me, and it wasn't him. I guess he was still bitter about that.

"And I don't like feeling like some charity case. I'd rather sleep outside on a bed of rocks than listen to this."

Brooks stepped forward. His smile was all teeth. "I'm sure the wolves would love the company."

Molly pushed on his shoulder gently. "Don't frighten her. There are no wolves in the woods."

He crossed his feet at the ankles. "Fine. Coyotes."

Now, I was getting irritated. Did he think I wanted to be here any more than he did?

I lifted my chin, not even trying to hide my little attitude. I've had a shitty day, and at this point, I'd rather sleep with the wolves and coyotes. They would be better company.

I turned to my friend. "I can sleep in your car if I have to."

"Perfect." Brooks stepped back. "Problem solved."

Molly groaned. "You two are impossible."

I shook my head, glancing at the porch swing. It was a nice swing. It looked sturdy and a hell of a lot more inviting than the bitter man standing in front of me. "It's fine, Molly. I'll figure something else out."

"No," she snapped. "Look, I get it. This isn't ideal, but it's one night, Brooks. Please. She has nowhere else to go. Look at her..." She pointed to me, standing there in my wedding dress. He studied me, as if taking in every tiny detail. His gaze lingered, like he wasn't sure what to do with me. "She didn't plan this. She ran from the church and called me for help. Just let her stay for the night. She is having her things sent in the morning."

He sighed heavily, running a hand through his hair. "What about the lake house?"

Molly shook her head. "Her key is back in New York, and the electricity and water have been shut off. Nothing can be done until morning."

His shoulders dropped in defeat. I had to hand it to Molly; she was relentless, which made her a really good attorney.

"Fine. One night," he snapped.

"Can you at least try to be nice?" Molly barked back.

He scoffed. "Don't you dare lecture me on being nice. You're the one who dropped her off here without even asking if I was okay with it."

She threw her hands up. "Because I knew you would say no."

He leaned against the doorframe. "You're lucky that your husband is my best friend."

Molly beamed, clearly happy that she had won this round. "I'm sorry for springing this on you at the last minute."

"Save it," he grumbled. "Next time, give me a damn warning. And don't think for one second that I'm happy about this."

"Hello." I waved my arms in the air. "May I remind you both again that I'm standing right here?"

Molly gripped my elbow gently. "Sorry, Harlow. I just want to make sure that you're going to be okay tonight. I know this isn't ideal, but it's only temporary."

He shoved a hand through his hair. "Damn right, it's temporary."

Brooks wasn't exactly known for his forgiving nature. I had a feeling this little arrangement would test both of our patience. Still, I was relieved that he was letting me stay.

"Thank you, Brooks. I promise to be out of your hair tomorrow. I won't stay one more second past my welcome."

"Of course, you won't, because leaving is what you do best." He pushed off the doorframe and stormed back inside the house.

I looked up at the sky and said a quick prayer, asking for patience and maybe a small miracle.

CHAPTER THREE
BROOKS

The door shut behind me as she crossed over the threshold into my house. Every breath, every little shuffle of her feet made me want to spin around and tell her to leave. But I wasn't the type of guy who would leave a woman in need stranded without a place to sleep. No matter how much her presence angered me.

I walked over to the back door to let Diesel in. A blur of black fur shot past me.

"Whoa." Harlow gasped, stumbling back as my black lab barreled toward her, his tail thumped with excitement.

"Diesel," I barked, but it was too late. The dog immediately started jumping on his paws, like he was ready to knock her over.

"Oh, my goodness. Aren't you adorable?" Harlow crouched down, laughing as Diesel licked her face like he had just found his long-lost friend.

"You got a dog." She glanced up at me with a soft expression on her face. "You always wanted a dog."

"Yep," was all I said.

I got Diesel two years ago, right after I finished building this house, to keep me company.

"He's so friendly."

"He's going to slobber all over your dress." I was annoyed that my dog was showering her with so much attention.

She scratched behind his ear. "I don't mind. I'm planning on throwing this gown in the trash anyway." She stood up and continued petting my dog, who didn't appear to be leaving her side anytime soon. "It looks like I made a new friend."

"Don't get used to him. You'll be gone tomorrow." I snapped my fingers. "Diesel, come." The dog gave her a lingering glance before trotting over to come stand at my side. I walked over to the cupboard to grab a bone to keep him busy.

The second I placed it in his mouth, he happily trailed to his dog bed in the corner.

"Thanks again for letting me stay." Harlow's soft voice floated over my shoulder. I turned to face her, and for a split second, I almost dropped the act. Seeing her in that dress messed with my head. I wanted to believe that she wasn't just running from him, but back to me, but I wasn't that young, stupid kid she left behind. I would be lying if I said I wasn't curious about what happened.

Did she finally come to her senses and escape from under her old man's thumb, or did something else send her running back here?

"It's not like I had much of a choice." I gritted my teeth and stepped into the kitchen. I needed a drink.

I thought maybe she would take pity on me and leave, but then I heard her footsteps come up from behind. "This isn't easy for me either, you know."

I grabbed my beer and slammed the door. I spun around to face her. My kitchen suddenly felt small. Her presence took up way more space than it should have.

"We need to set some boundaries."

"Okay." She leaned against the counter in her big, fancy white dress. I wasn't even sure how she fit that thing through the door. Her hair was messy, her makeup was smudged, but she was still the most beautiful thing I had ever seen.

No matter how much I tried to fight it, my traitorous body reacted to her. I tightened my jaw and reminded myself why she was there.

I popped the cap off my beer. "We're not going to rehash the past. What's done is done. My bedroom and my office are off-limits. You can stick to the guestroom and the common areas. Don't expect me to hang out and keep you company. You can stay tonight, but you will have to find someplace else to go tomorrow."

Her lips were pursed in anger. She was annoyed. "I get it, Brooks. You're still pissed at me. You have every right to be, but let's skip the part where you keep trying to intimidate me with your rules."

I raised an eyebrow. "Intimidate you? I don't want you to get the wrong idea and mistake my kindness for anything more than basic human decency. That's all this is."

She pinned me with a look that could set off car alarms. "Don't flatter yourself. I'm not here to pick up where we left off."

Her sass was pushing my buttons.

"Good, because that won't be happening."

"Agreed. So, are you done trying to scare me away?"

My lips flattened as she continued staring at me. "That depends. Do you agree to the rules?"

She folded her arms and tapped her fancy heels against my floor. "Yes, Brooks. I'll stay out of your room, keep to myself, and pretend we are strangers. But don't think for one minute that I'm going to walk on eggshells around you. You can act tough and demanding all you want, but I'm not afraid of you."

I took a sip of my beer. "I'm not asking you to tiptoe around me. I'm asking you to follow a few simple rules, so we don't end up killing each other."

She gave me a slow, deliberate stare like she was sizing me up. "I don't want to fight with you. So, I'll agree to your stupid rules. I'll stay out of your way, and you stay out of mine. Anything else, Your Highness?"

I cocked my head to the side. "Yeah, try not to breathe too loud, either."

"I wouldn't dream of it." She gave me a mock salute. "Are you done acting cold-hearted now? Are we finished?"

"I think that's all for tonight." I took a sip of my beer and stared at her like she was my enemy.

I wasn't trying to be a dick. I didn't mean to treat her like a pest, but I was mad at myself. I was pissed that I still cared after all this time. Annoyed that I even let her walk through my door in the first place.

I wanted her gone.

"Great." She pushed herself off the counter. "Any chance you'll feel generous enough and let me borrow something to sleep in?" She gestured down at her dress.

I couldn't help but smirk. "Didn't think of packing an overnight bag before bolting from the church?"

She shifted from one foot to the other as if she couldn't wait to get away from me. "Very funny."

I pushed off the counter and headed toward my bedroom. I opened my closet and rummaged through my clothes. Nothing was going to fit her, so I grabbed the first thing I could find.

I walked back into the kitchen. She was sitting on the floor. White lace was everywhere. Diesel was sprawled out on her lap. It was quite the sight.

"This is all I could find, so you better not complain," I said, tossing the clothes on the counter.

She stood up, walked over, and picked up the flannel and sweatpants. "Thank you."

I leaned against the fridge and crossed my feet at the ankles. "Try not to ruin them."

Her eyes narrowed. "Just when I thought we reached a truce." She stormed off, Diesel's tail wagging right behind her.

I sighed, running a hand through my hair.

What the hell was I doing? Letting Harlow stay here wasn't just inconvenient. It was dangerous. This situation was a pile of dynamite waiting to explode. Not just to my peace of mind, but to my self-control, too.

It was one night. I didn't need to make this more complicated than it already was.

The sound of the shower turning off echoed through the house. I sat in my recliner, nursing my beer with ESPN playing in the background. I scrolled through my phone, trying to distract myself from anything other than Harlow Bennett in my bathroom shower. Naked.

It shouldn't have mattered. Her staying here didn't mean anything. She'd be gone tomorrow. Then, I'd have my life back.

The door creaked open. I could hear her footsteps pad

across the room. I nearly choked on my beer when I spotted her.

She stood there in my black and white flannel. The fabric hung loose down to her knees. She had the sleeves rolled up awkwardly, and my sweatpants were so big and long on her that they dragged along the floor as she walked.

Her hair was damp, and her face was scrubbed free of the makeup she'd worn earlier. Somehow, this look felt more dangerous than the damn wedding dress.

This felt too intimate, and I didn't like it.

"Thanks for letting me borrow your clothes."

I cleared my throat and looked away. "Don't mention it."

She fiddled with the white buttons on my shirt. "I know you don't want me here. I promise I'll be gone tomorrow."

When I didn't say anything, she set her glass down and gave Diesel a scratch behind the ear. "I'm beat. It's been a long day. I'm going to bed."

I waited until I heard the door click shut before letting out a breath.

Diesel's eyes flicked from the hallway to me.

"Don't look at me like that," I said, rubbing a hand over his head. "She's only staying the night, so don't get used to it."

He looked at me like he didn't believe me. "Come on." I stood up to let him out for the night. "Come tomorrow, she'll be gone."

I wasn't sure if that reminder was for his benefit or mine. All I knew was when I lay in bed that night, staring at the ceiling, visions of Harlow sleeping in the next room, surrounded by my things, and dressed in nothing but my clothes, lingered in my mind longer than they should have.

CHAPTER FOUR
HARLOW

The smell of coffee hit me first as my eyes fluttered open. I stared up at the ceiling fan, momentarily forgetting where I was.

I groaned, throwing a hand over my eyes. I had trouble sleeping last night because my thoughts wouldn't let me rest. I knew it was hard for him to have me here. It was hard for me, too.

I wanted to apologize for leaving him, but he was so upset that Molly dropped me off without a warning, so I didn't want to make things worse. I was curious, though. Would he soften up toward me, or continue hating everything about me being back here? I squeezed my eyes shut, already knowing the answer to that question. I had to remind myself not to get too comfortable staying in this house. He made it perfectly clear that I wasn't welcome.

There was a knock at the front door, so I picked up my phone to look at the time. Brooks' heavy footsteps echoed throughout the house.

"Is she awake?" asked the soft, familiar voice.

"Not yet." Brooks' tone was hard. I could feel the tension seeping through the walls.

I threw the plaid quilt off my body, knowing I would eventually have to move from this spot and popped off the bed. I promised myself that I would be polite and not kill either one of them today.

The bedroom door creaked as I dragged my reluctant feet to the kitchen. I yawned and ran a hand through my hair, trying to tame the tangles.

"Good morning." Molly's voice was bright and cheerful as her husband stood beside her with a black duffel bag slung over his shoulder.

"You brought me clothes," I said, my entire body filled with relief.

Molly's eyes caught on what I was wearing.

"I can't let you walk around town wearing Brooks' flannel. People will get the wrong idea."

Leave it to Molly to make things awkward.

"Thank you."

"You're welcome." She smiled. If I didn't know any better, I would think she was enjoying this. "I just brought a few things to help get you through the next couple of days."

"I appreciate it." I wrapped my arms around myself, hoping that if I played nice with her husband, maybe he wouldn't be such a jerk to me. "Hey, Finn."

"Harlow," was all he said, and he went back to crossing his arms. He looked at me like I was a bug he wanted to squish under his shoe.

It didn't take a genius to figure out why Molly's husband hated me. I would always be the girl who broke his best friend's heart, and he'd been carrying a grudge ever since.

Finn and I had only seen each other a handful of times over the years. Whenever we were in the same room, we kept our distance. He never said it to me outright, but I could tell he wasn't a fan of mine.

"How did you sleep?" Molly asked, pulling a chair out for Finn to set the bag down. I didn't miss the warning look she shot him or how he ignored it.

"Fine."

Molly stepped closer. "So, what's the plan?"

I glanced at Brooks, who stood over the stove, shirtless. He hadn't said a word. Hadn't moved. The tension was so damn thick I couldn't wait to get out of here.

"I'm going to have my things sent overnight from New York. Would you mind giving me a ride to the lake house?"

Finn shoved his hands inside his pockets. "How do you plan on getting in without a key?"

"I was hoping one of you guys knew how to pick a lock, or I could always climb in through a window."

"You're going to break in?" Brooks asked, taking a sip of his coffee.

"I'm not breaking in if it's my house. Besides, do you have a better idea?"

He held his hands up with a smirk. "Your house, your rules."

"We can help." Molly sat at the kitchen counter and tried to pretend that there wasn't five years of bad blood simmering in this room.

"No, we can't," Finn announced, surprising us all. He was making it very clear that I wasn't welcome in this town.

"Finn," Molly scolded. "Stop with the attitude."

He looked down at his shoes. "I don't have an attitude.

All I meant was we can't leave Emma with my mom for too long. She has things to do today."

I twisted my hands together, trying to mask the hurt that was impossible to ignore. No matter how much time has passed, Finn would never forgive me for what I did.

What made it sting even worse was that Finn was a nice guy. If an old lady needed help carrying groceries to her car, he didn't hesitate. If a stranger were stranded on the side of the road with a flat tire, he would jump in to help without a second thought.

When it came to me, he would run me over without even attempting to hit the brakes. Okay, maybe not actually run me over, but he would take his sweet-ass time debating whether or not to stop.

The worst part was that I couldn't blame him. Maybe that was why it bothered me so much.

Brooks set his coffee down. "You guys go take care of Emma. I got this."

Finn raised an eyebrow. "You sure? You've been generous enough to let her stay here."

"Finn, stop being rude." Molly smacked her husband on the arm. "If he wants to help, let him help."

He gazed down at his wife. "Don't get snippy with me. Maybe if she didn't burn every damn bridge she crossed, she'd have more people willing to help her."

I knew my actions had consequences, but knowing how much Finn hated me, hit ten times harder. In spite of that, I still respected him. I always would.

"All right. I think that's enough for today." Brooks shocked me by stepping up to my side. "I appreciate your concern, Finn, but I'm a big boy; I can take it from here."

Finn held his hands up and started heading toward the door. "Fine. Don't say I didn't warn you."

Brooks crossed his arms and let out a frustrated sigh.

Molly gave me a tight smile as she pulled me into her arms. "I'm sorry. I'll talk to him. I promise."

I squeezed her hand. "Don't worry about it. I don't want to cause any more problems with your marriage. I appreciate the clothes. I'll call later, after I get settled."

Once she was gone, Brooks handed me a coffee mug. "Don't take it personally. Give him a bit of time. He'll come around."

I laughed weakly. "Now, do you see why Molly brought me here? Could you imagine how he would be if I were under his roof instead of yours?"

His eyes thinned into slits. "You hurt a lot of people, Harlow. You can't expect everyone in this town to forgive and forget so easily." He turned to walk away. "I'm going to get dressed. Be ready to leave in thirty."

I sighed once he was gone. If there was one thing I'd learned since I've been back, it is that running away all those years ago didn't solve anything. It only made things much worse, and after yesterday, I was officially done running.

***

THE SECOND we pulled up to the lake house, I got out of Brooks' truck and breathed in the crisp morning air. A sense of peace washed over me.

But that peace didn't last.

Brooks was already walking to the front door when he stopped in his tracks. His gaze dropped to something on the porch.

"Uh, we have a problem."

"What's that?" I asked, hurrying to catch up to him.

He pointed to the ground, where a puddle of water was seeping out under the door.

He placed his hands on his hips and glanced around. "I think your pipes burst."

I shook my head, fighting the urge to cry. "Please tell me you're joking."

He pointed to a puddle of water. "I'm dead serious."

My stomach dropped. This couldn't be happening.

"This isn't good, is it?" I asked, defeat creeping into my voice. Everything that could possibly go wrong had gone wrong. I must have pissed somebody off in my former life.

Without uttering a word, he moved to the door and pulled out a paperclip and a small screwdriver.

I started pacing back and forth. I only needed one thing to go right. Just one thing.

After a few minutes, I heard the click, and the lock gave way. Brooks swung the door open. I clamped a hand over my mouth and took in the damage.

This was worse than I imagined.

Our feet sank into what was probably an inch of water, but it still felt like a swamp.

"Oh, my God."

Brooks cursed and walked deeper into the house, trying to figure out where the water was coming from. I followed him, trying not to cry as I surveyed the damage.

The wood floors were ruined. The ceiling was coated with water spots and paint blisters, and the dining room wallpaper was peeling off the wall. The area rugs looked like little floating islands.

Once we reached the top of the stairs, we could hear exactly where the water was coming from.

Brooks pushed the door to the laundry room open and

rushed over to turn off the valves connected to the two cut water hoses.

"Please tell me this was some freak accident."

He pointed to the wall. "Hoses don't magically split apart on their own."

"Who would do this?"

"Well, let's start with the obvious."

I stared at him. "You think Baz did this?"

"Unless you pissed off someone else in the past twenty-four hours, I can't think of anyone with a stronger motive."

I swallowed hard, my gaze darting around the room. This wasn't just a house with four walls. This was my mother's home. It was all I had left of her, and now it was completely destroyed. I felt like someone ripped away the last bit of peace I could have.

"Now, what?"

Brooks crouched by the steel braided hoses again, running a hand along the length where they'd been cut. "We can call Tuck and file a report." He stood and wiped his hands on his legs. "For now, you'll have to find someplace else to stay."

I followed him outside, pacing the front yard while he called his brother. The back of my eyes burned with tears. I couldn't believe someone would actually do this.

Brooks slid his phone into his back pocket. "Tuck is on his way."

"He's the sheriff now, huh?"

"One of them," he clarified. "Let's take a look around and see what we have on our hands."

We took our shoes off and rolled our pants up as we walked through the house. I found myself getting emotional. This was the one place where I always felt at peace. This was supposed to be my safe haven.

Why was this happening? Why couldn't I catch a damn break?

"You, okay?" Brooks asked, gently touching my elbow.

I blinked and looked up to see him watching me.

"This was all I had left of my mom." My voice broke, and I hated how vulnerable I sounded. "Now, look at it."

He stepped closer, his expression softening. "I know how much this house means to you. I'll get my construction crew out first thing this week."

I wiped at my eyes, willing myself to keep it together. "You have your own construction crew?"

"Yeah." He stepped back and ran a hand along the back of his neck. "Pops recently retired, transferring all the work over to Hayes and me. And you know how Hayes doesn't like to get his hands dirty, so that leaves me in charge of all the hard labor."

"That's great."

He has always wanted to take over the family business. My heart swelled with pride for him.

"Hayes is our lead architect and handles the designs while I focus on the bidding and the job sites."

"Oh, my God. How old is he now?"

"Twenty-six, but he still acts like a little shit."

For the first time since I got here, I laughed. The Dawson brothers were always tight. Tuck was the oldest, Brooks was the middle child, and Hayes was the youngest. I was about to ask about the rest of his family when Tuck stepped through the door wearing a pair of rubber boots.

"Well, I'll be damned. Harlow Bennett is back in Marcellus Falls. I heard you've made quite a splash already."

Tuck Dawson was an older version of his brother. They both had the same dark eyes, sharp jaw, and build. Tuck's laugh lines around his eyes were deeper and a bit more pronounced, like he'd seen his fair share of late nights. He was also wearing a badge on his chest that wasn't there the last time I saw him.

His smile was easy as I walked into his open arms. "I heard there was a new sheriff in town."

"You got that right, sweetheart, so you better behave." He folded me to his side and shot his brother a grin.

I patted his chest. "Same goes for you, buddy. So, don't even think about writing me any tickets, or I'll tell your mom."

He snorted and squeezed me tight. "Speaking of telling, there is a rumor going around that you're shacking up with my little brother."

I shook my head. I should have known he would bring that up. "He was gracious enough to let me stay in his guest room."

"I bet he was." He smirked. "I know the options are limited around here, so if you need someplace else to crash, I'll leave my door unlocked."

Brooks' jaw tightened as he stared at his brother's hand on my shoulder. "Can we skip this little flirt session and get to the reason why I called you?"

He stared down at me with a raised brow. "I was hoping he would be in a good mood after playing host to you last night."

Brooks scowled. "Tuck, I swear to God..."

Tuck raised his hand in surrender. "All right, let's focus on the plumbing and see what we're dealing with here."

At least someone in this town, other than Molly, didn't despise me. I shouldn't have been surprised because Tuck was a good guy, but I wasn't expecting him to welcome me back with a hug and a smile.

They both crouched down to inspect the damage. Tuck looked back at me. "You think this is your ex?"

I wrung my hands in front of me. "I don't know who else it could be. He's probably pretty upset about what happened, so I wouldn't put anything past him."

While it was hard to imagine him taking his anger that far, I couldn't dismiss the possibility. Marcellus Falls was only a little over four hours from the city when driving the speed limit, so it wouldn't have been impossible for him to make it up here last night, cut the hoses, and make it back to Manhattan before anyone noticed.

He pulled out a notepad and jotted down a few notes. "There doesn't appear to be any forced entry, but that doesn't mean they couldn't find a way to get in. I can check with a few neighbors and ask to look at their security cameras."

"What about dusting for prints?" Brooks asked.

Tuck rubbed his jaw. "I can call Chief and see what he wants to do. We don't have an available team, but the state police might be able to send their technicians out. Every agency handles things differently."

"Okay," I said. "We won't touch anything."

"I'll get started on the report. I'd suggest calling your insurance company to assess the damage and file a claim."

I rubbed my hands along my jeans. "Thanks for coming out."

He glanced down at the puddle of water and squeezed my shoulder gently. "We will get to the bottom of this."

I'd imagined Tuck giving me the cold shoulder, maybe act a little bitter toward me for breaking his brother's heart, but this level of kindness caught me off guard.

"I appreciate it. I'm sure you have a lot more important things to deal with."

"Nonsense. Your safety is a priority." He straightened. "Do you have a place to stay until the repairs are done?"

"I'll probably book a room at the Stanford Inn until I come up with a more permanent plan. Hopefully, the repairs won't take long."

"How long do you plan on staying in town?" Brooks asked, angling his head to the side to study me.

I shrugged my shoulders. "I don't have a plan. I'm figuring things out as I go along."

There was something in his expression, something I couldn't quite read. "But you're going back to New York, right?"

Was he asking me simply out of curiosity, or was he hoping I would say yes?

"I don't know what I'm doing, Brooks, but I'm not going back anytime soon."

When he frowned, I knew I had my answer. Fixing up the house wouldn't bring back my mom or make him hate me any less. This was all too much. "I need a minute," I said and headed toward the stairs.

Coming back to this town was supposed to bring me contentment. A place for me to figure out who I was and what I wanted to do next. Instead, all I could feel was a constant ball of tension curling in my stomach. It felt like I was being forced to face things I didn't want to deal with. Him. The past and every mistake I'd ever made.

I walked through the house and ran my fingertips along the walls. Every corner held a memory. This house was my mom's pride and joy before she passed away from complications from a stroke when I was sixteen.

I walked over to the window and stared out at the backyard. The garden, which used to be so full of color, was now overgrown with weeds. She was meticulous about her garden and would spend hours out there tending to her flowers and plants. I could almost hear her humming as she worked.

This is where she would go when she needed to get away from my dad. They didn't have the best marriage, but I think she stuck with him for my sake, because she thought it was the right thing to do. She was always happier when she was away from him. I didn't understand it then, but I got it now.

Tears built up in my eyes, but I wiped them away quickly. The loss of life in this house was almost too much. Everything felt out of place. The things that used to make sense to me no longer did. I'd never felt as lost and alone as I did at that moment.

The creak of the floorboards made me stiffen. I didn't need to look over my shoulder to know it was him. My body tensed, like it always did when he was near.

"Are you all right?" he asked, his voice much softer than it was earlier.

I brushed a hand across my cheek, keeping my gaze fixed on the outside. "This house is all I have left of my mom, Brooks. I came here to think. I came here for peace and quiet. Now, I feel like I have nothing."

"Hey." He stepped up to my back. "I understand how much this house means to you. That's why we're going to figure out what happened and fix it."

I cleared my throat and looked around. "I'm going to see if I can get a room at the Stanford Inn."

"No," he said abruptly.

I blinked and turned to face him. "Excuse me?"

He sighed and pulled on the brim of his hat. "That place is haunted, and it just failed a fire inspection from the code enforcement officer."

"Then what do you suggest, because there aren't any other options in town?"

His jaw tightened. "You can stay with me."

"What?"

Was it wrong that my heart quickened at the idea?

"You heard me. I've got the space, and it's only temporary."

I opened my mouth to argue, but he put his hand out, stopping me. "You have no other choice. So, unless you have some other brilliant idea, it's me or nothing."

Well, when he put it that way.

"Thank you." I shifted on my feet. He continued to surprise me.

He grumbled, "Don't thank me. Just don't make me regret it."

I would not cry in front of him. I would not cry.

As much as I resented his coldness toward me, I had no one to blame but myself. I didn't just leave this town behind all those years ago. I left him, too.

Instead of going back and forth with him, I decided to swallow my pride and accept his offer. Like, he said, what other option did I have?

CHAPTER FIVE
BROOKS

Dirt and gravel flew in the wind beneath my truck as I hauled ass out of my driveway. I had to get out of my house. I just dropped Harlow off after a quick trip into town to grab a few essentials, because all she had was a bag of borrowed clothes.

What the hell was I thinking, offering her a place to stay? I should have told her no from the jump. Let her figure it out on her own. My reaction to seeing her standing there, looking lost and defeated, scratched at something inside me. I reacted on instinct, and now I was questioning every single decision I'd made over the last twenty-four hours.

Harlow Bennett would be living in my house. Sleeping right down the hall, sharing my space like some twisted version of a future that could have been.

I pulled up to the Lakehouse Pub and followed a couple of guys in suits into the bar. It was right in the center of town, serving both townies and tourists. The place was known for cheap drinks and good food.

I sat at the bar and rested my hands on the wood countertop. My buddy, Ryan, who I went to high school with, slid a bottle of Labatt's Blue Light my way. There was a ghost of a smile on his lips as he watched me closely.

I adjusted myself on the worn stool. "Whatever it is you want to say, go ahead and spit it out."

"I didn't expect to see you in here tonight."

I ignored his smirk. "Why is that?"

He cocked his hip against the bar and ran a hand through his dark, blond, curly hair. "Heard you were shacking up with your ex."

Tuck had a big mouth.

I took a swig of my beer as the jukebox in the corner played some sad country song that kind of fit my mood. "Rumors, in this small town, sure do travel fast."

"People in this town are already talking."

Of course they were. Nothing stayed quiet.

"What was I supposed to do, Ry? Slam the door in her face?"

She had nowhere else to go. And no matter how many times I told myself I didn't care anymore, I couldn't leave her stranded.

Even if it felt like I just threw a lit match at a can of gasoline that held the rest of my sanity.

He exhaled sharply. "I don't know, dude, but you better make damn sure you know what you're doing."

I didn't reply because we both knew that there wasn't a single part of me that had ever truly moved on from her.

I've dated over the years, but nothing ever stuck. I compared every smile, every laugh, to hers. The truth was, when you had that type of connection, you could spend your entire life trying to find it again with someone else, but you never would.

"She's only staying with me until the renovations are done."

He leaned both hands on the bar and stared at me like I was dense. "Do you really believe you can keep your distance?"

I scrubbed a hand down my face. "Yes, because it's only temporary."

He raised an eyebrow. "Someone really flooded her house?"

"If I were a gambling man, I'd say it was the ex."

He whistled. "Damn."

Yeah. Damn was right.

It was hard to wrap my head around that she almost married a guy who would do something so extreme.

It was clear this was personal the second I stepped inside the laundry room.

Whoever did this wanted to make sure she had no place to go.

Ryan dragged a rag over the counter. "You think he knew she would run back here?"

I took a slow sip of my drink. "That would be my guess."

He shook his head and rolled up his sleeves. "That's a whole new level of crazy."

He wasn't wrong. I was starting to wonder if it was more of a warning than an act of revenge.

I hadn't seen the guy since Molly's graduation party. But I remembered the look on his face like it was yesterday. Smug and cocky. He cozied up to her dad like he knew he had already won.

And I guess he had because she chose him over me.

But now, she was back at my house, and I wasn't sure how to handle that.

Ryan crossed his arms. "Maybe Tuck can find some evidence of who did it."

I set my beer down a little harder than I intended. "That would be nice, but I'm not getting my hopes up."

The guy had money and influence. He might have been a jackass, but he wasn't stupid.

Ryan wiped his hands off on the rag and pointed to my beer. "Do you want something stronger than that?"

"It's probably best if I stick to beer."

He leaned forward, resting his elbows on the counter. "How long is Harlow in town for?"

That was a damn good question.

"No clue." I shrugged.

"Seems like there are a lot of things about your ex that you don't know."

My eyes narrowed. "Where exactly are you going with this?"

Ryan exhaled. "Brother, you've been in love with the girl forever. I know you've always had a soft spot for her, but after skipping town and leaving you in the dust and now magically showing up out of the blue..." His eyes softened. "I'm worried about you. And it's nothing personal against Harlow, but it's been five years. People change. You know nothing about what her life has been like since she left."

Ryan was just being a good friend. He was worried about me and what this would do to me mentally. After Harlow left, I shut down. It took me a long time to pick up the pieces and move on. He didn't want to see me go down that road again. Hell, I didn't want to either.

Was there a small part of me that wanted to know every little detail about her life? Of course, there was. But another part was afraid to let her get too close to me. I spent years trying to get those wounds to heal. I wasn't interested in having them ripped open.

"I'm not the same guy I was back then, either."

He looked like he didn't believe me. I meant what I said. I wasn't the same inexperienced kid who felt love was all that mattered. I'd been through enough and seen enough to not believe in that fairy tale anymore. But that didn't mean I wasn't curious and wondered what might have happened if she had stayed?

He leaned forward, lowering his voice, when two older ladies took a seat next to mine. "Come on, Brooks. Are you going to sit there and tell me you don't still have a thing for her?"

I shook my head and took a sip of my beer. "Don't start, okay. What we had was a long time ago."

"If you don't still care about her, why is she sleeping under your roof?"

I stared at my beer bottle. "Because I'm a decent human being."

"Really? Is that all?"

"Yes. She didn't have anywhere else to go."

I can't believe I actually came here to unwind.

"Maybe." He shrugged. "But based on how moody you are, it seems there is more going on here than you're letting on."

Of course, I still cared about her. How could I not? Harlow wasn't just anyone. She was the girl I planned on marrying someday, until she walked away and decided she wanted to marry someone else instead.

"Her staying with me doesn't mean anything."

Ryan snorted. "Right. Keep telling yourself that."

I shot him a glare, but he just laughed it off and moved down the bar to take care of another customer.

I sighed and ran a hand through my hair. I hated how much she still got under my skin. How, after five years, she still had the ability to stir up old feelings that I thought I had moved on from.

No matter how tempted I was, I would not let myself go there again.

I wanted to pretend that her being back in Marcellus Falls didn't matter, but the truth was, it mattered way too much. Having her in my house, in my space, would make it a hell of a lot harder to keep those feelings locked down.

I finished my beer and signaled for another. If I were to survive the next few weeks, possibly months, I would need more than a cold beer. I was going to need a damn miracle.

CHAPTER SIX
HARLOW

"Tell me everything," Molly said when I sat next to her on the couch.

I propped my feet on the edge of the table. "I don't have a clue where to start."

She pulled a knit blanket over her lap. "You've been back in town for three days now, and you still haven't talked about why you ran out of the church, seconds before you were supposed to walk down the aisle. Why don't we start there?"

I stared at my wine, swirling it around in my glass. I didn't want to discuss this, but Molly was my best friend. She was there when I needed her most. I owed her the truth.

"I didn't love him."

She rolled her eyes. "Can you at least tell me something I don't already know?"

My head snapped to hers. "If you knew I didn't love him, then why did you ask?"

She smiled. "Because I wanted to hear you say it."

I groaned, letting my head fall back against the cushion.

"I thought if I had a long engagement, it would give me time to fall in love."

When I agreed to the arrangement, the only thing I asked for was time. I told my dad we didn't want it to look rushed, but the truth was, I needed to get used to the idea. I thought if I dragged my feet long enough, maybe it wouldn't actually happen. Or at the very least, make it seem less real.

She frowned. "Harlow, that's not how love works."

I played with the ends of my hair. "I know that, but I convinced myself that my happiness would come later if I kept playing the role, but deep down, I always knew how wrong it was."

I only said yes to help my dad secure a government contract. He was counting on me and I thought I could handle it. Senator Zimmerman was looking for a favor and I found myself caught up in something I never wanted.

Baz was involved in a hazing scandal in college that almost cost his father his political career. That was where I came in. I would make him seem more responsible and restore his public image.

The deal benefited everyone but me. And to make matters worse, somewhere between all the planning, I met Brooks. He was someone I never saw coming. And walking away from him was the hardest thing I'd ever done.

She sighed, tucking the blanket around her legs. "I always understood why you went through the engagement. I'm honestly surprised it took you so long to come to your senses."

I opened my mouth, but the words got stuck in my throat. I knew what I wanted to say, but it sounded more pathetic when I said it out loud. No one knew the real reason, not even Molly. She believed that the arrangement was all about my dad trying to control me, but it was much more complicated than that. I wanted to tell her, but Brooks could never know the truth, and I would never put her in a position to keep a secret from her husband.

"I kept hoping that it would get better, but the closer I got to the wedding, the more I questioned if I could go through with it."

She shook her head. "You always felt obligated to do what your father wanted, and he always made sure that you felt that way, too."

She wasn't wrong. I'd been told what was best for me since I was a little girl. My dad was a man who thrived on control.

I was raised to be the perfect daughter. The one who would toe the line, make good decisions, and marry well.

And Baz Zimmerman suited the plan perfectly.

Right after my mom passed away, my dad planted the idea in my head that Baz would be perfect for me.

I convinced myself that I could handle it. That Baz was at least tolerable, and eventually, I would grow to love him, but toward the end, I realized I was in over my head.

I swallowed hard, wishing I could take it all back. "I made a mess of everything, and now I don't know how to fix it."

Molly's eyes softened with concern. "I always hoped you would wake up and realize you didn't owe your dad anything, and you deserved more than what he wanted for you, but I knew you would have to get there on your own."

I blew out a big puff of air. "I have no idea who I am anymore."

It felt like all the sacrifices I've made over the last five years have been for nothing.

She squeezed my hand. "Then perhaps it's time you figure that out."

I gave her a weak smile. "You make it sound easier than it is."

She was quiet for a minute before she asked, "Do you think you'll eventually go back to New York?"

"I have no idea." Just thinking about it stressed me out. That's where my home and my job were. I hadn't let myself think that far ahead.

"You could always stay in Marcellus Falls."

I blinked, surprised she would even suggest that. "What would I do about work?"

She reached for the wine bottle and poured more into my glass. "The same thing everyone else does. You start by looking for a job."

She made it seem like it was no big deal.

"Where am I going to find a director of finance job here in Marcellus Falls?"

Her brows lifted. "I'm sure there are opportunities close by."

"I don't know," I mumbled. "Are there any Fortune 500 companies around here that I don't know about?"

"If there are, I'm sure they will scoop you up in no time." She smirked.

I closed my eyes and dragged a hand down my face. "Maybe I'll apply at the hardware store. God knows I'll be spending enough time there trying to repair the house."

She sat up and rested her hands on her thighs. "Let me ask you something. If you had the power to do anything, what would it be? What would make you happy?"

That was a good question. I'd spent the last five years structuring my life around schedules and deadlines. It was weird not having an office to go to, meetings to attend, or emails to return. I know that was part of the reason why I came here, to take a break, but now what was I supposed to do?

I spent years chasing a life I was supposed to want: the corner office, the job title, the constant hustle. Now, just thinking about it made me exhausted.

"I have no clue, Molly. I've been so focused on doing what was expected of me that I never really considered what I want to do."

She leaned back and took another sip of her wine. "Okay, then. Let's start with your hobbies."

I peered at her over the rim of my glass. "What hobbies?"

She nudged me with her foot. "Come on, Harlow. I've known you forever. You weren't always a corporate robot. What did you love before you started working for your dad?"

I opened my mouth to argue, but she was right. Working long hours and trying to meet deadlines never made me happy. The only time I was happy was when my mom and I would garden together.

I could still picture her in the dirt, with streaks of mud across her cheeks. She would hum some eighties song while planting wildflowers, and I always admired the simplicity of it, but it didn't stop there. She had an eye for design, too. She would help neighbors plant their flower beds. She had a gift and enjoyed every second of it.

"I forgot how much I loved gardening," I said, surprising myself.

She smiled. "Maybe that's your answer."

I scoffed while staring down at my perfectly manicured nails. "It's a hobby, not a job."

It was something I did for fun. It wasn't a business.

"Says who? Lots of people turn hobbies into careers. You don't have to get down and plant your hands in soil all day long. You could design open spaces. You have enough passion and skills to start a small business."

I shook my head, feeling a tiny flicker of hope. She made it sound doable, but I wasn't convinced. "My options here would be very limited. I wouldn't even know where to begin."

"Well, lucky for you, you have an entire town full of overgrown yards that could use a little love. I'm sure Finn could help you get started."

I snorted. "He would probably kill me with a shovel."

She laughed. "I'm serious, Harlow. Think about it. If I can pull off juggling law school with a baby, you can figure out a way to make it happen."

I never considered creating something from the ground up, but now that she'd put that idea in my head, I didn't see it going away anytime soon.

"I guess I could give it some thought."

After all, I had nothing but time on my hands.

CHAPTER SEVEN
HARLOW

Heavy footsteps vibrated through the walls as Brooks entered the living room. I sensed the tension rolling off him before he appeared in front of me.

"Have you eaten?" he asked, setting a brown paper bag on the coffee table.

"I had one of your protein bars earlier."

He looked like that answer didn't make him happy. I wasn't sure why he even cared.

Instead of replying, he reached into the bag and pulled out two containers. He flipped the lid open on one and pushed it across the table. "You need to eat something."

I sat up straighter, my eyes widening in surprise. "No way. Beef on a wick from the pub?"

He reached over and grabbed the other container. "I stopped after work and brought food back. It's not a big deal."

My stomach growled, reminding me that I barely ate anything today. The only things I found in the fridge earlier were a sad-looking container of lettuce and a questionable block of sharp cheese.

I set my phone down and glanced at the time. It was almost eight p.m. "I was starting to think you forgot about me."

He glanced at me out of the corner of his eye. "Why didn't you eat one of the frozen meals in the freezer?"

"Because I wasn't sure if I was allowed to."

His glare hardened, and for a moment, I wondered if there was anything I could say or do to get him to not hate me so much. "You can help yourself to whatever you want. I don't want you to starve on my watch."

"Right." I reached over and grabbed my container. The smell hit me immediately, and it was warm and comforting. This used to be my favorite sandwich because the roast beef was full of flavor and would melt in your mouth.

Brooks sifted through the bag and dug out the utensils and napkins. As I bit into my sandwich, I felt his eyes on me.

I chewed carefully, trying not to spill anything on my lap. "Thanks for bringing me dinner."

He moved to sit beside me on the couch; the cushions dipping slightly under his weight. "I wasn't sure if you still like to eat that kind of stuff, so I got a salad in there too, in case."

The sandwich paused on the way to my mouth. "What's that supposed to mean?"

He scratched the side of his cheek. "We don't really know each other anymore. For all I know, you only eat kale and drink green smoothies."

My eyes narrowed. He was hinting at something; I wish I could figure out what.

"I can assure you that I will pick meat and carbs over kale and a smoothie any day. Just don't ask me to cook anything."

A smile tugged at the corner of his mouth. It was a small one, but it was genuine, and it felt like a tiny victory.

"Good to know that some things about you haven't changed."

We ate the rest of our meal in silence. It wasn't comfortable, but it wasn't awkward either. It was neutral, like we were both wrapped up in thoughts and not sure how to act around each other.

"Can I ask you something?" I asked as we gathered the empty containers and brought them to the trash.

"Uh, yeah," he replied, bending over to shut the disposal off.

"What did you mean when you said, 'you were glad some things about me haven't changed'?"

He hesitated for a moment before looking out the window. "It was nothing."

"It was obviously something," I said, not accepting that answer.

"We were kids back then, and it's not like we kept in touch over the years. I have no idea who you are today."

"I'm the same girl I was back then, just a little older and a lot wiser."

He shoved his hands into the front pockets of his worn jeans. "Maybe, but you look different now, too."

I cocked my head to the side, trying to determine if he meant it as a compliment or a dig. "Don't we all change over time?"

"I guess." He rubbed the back of his neck like he used to do when he was irritated. "But I never left to go pursue my dreams like you did. I stayed here, in the same town I was raised in. Took over the family business and still hang out with the same group of friends since I was ten. Not much about me has changed since you left. I'm not so sure you can say the same."

I crossed my arms. "Of course, I changed. I had to. But I'm still me in the ways that matter."

He folded the towel and set it beside the sink. We both stood there facing each other. "Did you ever think about me?"

Slowly, I was starting to understand where some of his hesitation was coming from. "Yes," I said, stopping myself from saying more. I was tempted to tell him that I missed him, and wondered every day what it would have been like if I had stayed.

His hands flexed at his sides. "And yet, you still left."

I forced myself to hold his gaze, even if it hurt. "I didn't know what else to do."

He scoffed. "That's bullshit. You had a choice, and you chose him."

I shook my head. "I didn't choose him. Everyone had expectations of who I should be. I was young and naive, so I chose the path that was laid out for me."

If he only knew the whole truth.

His eyes were hard. "We all have expectations in life. Did you think you were the only one?"

"Of course not, but you don't understand the pressure that was put on me."

Or the extremes I would go to in order to protect you.

He grabbed a sponge, dropped it in the soapy water, and rested his hip against the counter. "You can rationalize it any way you like to soothe yourself. It won't change what happened to either one of us, will it?"

No, it wouldn't because life was messy, painful, and full of regret. At least mine was. And I was starting to wonder if

I would ever be able to fill in the gap between us. "I'm sorry for leaving the way I did."

Brooks stared down at his hands. "I got over it."

A knot formed in my stomach, and I had to force myself not to cry. Sure, we were young and clueless, but I'd made a choice. A choice that took me away from the only man I ever loved and a town that meant everything to me.

"I hate that I hurt you, but let's be honest. You were happy here. This town is your life. I never would have asked you to give it all up for me."

Nor would my father have ever allowed it.

His head snapped to mine. "That wasn't your decision to make."

I could feel his anger, his pain, and the betrayal that still lingered after all these years. "I would have ruined your life, Brooks. I wanted you to have a chance to find real happiness, even if I wasn't the one who could give it to you. That's all I ever wanted for you. Please tell me you were happy."

He met my eyes and hesitated for a minute. "There are times when I thought I was. I know I want to be."

I opened my mouth to say something, but I had no idea what. It wouldn't matter anyway, because nothing would change the past. I couldn't go back and make different choices, no matter how much I wished I could.

When I looked at Brooks, I saw the man he had become —the man who stayed true to himself and built a life centered around his family and friends. I saw what he's accomplished. I saw his loyalty and his pride, and it's so different from what I was used to.

The weight of everything I lost and all I could have had if I had stayed pressed down on my heart.

"What about you?" he asked, as if he wasn't sure he had a right to know the answer. "Were you happy with your decision? Were you happy at all after you left?"

"I was content doing what I was doing. I mean, I didn't have time to focus on myself because I was too busy building my career."

That wasn't the question, and we both knew it.

"I'm not talking about your career."

Right. He was talking about Baz.

Silence settled between us. Heavy and thick, and I hated it. Neither one of us knew what to say, and it felt like we were only making things worse.

He pushed away from the sink and stepped toward me. "I don't get it, Harlow. You left and were ready to commit your life to a man you didn't love. Make that make sense."

I sat down and brought my knees to my chest. "You don't understand."

"Then make me understand, because I can't wrap my head around it. I can't figure out how a girl who used to be so full of life would settle for something so empty."

I wrapped my hands around my legs, my nails digging into my skin. "I wasn't looking for love. I already had it and lost it."

"Correction. You didn't lose it. You threw it away."

I tilted my chin up in defiance. "That's not fair."

He leaned against the sink and crossed his arms. "Fair? You want to talk about fair? You were ready to sign your life away just to make Daddy happy."

"You are right, and I have to live with that. But it's easy to judge and criticize when you're not the one making the sacrifice."

It was hard to ignore the look of pity and

disappointment in his gaze. "I guess things didn't turn out quite like you planned, huh?"

I hung my head and stared at the floor. "No, and I realize now it was a mistake."

"Why did you run from the church?"

I picked up the glass of water and took a sip. I wasn't expecting this conversation to get so heavy. "Lots of reasons, but the one that struck me most was when I would go to dress fittings. I would be surrounded by happy brides. They would talk about how happy and in love they were, and then I stepped out of the fitting room and looked at myself in the mirror. I was the furthest thing from happy. I felt empty. I saw the rest of my life flashing before my eyes, and it seemed so cold and bleak. Our marriage would have been nothing more than a business arrangement. The closer the wedding date got, the more I questioned my decision."

His brows furrowed, like he was searching for a piece of the girl he once knew. I thought maybe he would say something, but he didn't.

"Talk to me," I pleaded.

He clenched his jaw and looked away from me. "I can't do this."

"Brooks," I called out, but he was already around the corner. "Wait."

He paused for a moment when I finally caught up to him. His shoulders were rigid. "What do you want from me, Harlow?"

I swallowed thickly, wishing I had the nerve to tell him how I really felt. "Will I ever be able to fix this? Will you ever be able to forgive me?"

He raked a hand through his hair. "You can't expect one conversation to fix everything."

"I don't, but I have to start somewhere, right?"

He paused for a moment and glanced back at me. He looked like he wanted to say something, but he nodded and walked away. I sat in the empty kitchen, wondering if I would ever get the chance to make things right with him.

CHAPTER EIGHT
BROOKS

I was staring out my kitchen window when my phone started ringing.

I picked up when I saw Tuck's name. "Perfect timing. I was about to call you."

"I would have called sooner, but I had to bring Marty to his doctor's appointment."

My chest twisted. "Any updates?"

Marty was our grandfather. He was recently diagnosed with stage-four lung cancer. The doctors gave him thirteen months. Losing him was going to be tough.

"They want to adjust his meds. Recommended some vitamin C infusions to help with his fatigue."

I shifted the phone to my other ear. "Good. He looked wiped out when I was there the other day."

I promised to take Marty fishing this weekend, but the forecast called for rain, so I wasn't sure what my backup plan was going to be. My brothers and I were the only things keeping the old man going. None of us were the type to talk about our feelings, but we didn't have to. We all knew the end was coming, and nobody in my family was ready for it.

Tuck cleared his throat. "I'm worried that the treatments aren't doing much. He's weaker than the last time I saw him."

A wave of dread washed over me because the doctors told us that his life expectancy would be determined by how well his body responded to the treatments. While there were other options still left on the table, his age and overall health were working against him.

I sighed, rubbing the back of my neck. "I'll head over tomorrow."

"He would appreciate that."

I walked over to the Keurig machine and dropped a pod in. "Do you have any updates on the investigation?"

He let out a sharp laugh. "I had a lovely chat with a couple of really nice men today."

Normally, I would laugh at his sarcasm, but I was too exhausted from the lack of sleep I had last night.

Harlow Bennet has been sleeping in my guestroom. Under the same quilt my grandmother made for me when I was ten. All because some asshole decided to flood her house by cutting the water supply line to her washer.

"And? What did they have to say?" I grabbed my coffee and let Diesel outside so he could go do his business.

"Her dad was as pleasant as you would expect."

I never liked the man, and the feeling was mutual.

"I imagine he's not very happy with his daughter right now."

He let out a low chuckle. "Yep. He's a total asshole. He's been trying to get in touch with her, but she's been dodging his calls. I wouldn't be surprised if he showed up soon."

I set my coffee down on the porch railing. "Sounds about right. Do you think he had anything to do with it?"

"It's hard to tell. He was too busy telling me how ungrateful his daughter was and how lucky she was that someone like Baz Zimmerman would even want to marry her in the first place."

I dragged a hand through my hair. "He's a miserable excuse for a human being."

"Agreed."

I rubbed my temple. "What about the ex?"

He paused. "Yeah, he was even worse. The guy is a real piece of work. He acted like he was offended that I even called. When I told him about the house, he didn't ask where she was or if she was okay."

I cradled the phone against my shoulder. "My money is on him."

He was quiet for a minute. "It's too early to tell, but his reaction raised a few red flags. He was furious with her. Played dumb when I questioned him about the hoses but made some comment about, she should come crawling back to him any day now."

I gritted my teeth and tightened my hand around the phone. "That won't be happening."

Tuck laughed, and I frowned.

It might have been five years, but I still felt this need to protect her.

"Listen, I'm calling in a few favors. Due to the amount of damage, Chief had the state police send their tech guys out to the house and dust for prints. We got nothing, but I promise, nothing is being ruled out. Those washer lines were intentionally cut. I promise I won't stop until we figure out who is responsible."

"I know he's responsible," I said. My theory about her

ex was gaining strength in my head. "She humiliated him. The guy has an ego bigger than the state of Texas. He's got money and influence to boot."

"I'm not saying you're wrong, but we have no proof. There were no security cameras installed. Right now, it's simply a hunch."

I stared across the yard. "What does that mean? How do we prove it was him?"

"It means I keep digging until I find something to connect him to the house, but I'm doing this mostly on the side, so I don't catch heat from Chief Scott. I'm a sheriff, not a detective. I'll lose control of the investigation if I get caught using the department's resources."

That sounded like Chief Scott. He did everything by the book. He didn't bend the rules for anybody, no matter who you were.

"I understand, and I appreciate it."

"Can you promise me something, Brooks?"

"What?" I asked, feeling the third degree coming on.

"Promise to keep your head on straight. I mean, don't get me wrong, I think you're doing the right thing. My only concern is that it might come back and bite you in the ass later. Her staying at your house means something, whether you want to admit it or not."

"I'm only letting her stay here because she has nowhere else to go. The sooner we get that house cleaned up, the sooner she can leave."

"Just don't do anything stupid."

I let out a dry laugh, feeling the weight of the situation press down on me. "Define stupid."

"Like inserting yourself deeper into this mess. She pissed off some very powerful people, and I know you're still hung up on her, so don't do something you will regret."

"You know nothing," I said, picking up my coffee and wishing I had something stronger.

"Yeah, okay. Sure. Whatever you say. You are so keyed up right now, I can practically hear you vibrating through the phone."

I leaned against the porch railing and crossed my feet at the ankles. "Thanks for the pep talk, brother. I'll let you go back to work so you can go write some speeding tickets."

He exhaled audibly, the sound coming through like static. "Just be careful. I know you are pissed and want to help her. Don't let your anger cloud your judgement. If either of them shows up, you call me."

I glanced down at a scuff on my boots. "You don't need to keep repeating yourself. And stop making this into something it's not. I have no intention of picking up where we left off. I don't have feelings like that for her anymore."

The words tasted bitter on my tongue.

"Brother, I've known you my whole damn life. You're lying to yourself if you don't think you still feel something for her."

I rolled my eyes even though he couldn't see me. "I feel nothing. Whatever we had was a long time ago. The sooner she packs up and leaves, the better."

"You don't fool me, but I'll let you off the hook for now. Let me know if you hear or see anything. I wouldn't put it past either of them to try something."

I would like to see them try. They might have power and influence, but this was my town and my people. I would not let them intimidate me.

"You sound like you think I'm in danger."

"I think you're in danger of making a dumbass decision."

I picked up a ball and threw it across the lawn for Diesel to catch. "Have a little faith in me. I'm not stupid. I know what I'm doing."

That was a total lie. The truth was, I was in over my head, but it was too late to turn back now.

He snorted. "I gotta get back to work."

"Just keep me posted, yeah?"

"Will do. Try to get some sleep tonight. I'll check in with you later."

I hung up and blew out a long breath. The tension in my chest refused to let up.

I turned toward the door, ready to head back inside, when I saw her standing against the doorframe. She was barefoot and wearing my red and blue flannel that swallowed her entire frame. I wasn't sure why she was wearing it, considering she had other things to sleep in. Her arms were wrapped around her middle, and she looked like she was on the verge of crying.

My heart sank. She must have heard my conversation with Tuck.

"Sorry," she said, keeping her eyes glued to the ground. "I didn't mean to eavesdrop. I heard you talking and figured it was about the house."

"How much did you hear?" I asked, feeling guilt twist around in my stomach.

"Enough." She stood there, refusing to meet my eyes. She looked so small and fragile. It made my chest ache.

"Harlow..." I started, but she held her hand up, stopping me.

"It's fine. I don't want to cause any trouble. I can leave.

My stuff is supposed to arrive tomorrow. I can find a rental or a hotel outside of town."

She definitely overheard.

"You don't need to rush out of here. I told you. You can stay until we figure things out."

She rubbed her arms like she was cold, even though it was warm outside. "I'm grateful you're allowing me to stay, but I don't want to make things more difficult for you."

She only heard my end of the conversation, and I could only imagine how bad it sounded. I should have been more careful.

"Harlow." I stepped closer, wanting to say something, but I stopped myself. If I said too much, if I let my true feelings slip out, I wouldn't be able to take it back.

Instead, I settled for the safest thing I could say. "Having you here is no trouble. I have the space."

She let out a laugh. "I heard you, Brooks. I'm not welcome here."

"It's not like that."

She met my gaze head-on. "Then tell me what it's like, then?"

I had no answer. At least not one I was willing to admit to. I didn't know how to reassure her without exposing everything I was feeling.

She shook her head and pushed off the doorframe. "That's what I thought."

I ran a hand over my face. "Harlow, you are jumping to conclusions. You overheard one half of a conversation. You are not a burden, okay? I just didn't expect to be in this situation. I'm doing the best I can here, but know this: if I didn't want you here, you wouldn't be here."

She stood there, arms crossed, with a guarded look on

her face as if she was trying to decide whether she could believe me. "Okay. I'll stay. Thank you."

I nodded back and walked past her, heading to my room to get ready for work. I should have said more. I could have been honest. Instead, it felt like I screwed up.

I shut my bedroom door behind me, but it no longer felt like my space. Not with her right down the hall.

I peeled off my clothes and threw them into the hamper. I sat on the edge of my bed and dropped my face in my hands.

Every time I looked at her, I saw the girl I fell in love with all those years ago. I shouldn't still care this much. I shouldn't be so caught up in this shitstorm.

Yet here I was.

Tuck was right to warn me. But that didn't change how I felt.

I should want her to leave. Hell, I could help her find a place. It would make my life easier and less complicated.

But I couldn't bring myself to do it.

CHAPTER NINE
HARLOW

I pushed the door open with more force than necessary and kicked my wet shoes off on the mat. My entire body ached from spending the day trudging through my flooded house, listening to plumbers and contractors rattle off estimates, and spending hours on the phone with the insurance company. According to the trust, my mom's attorney, who was the trustee of her estate, was responsible for the upkeep and renovations. He responded to my email politely, letting me know he was on vacation and would look into the matter when he returned.

The house was all I had left of my mom. I would be dammed if I let it all turn to shit because her lawyer couldn't be bothered with making a phone call while on vacation.

The entire day was overwhelming, and the idea of spending another night at Brooks Dawson's house was sending me over the edge.

While I was grateful that he allowed me to stay, the man drove me crazy.

Speak of the devil. "You didn't need to slam my door open."

"I didn't slam it," I shot back and crossed my arms. "It's not my fault the damn thing is hard to open."

He raised an eyebrow and kicked his boots off. "Of course, my door is the problem, not your attitude."

"What do you expect? Your contractors told me it would take months—months! To repair the damage. If your guys are as good as you say they are, then they should be able to get it done quicker." The words slipped out before I could shut my mouth. I didn't mean them; I was simply frustrated. It wasn't his fault I was in a mood.

He smirked. "You're welcome to find someone else who can do the job on such short notice. Good luck finding someone, though, who can do a better job than me and my team."

I huffed and turned toward the kitchen. "Whatever. I'm too tired to argue with you right now."

I heard his steps follow me over to the wine rack. "Careful, princess. You're starting to sound a little ungrateful."

I spun around as he casually leaned against the counter. "I'm not ungrateful. I've been through hell these past few days. I went from living in a high-rise in the city and a thriving career, to being homeless, and you treating me like I'm some clueless little girl who can't make her own decisions."

His smirk disappeared. "I'm trying to help you. But, sure, let's make me out to be the bad guy. Does that make it easier for you?"

I huffed. "Nothing about this situation is easy."

"I'm not the one who fucked up your house," he fired

back, his tone matching mine. The tension between us was growing so thick that I almost choked on it.

We stood toe-to-toe in some type of standoff. His eyes were locked on mine. His jaw was tight with tension. For a moment, I forgot why I was even angry.

I sighed. "I'm sorry for snapping at you. I'm tired, and it's been a long day. Can we start over?"

"Fine by me." He brushed past me to get a beer from the fridge while I grabbed a bottle of wine.

We moved around the kitchen in tense silence and set the table for our takeout containers. We grabbed some Mexican food on the way back, but my appetite was nowhere to be found.

Brooks sat across from me and started eating his burrito while I cut into my quesadilla. He kept stealing glances at me when he thought I wasn't looking.

He took a sip of his beer. "Listen, I understand you're not happy with the timeline, but there was more damage than I expected."

I picked up my wine and brought it to my lips. "Can't your guys find a way to speed things up?"

"You obviously know nothing about construction. You need your electrical system fixed, floors redone, and walls replaced. You need to have patience."

"I need your guys to work faster, that's what I need."

He exhaled through his nose, trying not to lose his patience with me. "That's not how it works, unless you want me to cut corners."

I pushed the rice around on my plate with my fork. "I'm grateful that you're letting me stay here. I don't want to be a burden."

He pushed his chair back. "You are not a burden."

I kept my eyes on my plate, which I barely touched. "I

know you didn't sign up for this, and it's not easy for you. I can look for a temporary living situation."

He set his beer down with a thud. "You want to leave my house?"

I bit the inside of my cheek and looked over at Diesel, who was lying by my foot, waiting for a crumb to drop. "I don't want to overstay my welcome."

He leaned back in his chair. "I told you the room was yours for however long you need it."

"You did, but I know how much you hate having me in your space. You're used to living alone, and now you have to deal with me and my problems. I'm sure you would rather have your freedom back."

He kicked his feet out and crossed his ankles. "What kind of freedom are you referring to? What exactly am I missing out on?"

I poked at my quesadilla like an idiot. "I don't know, maybe bring a woman over. Date or whatever it is you do."

He folded his arms across his stomach. "Why don't you focus on your house and let me handle my personal life."

"I'm just saying, if you want to have someone over, I'll stay out of your way." The words didn't sit right, not even as I said them. I had no idea why I even had to bring it up? The thought of him with someone else made me want to puke, and I knew I had no right to feel that way.

"You don't need to worry about who I date or what I do."

"I'm not worried," I said, way too quickly.

It was a lie, and I was pretty sure he could see right through me. All I could picture was him with a beautiful woman, with perfect hair and flawless skin, sitting on the couch, laughing at jokes or, God forbid, hearing them in his bedroom.

I would die.

The jealousy that churned in my stomach had no right to be there. He wasn't mine. He hasn't been for a long time.

"So, you would be okay if I brought someone back here?"

I picked up the napkins on the table and started rearranging them. "I mean, it's your house. You can do whatever you want. I don't want to make things awkward for you."

His lips curved slightly. "Things are already awkward."

"They don't have to be. I can leave."

"Stop." His voice was firm, causing me to stiffen. "Just stop, okay?"

"Stop what?" I asked, playing dumb. I hated his ability to see right through me.

"Stop acting like you don't care."

"I don't."

Jesus. I was so damned stubborn. It was clear to both of us that it would bother me.

"You're seriously going to lie to my face?"

I didn't respond because I didn't trust myself to speak without saying something stupid. So, I stood up and brought my dish to the sink.

My heart started to pound when I heard him step up to my back. I hated that after all these years, those feelings were still there, that he still had the ability to get under my skin. My heart, which I worked very hard to keep safe, was in a dangerous place when it came to him. It always had been.

"Tell me again how it doesn't matter," he said, his hot breath against my ear.

I had to clench my eyes shut and shove my feelings down where they belonged. I couldn't handle him this close to me. In my personal space, making me feel things that I didn't want to acknowledge.

"It doesn't matter."

But it did matter. It mattered a lot. I just convinced myself that I didn't have the right to care.

"Liar," he said, moving closer. He brushed my hair to the side and pressed his chest against my back.

The plate I had been holding on to slipped out of my hands. My breath hitched when I felt the heat of him press further into me. All I could focus on was his scent. It was a mixture of soap and sawdust, and it was all him.

"I'm not lying," I said, feeling my pulse hammer against my ribs.

"Then turn around and face me. Look me in the eye and tell me the idea of me being with another woman doesn't drive you crazy."

I shook my head, not trusting myself to look at him. "What you do is your business."

"Turn around and face me, Harlow."

Against my better judgment, I did and suddenly regretted it.

His eyes searched mine as if he saw right through my bullshit. This was too much. He was too close. I wanted to back away and put some space between us, but I couldn't get my body to move. I stood there, tangled up in my emotions that were caught between logic and insanity.

"I'm facing you. Now, what do you want?" I tried to come off as snarky, but it came out breathless instead.

He swallowed hard. "Isn't that a loaded question?"

"Brooks." I shook my head. I thought I could handle this, but I'd never been more delusional in my life.

"I don't know why I still care so much about what happens to you. I should tell you to leave, help you find someplace else to stay." He leaned in, and his eyes fell to my lips. "Did you really mean it?"

"Mean what?" My head was fuzzy, and my knees felt like they would give out at any second.

"That you didn't care."

Oh, that. Damn it. How was I supposed to get out of that one?

I opened my mouth to say something, but he was making it impossible to think straight. The truth was right there between us. I did care, and the smart thing to do would have been to back away and ignore the pull that seemed to be getting stronger by the second, but my legs wouldn't move.

His hand gripped the side of my neck. "That's what I thought."

Before I could say anything else, he hauled me into his chest and kissed me. It was light and soft and barely a kiss. It felt like he was testing the waters and giving me a chance to pull away, which I didn't. Something unleashed inside me, giving me the courage to stand on my tiptoes and grip the fabric of his shirt in my hands.

The kiss was beautiful and devastating at the same time. It reminded me of how much I loved him before everything fell apart. Brooks took his sweet time, as though fully aware of what he was doing to me.

His hands moved to my waist, pulling me closer. Kissing Brooks felt the same as it always had, but there was something different about it, reminding me how we both had changed over the years. I wanted to cling to him and allow the last five years to fade from my memory.

Diesel barked and Brooks jerked back. My heart was racing, and my mind was all over the place.

It was only a kiss. It shouldn't mean anything, but I forgot how easily I could get wrapped up in this man.

His fingers brushed my cheek, and I quickly stepped back, needing a little breathing space. He stared at me for a moment, as if he was trying to figure me out. There was so much I wanted to say, but I didn't even know where to begin. There was too much history between us. So much pain.

I might have been the one who ended things, but the reasons why were still there.

For a moment, I thought he would say something, but then the doorbell rang.

Brooks cursed as he strode across the room. He swung the door open, and my heart stopped.

"Well," my father said, his hard eyes darting back and forth. "Doesn't this look cozy?"

CHAPTER TEN
HARLOW

"**D**ad." I crossed my arms, wishing I had more than a minute to prepare for this. I didn't even have time to catch my breath. I was still reeling from that kiss.

"I heard you were back in Marcellus Falls," he said, not even bothering with a greeting. No hello, or are you okay? Just straight to the point.

I fought the urge to fidget in front of him. "Yes, I was going to call you."

"May I come in?"

Brooks moved aside but stood at the door, silently watching.

"I'm assuming you know why I'm here?"

I twisted my hands in front of me. "I was planning on talking to you in person."

"Were you? Because it seems to me like you've been avoiding me."

Brooks slammed the door and came over to my side. "Nice to see you too, William."

My dad turned. The vein in his forehead pulsed. "I wish I could say the same."

My stomach twisted. The two of them never got along, and that's putting it mildly.

"Dad, I understand you're upset, but leave him out of this."

"Upset." He turned to face me. "Upset doesn't even begin to cover how I feel right now. You made a spectacle. You humiliated the Zimmermans. Do you have any idea what your little stunt has cost me?"

Brooks crossed his arms tightly. "Sounds like she finally came to her senses to me."

Dad stepped forward, ignoring him. "I spent years working on that deal. That marriage was supposed to secure our partnership. That contract would have brought in millions. Now, it's up in smoke because you couldn't keep it together for one day."

The deal. That was all he cared about.

Tears burned the back of my eyes. "I didn't want to marry someone I didn't love."

He shook his head in disappointment. "You're more like your mother than I ever gave you credit for. You are too soft."

"Please don't talk about my mother like that." I raised my voice, letting him know I wouldn't tolerate his petty comments. "You expected me to commit the rest of my life to a loveless marriage, all so you could get your hands on another piece of property."

He jabbed a finger in the air. "Don't you act like a child and talk back to me?"

My back straightened. "Then stop treating me like I am a five-year-old having a temper tantrum. Does my happiness not matter to you at all?"

He didn't even try to pretend to care about me. I expected him to be mad, but this was on a whole other level. One that I would never understand.

"This is business," he said coldly. "There are worse people for you to marry than Baz Zimmerman. You have known him for years. You are acting like I tried to marry you off to a stranger in a foreign country."

"Dad, I don't want to fight with you. I came here because I needed some space. My intention was to go to the lake house. But it's flooded. I'd like to take some time and get the house repaired and figure out my next steps. I can work remotely once I get the rest of my things."

He unbuttoned his suit jacket and placed his hands on his hips. "You won't be working remotely, because you're fired."

I felt the floor tilt beneath my feet. I couldn't believe what I was hearing. I worked my ass off for that job. I've spent years proving myself, fighting for every opportunity that was put in front of me.

"You are seriously going to fire your own daughter?"

He was punishing me. Plain and simple.

"I don't want to fire you, but you've left me with no choice."

Brooks scoffed because we both knew he wasn't giving me a choice. He was giving me an ultimatum. "You're a piece of work, you know that."

He wanted me to cave. He was playing hardball, like I'd seen him do in the boardroom.

I shook my head, standing my ground. "I'm staying here in Marcellus Falls until the repairs are finished on the lake house."

"No, you're not," he barked.

"Mom put that house in trust for me."

His lips curled. "Which you only get if you are married, which you are not, may I remind you."

I shifted on my feet, because damn it, he was right. That house was left to me by my mother. It had been in her family for decades, but there was a catch. I had to be married in order to inherit the property. Until that time, it would be held in a trust. At first, I thought it was messed up until I learned why she did it.

She was worried that my dad would try to hold the property over my head or sell the house from under me. However, if I were married and had someone to stand up for me, then it would make it harder for him.

I guess she knew him well.

"I am your daughter. Why are you trying to make things difficult for me?"

Why couldn't he be a normal father and want what's best for me? Why did he have to be such an asshole?

"Just because you're my daughter doesn't mean you're entitled to that house."

This was my punishment for going against him.

"You don't want anything to do with that house."

He lifted a shoulder. "Maybe I'll sell it."

It felt like I was going to puke. My mom inherited the lake house when my grandmother passed away. She wanted me to have a place where I could feel safe. Where I could breathe. It was my last connection to her, and I would not allow him to take it from me. "Mom did not want you to have that house. That's why she set it up the way she did and had her lawyers handle everything."

"Who do you think paid the taxes and handled the upkeep on that property when we were married? I did. Maybe this will be a good way to earn back some of my investment."

Oh, my God. He was actually serious.

"That house is legally mine. You don't have the authority to sell it."

I would be calling Molly as soon as he left. There was no way he would get his hands on the only thing I have left of my mom. Because if anyone could find a loophole, it was him.

"I'll tell you what? I'll make a deal with you. Come home and marry Baz, and you can have the house today."

Brooks stepped closer to my side. "She's not going anywhere."

It was rare for anyone to challenge my father like this. In fact, it was a big no-no. The whole situation made me uneasy.

"This is none of your business. She is my daughter."

Brooks let out a bitter laugh. "I think it's funny how you try to act like that title gives you some type of claim on her."

"You know, you've always been nothing more than a—"

"Dad, please stop," I said, cutting him off from finishing that sentence.

Brooks has always been protective, maybe a little too protective, at times. But the thing with my dad was that if you pushed him, he only pushed back harder. He wasn't going to give in, and Brooks wasn't known to back down from a confrontation. This was an absolute nightmare.

"Stay out of this." He yanked on his tie and turned to me. "You need to come home with me. We can sit down and negotiate some new terms if that's what it takes, but this wedding needs to happen."

"It's too late for that." Brooks reached for my hand, lacing our fingers together. "Because Harlow and I are already engaged."

My head snapped to his so fast I almost gave myself whiplash.

Was he out of his mind?

My dad's eyebrows popped up. "What did you just say?"

"You heard me. I asked Harlow to be my wife, and she said yes."

I blinked, thinking maybe I had misheard him and was waiting for the punch line until I saw the murderous look on my dad's face.

His sharp gaze darted back and forth between us, not looking very convinced. Why would he be? I haven't spoken to Brooks in years. Yet he was trying to sell my dad a lie like it was something he did every day. As if it was no big fucking deal.

My dad's eyes narrowed. "Bullshit."

Brooks looked perfectly at ease, while it felt like my world had just tilted sideways. "It's no secret that I've been in love with your daughter for years."

My heart pounded in my chest.

It was a lie. He didn't still love me, did he?

His gaze was sharp and assessing. "I don't know what's going on here, but I don't believe it."

Brooks brushed his thumb across my knuckles. "Believe it, because it's the truth."

I had no idea what he was doing or how he could keep a straight face. I don't remember him being such a damn good actor before.

He could feel me freaking out, so he squeezed my hand, trying to get me to relax.

He was too good at this. So good that I was almost convinced that this was real.

"Is he telling the truth?"

Hell no, he wasn't.

Nothing about this was true. There was a time when I wanted it to be, but that was a long time ago.

Brooks' warm hand folded along mine. It was strong and comforting, but it did nothing to quiet the noise in my head.

I should say something, but what was I supposed to say?

My lips parted for a second before I hesitated, and then the words, by some small miracle, came from my mouth. "Yes."

My dad scoffed. "This has to be some sick joke."

"No joke," Brooks said calmly. "Harlow has made her decision. You need to respect it."

My dad's face turned beet red. "I don't have to respect anything. You are a nobody. I don't know how you weaseled your way back into her life, but you weren't good enough for her then, and you sure as hell aren't good enough for her now."

His face fell, and my heart shattered for him. My dad hit his target. Exactly like he did five years ago.

"You know what, Dad, I think it's time you leave. This is his home. I won't allow you to come here and disrespect him."

My father curled his hands into fists. "If you think this is over, you can think again."

With that, he stormed out the door, slamming it so hard I flinched.

I blew out a breath and tilted my head. "I can't believe you just told him we are engaged."

He ran a hand through his hair. "Neither can I."

I stared at him, wondering if he had injured his head. "What in the ever-loving hell were you thinking?"

"Obviously, I wasn't."

I looked up at the ceiling, praying for patience. "Now, what are we supposed to do?"

He stuffed his hands in the front pocket of his jeans. "I guess we fake it till we make it."

"Brilliant plan," I said flatly. "And then what do you suggest?"

He lifted his shoulder and stared out the window. "We cross that bridge when we come to it."

My mouth popped open. It felt like I was missing something here.

He stared at me, and I stared right back.

"Why would you want to help me?"

He started pacing back and forth. I silently watched him, giving my brain a minute to calm down. "Because I need a favor."

I blinked. "What kind of favor?"

"I've been talking to an investor. I need to purchase some new equipment so I can compete for bigger projects. When Pops retired, we advanced him some cash. The guy I'm talking to is old-school and very family-oriented. He will only invest in businesses with values that align with his."

"How would this even work? Would we pretend to be madly in love, tell them we are getting married, and he just writes you a check?"

He shrugged. "Pretty much."

I scoffed. "You can't be serious. There is no way this would work."

"Why not?"

I threw my hands up. "Because this is crazy. I just left a man at the altar a week ago. How are we supposed to convince everyone that I'm already planning another wedding?"

He raised an eyebrow. "Do you want your house?"

I glared at him. "You know I do."

It was the main reason why I came back to this town in the first place.

He let out an exasperated sigh. "Look, Harlow, I get it. This isn't exactly ideal for either one of us. But you need something, and I need something. That's all this is, plain and simple."

I closed my eyes, fighting the urge to cry. My life had been turned upside down. I went from running from the church to staying with my ex to finding my lake house flooded. My father was pissed, and I was out of a job. I wasn't sure how much more I could take.

"What if people can tell it's fake? What if they don't believe us?"

He shrugged. "Simple. We make it believable."

This town thrived on gossip. There were probably already rumors going around about me. Heck, I wouldn't be surprised if they hadn't stopped talking about me since I left.

This had disaster written all over it, but I'd known Brooks long enough to know he wouldn't do this if he weren't desperate. And the worst part, the idea of living with him, and pretending we were still in love, made my heart pound for all the wrong reasons.

"I can't believe I'm actually considering this."

"You better make up your mind quick. We don't have a lot of time."

I shot him a glare. "Can you give me more than a second to make a decision?"

"Fine," he snapped and looked down at his watch as if to remind me that the clock was ticking.

The irony of this situation wasn't lost on me. I just walked away from an arrangement because it wasn't about love, and now, I was contemplating walking into another one. What did that say about me? That I was a hypocrite?

Maybe, but this felt different. I didn't feel like I was selling my soul. It felt more like I was getting it back.

I rubbed my temples as if that would make this less real. "Okay. I'll agree to it."

His gaze traveled down to my mouth. Was he contemplating kissing me again? Did I want him to? Yes, yes, I did, until he said, "If we do this, just remember this is strictly business. Got it?"

I crossed my arms and forced myself to nod. I needed this arrangement to be practical and logical. I refused to let old feelings get in the way. And I definitely wouldn't allow him to kiss me again. "You've made yourself crystal clear. So, now what?"

"Well…"he spun his ball cap around his head and flipped it backward. "Now, we start playing the part of the happy couple who got a second chance at love. We also need to get you a ring."

"This is insane, but if you insist, then we can get something cheap."

"Do you want this to look real or not?"

"Of course I do."

"Great, because we can't have you walking around town with one that looks like it came from the Dollar Store. It's just for show. Don't overthink it."

"Oh, trust me. I won't. While you're prattling off lists, I have a few of my own."

He grinned. "I can't wait to hear them."

"Number one, we can't let old feelings get in the way. Number two, we need to remember what this is. And last, we cannot blur any lines. No more kissing unless we are in public and it's all for show."

His eyebrow raised. "It sounds like you're the one who needs those reminders, not me."

CHAPTER ELEVEN
BROOKS

Trees blurred past the windows of my truck as I drove to my parents' house for Sunday dinner. Harlow was stiff as a board next to me. Her hands were clenched in her lap while I kept one on the wheel and rested the other on the console between us.

"Do you want to pick something on the radio?"

"I'm fine," she said, which was a total lie. She was the furthest thing from fine.

"You look like you are spiraling over there." I gestured to where she was, twisting her hands nervously in her lap.

She huffed, trying to laugh it off. "Are you sure your parents don't hate me?"

My parents were upset. Her leaving didn't just hurt me. It hurt them, too. They hated seeing me so broken, but they always had a soft spot for her.

"They don't hate you, Harlow. They might not have been happy with what you did, but they have always cared about you. Look at how happy Tuck was to see you. I'm sure Hayes will be just as thrilled."

"Your brothers don't count."

I laughed. "I can't wait to tell them that."

"You better not."

I drummed my fingers on the steering wheel while she stared blankly out the window. She looked like she was ready to jump out of my truck.

"You need to relax, or they will know something is up."

She twisted in her seat to face me. "I hate the thought of lying to them."

"I'm not crazy about it either, but the more people that believe our story, the more real it looks to everyone else."

She tilted her head to the side. "I know we have to keep up with appearances, but this is your family."

"I'm aware, but my mom would not be able to keep this secret, so she has to believe it's true."

I loved my mom, but she was the last person I trusted when it came to keeping things quiet. She would call her best friend, Laura, who would then call their friend Janet. Then, the next thing you knew, the entire town would know before we even finished dessert.

"What about your dad and brothers?"

"Tuck and Hayes, yes, but not my dad."

If I told him this whole thing was fake, he would worry. Things were still new and uncertain. I needed to keep the real reason why we were getting married close to the vest. I didn't want everyone I cared about weighing in and giving me their opinions.

The truth was, I wasn't the type of guy who avoided tough conversations. I dealt with crap head-on, but this was different.

"I still feel guilty, but you know your family better than I do, so I'll follow your lead."

I'd spent the entire car ride trying to reassure her that everything would be fine. However, by the time I turned into my parents' development, an unexpected tidal wave of nerves rolled over me.

Their driveway was packed with cars, so I found a spot on the street behind Tuck's squad car.

I killed the engine and glanced over at her. Harlow wore a pretty blue sundress that reminded me of summer and old memories. She looked carefree and beautiful, more like herself than in those pictures I saw of her online. Dressed to the nines, expensive-looking jewelry, perfectly styled hair, and manicured nails. I could almost see the girl she once was before becoming a pawn in her father's twisted world. There wasn't a trace of makeup on her face, and no dark shadows under her eyes.

I forced myself to glance away. Seeing her like this and with the soft scent of her familiar perfume stirred up old memories.

Memories of late-night kisses under the stars, stolen kisses down by the creek, and dreams we shared, before life took her away from me.

I cleared my throat, trying to shake off these feelings. Taking a trip down memory lane wasn't helping me keep my emotions in check. I was still trying to get over kissing her the other night in my kitchen.

I didn't know what the hell I was thinking.

"Come on, let's get this over with." I opened the door and slid out.

She fell into step beside me, so I threw a hand over her shoulder as we walked toward the house. It was the same house we moved into when I was fourteen, right after Dad's construction business took off.

Rocking chairs sat on the wraparound porch of the large two-story white colonial, which was decorated with an American flag on the post.

It was warm and inviting, but the closer we got, the more nervous I became. I had to remind myself that it was just my family. The same people I've known my entire life, but with Harlow by my side, nothing about this felt normal.

I tried to ignore the heat from her body and the scent of her perfume as she glared at my hand on her shoulder. She tried to move out of my hold, but I only tugged her harder.

I looked down at her with a scowl. "You need to act natural and not recoil whenever I touch you in public."

Her steps slowed. "I'm not recoiling. I'm nervous because every word we speak will be examined under a microscope."

"Just try your best and remember why you're doing this," I said, dismissing her glare as we made our way up the driveway.

I didn't like the way she tried to pull away. If we were going to pull this off, she would have to warm up to this arrangement, or it would be over before it started.

"Sorry we're late," I said as we walked into my parents' living room. My younger brother, Hayes, was on the couch, typing on his phone, Dad was in his recliner watching a Yankees game, and Tuck was in the other chair.

Tuck studied us momentarily, taking in my hand on her shoulder. Hayes looked up from his phone, and a huge-ass smile split his cheeks. Hayes loved to stir up trouble, and I could already see the wheels turning in his head.

"Holy shit. It looks like the rumors are true."

She barely had time to react before he pulled her into a hug and lifted her off the ground.

She laughed when he finally set her down. "Wow, you've grown like two feet since I last saw you."

He grinned. "I look good, right?"

I stepped up between them and gave him a stern look. "Will you knock it off?"

Hayes, being Hayes, completely ignored me. "Seriously, Harlow Bennet is here in the flesh, looking like a million bucks."

Harlow laughed. "And you're still full of it."

His grin widened. "I can't let all my charm go to waste. I gotta use it on somebody."

I gave Hayes a good shove toward the chair. "Don't mind my brother. He sometimes forgets how to behave around adults."

Hayes was still grinning. "He is so easy to rile up. If you get tired of his grumpy ass, you know where to find me."

She smiled back. "I'll keep that in mind."

"All right, we're done here." I steered her over to my dad. He had one leg crossed over the other, holding a cup of coffee.

"Nice to see you, Keith." I could see her fingers twitching, like she was trying to decide whether to tuck them in her pockets or shake his hand.

Dad didn't move for a second. He merely studied her with a blank expression. Then, to my surprise, he stood and held his arms out.

"Long time no see, beautiful. How have you been?"

"I know, it's been too long." Harlow stepped into his arms while my two brothers watched me. I could see the relief in her eyes that things weren't going as badly as she thought they would. I wasn't the least bit surprised that my family was rolling out the welcome mat for her. They always saw the good in people.

"It's been ages. You don't look like you've changed a bit." He patted her back before stepping away.

"Dinner is almost ready," Mom called from the kitchen.

I leaned in and whispered in her ear, "Are you good?"

She glanced at me briefly before looking toward the kitchen. "I'll let you know in a few minutes."

I almost laughed as we made our way into the other room, where my mom was stirring her Sunday sauce in a huge-ass stock pot. The smell of garlic and fresh tomatoes made my stomach rumble.

"Please, tell me there are meatballs in there." I set the Italian bread that Harlow and I had picked up at the bakery on the counter.

Mom rounded the kitchen island to hug me. "And sausage." She kissed my cheek. "Thanks for picking up the bread."

It was then that she noticed Harlow standing behind me. My mom's eyes softened. "So, it's true? I heard you were back in town, but I didn't believe it."

A cautious smile lifted Harlow's lips. "It's good to see you, Josie."

My mom, who was a foot shorter than me and weighed no more than a hundred and thirty pounds, shoved my ass aside.

Mom wrapped her up in a big squeeze. "I can't tell you how happy I am that you are here." She pulled back, holding her at arm's length.

Harlow smiled warmly. "How have you been, Josie?"

Mom looked her over. "I'm good, but you're too skinny. Is my son not feeding you?"

I snorted. "She's been in town for a week, Ma."

She glared at me. "That's not what I asked."

I rolled my eyes, but Mom was already moving toward the fridge. "Do you want something to drink, sweetheart?"

"What about me?" I asked, picking up the spoon on the

stove. Mom's meat sauce was my favorite, and I couldn't wait to dig in.

Mom grabbed a glass from the cupboard and pointed at me. "You know where everything is. You can help yourself, and don't you dare think about touching that sauce."

I held my hand up and started backing away. "I'm hungry."

"You're always hungry, so why don't you go help your brothers set the table so Harlow and I can catch up?"

I glanced at Harlow, who gave me a nod, letting me know she was fine.

"All right," my mom said, pouring her a glass of iced tea. "Now, tell me everything, starting with how you ended up back in Marcellus Falls."

Harlow hesitated. "It's a long, messy story."

Mom walked over and started stirring the sauce in the pot. "Well, it just so happens I have time, so take a seat."

Maybe this would go easier than expected.

I stood off to the side, watching the two of them together. Mom had a way of making people feel at ease, even if they didn't deserve it.

My folks were warm and genuine, but they were also loyal. They witnessed firsthand how devastated I was when Harlow left me. I felt a smidge of relief that my family wasn't holding any grudges.

I might have been almost thirty years old, but the people in this house meant everything to me. And seeing Harlow with my mom filled me with emotions I wasn't ready to process or understand. For a brief second, I almost forgot that this was all fake.

WE SAT AROUND THE TABLE, stuffed from dinner, while Harlow answered my family's endless questions. Mom grinned like she had just won the lottery, and Dad fired off question after question about her life in Manhattan.

Mom sighed dreamily and clasped her hands under her chin. "I always hoped you two kids would find your way back together again."

Harlow smiled politely. "Thank you for saying that and for welcoming me back and making me feel at home."

Mom patted her hand while Dad poured her a cup of coffee. "You will always be part of this family."

I cleared my throat, figuring this was the right time to announce our engagement.

"I'm glad you feel that way, Ma, because Harlow and I have news."

The room went silent. I felt Harlow fidgeting next to me.

Hayes was stuffing a chocolate chip cookie in his mouth. "What kind of news?"

I grabbed Harlow's hand under the table. "Harlow and I are engaged."

Hayes choked on his cookie while Tuck's head whipped to mine. "I'm sorry... you're what?"

"You're engaged?" Mom squealed as Dad dropped into his seat.

"Am I missing something here?" Tuck seared me with a look as if I'd lost my mind.

Harlow's hand was cold and clammy. I brushed the top of her knuckles with my thumb. My eyes begged her to follow my lead.

I probably should have eased them into it, complimented Mom on her dinner, or talked about the weather, instead of just ripping off the Band-Aid. But it was important for me to tell them before word got out. Which wouldn't be long.

I straightened in my seat. "I'm sure this is a shock."

"That's an understatement," Tuck sputtered out.

Harlow glanced at me like she was debating on stabbing me with a fork or bolting toward the door.

Dad leaned back in his chair, arms folded, and eyebrows raised in doubt. "She's been in town for a week, and you proposed already?"

Hayes was grinning from ear to ear like he knew I was up to something. "So, when is the big day?"

"We don't have one yet," I said quickly. "We are still figuring things out."

Dad didn't move. Didn't smile. Simply stared. "You're serious?"

"Yes," I said, noticing that not one person sitting at the table had congratulated us yet. I suddenly second-guessed my decision.

Tuck leaned forward, clasping his hands in front of him. "When did this happen?"

My pulse was too loud in my ears to think straight. "Yesterday."

He leaned forward and narrowed his eyes. "So, let me get this straight. It's been five years since you two last saw one another. She's recently coming off the heels of a very public breakup, and now you guys are magically engaged?"

I rubbed a hand along the back of my neck, which was breaking out in a sweat. "You all are familiar with our history. I figured we had already wasted enough time. Why waste another day? Life is too short."

Dad looked between us. "I can understand that, but what's the rush? Why not date for a little while to make sure you both are compatible?"

"Because this is what I want, Dad."

He scratched the side of his head while Tuck muttered something about this being convenient.

Mom seemed to be the only one excited for us. "I don't care how fast this is. This is the best news."

"Thanks, Ma." I smiled and tried to ignore the tension in the room.

Dad rested his elbows on the arms of his chair. "This is what you really want?"

"Yes," I said without hesitation. My gaze darted around the room, never landing on one spot.

Silence fell over the table. My black T-shirt felt like it was sticking to my back.

Dad watched us like a hawk. "All right," he said, not looking too convinced. "If you're happy, then that's all we want for you. I'm just shocked. This seems sudden. You both understand that marriage is a big commitment, right?"

Harlow did her best to give him a reassuring smile. We both knew that question was directed toward her. They were probably worried about her leaving again. They weren't the only ones.

"Dad, we wouldn't take this step unless we were ready."

Dad nodded and glanced at Harlow. "Please, don't take any of this personally. This is just sudden."

She pulled out of my grip and placed her hands on her lap. "I understand. Really, I do. You have every right to be concerned."

That seemed to satisfy him, but I could tell it still bothered her. Her shoulders dipped, and her smile didn't quite reach her eyes. They were subtle gestures, but I knew her well enough, especially with the way she went quiet.

Hayes picked up on it, too. He teased her once or twice,

trying to get a laugh out of her, but I could tell, with her eyes darting toward the door and with the way Tuck and Dad kept staring at me, that it would take some time.

Things would be awkward for a while, but my family would come around.

Now that the proverbial cat was out of the bag, I should have felt relief. Some type of victory, but a pile of guilt hit me square in the chest.

I was lying to the people I loved. I wasn't proud of what I was doing, but I had my reasons, and if it meant keeping her out of her father's grasp, then it was worth it.

Because, despite everything, I still cared about her. Probably always would.

We managed to make it through the rest of the dinner without further interrogation. Harlow sat beside me, quiet and trying to fake her way through this. She handled my family like a pro. When I reached for her hand again under the table, and she wrapped her fingers around mine, I had the urge to hold on to her for just a little while longer.

CHAPTER TWELVE
HARLOW

When we walked through the door of Gilda's, I was hit with a wave of nostalgia. It was small, but exactly as I remembered it. There were only ten tables in the restaurant, so we sat at the bar and had a drink while waiting for a spot to open up.

I didn't usually drink alcohol in the afternoon, but today wasn't a typical day. Brooks and I were going to pick out rings.

I stole a glance at him from the corner of my eye. He sat beside me, one arm draped along the back of my chair.

We probably looked like a normal couple enjoying a drink together, unlike two people who could barely stand to be in the same room together.

"Are you sure you want to do this?" I asked, giving him one last chance to bail out of the plan.

After having dinner with his family, I was second-guessing everything. I liked the Dawsons, and I hated lying to them.

He took a sip of his drink. "We need to make it official. Show everyone in town you're still madly in love with me."

I rolled my eyes. "We've already told enough lies, let's not add any more."

"Oh, come on. It's kind of romantic, don't you think?" he teased.

"Yeah, sure. Nothing says romantic like a fake engagement and a flooded house."

I was sipping my chardonnay when Shannon, who owned one of the shops in town, came over to say hello to Brooks. She did a double take when she looked at me. Her eyes lit up in recognition.

"Well, I'll be dammed. Harlow Bennet, is that really you?"

I turned in my seat to face her. "Yes, ma'am."

Shannon Anthony was an ex-beauty queen. She had to be in her late fifties now, but the woman was always dressed in beautiful pastel colors and wore pretty jewelry.

"I can't believe my eyes." She glanced between us. "I never thought I would see you two lovebirds back together again."

Brooks flashed her a charming grin. "What can I say, Shannon? God blessed us with a second chance. Harlow was always the one who got away. I told myself if I ever got another shot, I wouldn't let her slip through my fingers again."

I almost choked on my drink.

She patted his hand. "I remember telling your mama that you two would get married someday. I just knew you needed a little bit of time to get there."

She smiled and looked me up and down. "You are just as pretty as you were last time I saw you."

A blush crept up my neck. "Thank you, Shannon. You look great, too."

She waved me off. "It's the Botox. I refuse to accept my age."

Brooks placed his foot on the edge of my stool's footrest. "You don't need all that crap. You have natural beauty."

She clutched her pearls, literally. "You always were a charmer, even though you lay it on thick sometimes."

Brooks grinned. "And you love it."

She shook her head. "I swear I'm going to cry. I just want to tell you how happy I am. You made this old lady's week."

Brooks grabbed my hand. "I'm thankful she smartened up and came to her senses."

I squeezed his fingers a little too tightly. "And I'm so glad I finally gave in after he spent years trying to win me back."

Brooks scowled, and Shannon swooned. "I truly enjoy it when love gives you a second chance in life. My Thomas and I broke up a few times before we got married. Sometimes men need to grow up and let puberty catch up to them before they can think clearly."

Brooks smiled. "That's why I'm not waiting another second to make this beautiful woman my wife."

Her eyes lit up like a Christmas tree. "Oh, my stars. You two are getting married?"

Brooks wrapped his arm around the back of my chair. "We sure are. We figured it was long overdue."

She let out a delighted sigh. "Well, isn't that something? You both look so happy. It just makes my heart sing."

Shannon was practically bouncing with excitement. I suppose for a small town, this was a love story for the ages. "Oh, this is wonderful news. When's the wedding? Have you picked out a venue? I can talk to Father Austine. I'm sure he would be more than happy to perform the ceremony. And the ladies at the church love to put on a good potluck. You could even have the reception in the rectory basement."

Jesus, take the wheel.

Brooks scratched the side of his head. "We haven't nailed down a date yet. This is all new. We are going shopping for rings after lunch."

She patted his leg. "You always were a good boy." And then she turned to me. "And Harlow, you let me know when you decide on a date. I'd be more than happy to help you plan the wedding."

I forgot how overly friendly people in this town could be. There was a good chance that everyone who lived within a five-mile radius would know by dinner time.

"Thank you, Shannon. I'll keep you posted, but we are trying to keep things simple."

She winked at me. "You let me know if you need anything, dear. I have a lot of time on my hands, and I love a good old-fashioned wedding."

"Thank you. I appreciate it."

She clapped her hands together. "I won't keep you two, but you can bet I'll be telling everyone the good news."

I groaned internally because I had no doubt she was heading off to spread the news as fast as humanly possible.

"You two take care now." She smiled at us one last time before sauntering away.

As soon as she was gone, I smacked him on the arm. "What the hell is wrong with you?"

He shrugged, seeming completely unbothered. "You want this to be believable, right? Isn't that the whole point?"

I drained the rest of my drink. "Yes, but you just told her we're engaged. The whole town is going to know before we even have a chance to come up with a solid plan. You might as well put a billboard sign up."

He leaned in with a grin. "At least you don't have to pick out a wedding venue or worry about food. I've heard Shannon won the chili cook-off last year. I'm sure I could convince my mom to make her famous cornbread."

"I hate you."

"Relax." His voice dropped to that annoying, smooth tone that always seemed to get him whatever he wanted. It was the same tone he used to charm his way into my heart. "Maybe this little charade will be easier than we thought."

I looked down at my left finger. I couldn't believe it had been a little over a week since I ran from the church. I was supposed to be in Barcelona, sipping on sangria. Instead, I was having lunch and shopping for an engagement ring with my ex. Talk about whiplash.

"Why did I ever think this would be a good idea?"

He stood from the stool when the server called us over. "Because you were desperate."

He wasn't wrong. I was desperate. So, when he threw me a lifeline, I took it. Time will tell if it was a smart idea or if I was a complete idiot for even going along with this.

AFTER LUNCH, we wandered down the main drive. Brooks' hands were shoved in his pockets, and his strides were long and determined. He hesitated for a moment when the jewelry store came into view. "Are you ready to do this?"

I shook my head with a laugh. "Not really, but I guess I'm doing this anyway."

He stopped walking and stared down at me. "You act like being married to me is a bad thing. I'm quite the catch, so try to act a little more excited."

I scoffed. "Oh, that's right. How can I forget? I'll try to remember how lucky I am."

"Glad to see you're finally catching on." He winked as we reached the store.

The reality of what we were about to do caught up to me. Pretending to be in love with him would be easy—too easy. That's what made this so risky.

He slid his hand into mine. "Show time. Try to be convincing."

I swallowed, hating how holding hands with him felt like second nature. "I'll do my best."

"Just don't crinkle your nose. That's your tell that you're lying."

I frowned. "I don't have a tell."

"You do," he said, tapping me on the nose. "Now let's go get you a ring."

The bell over the door chimed as we walked in. An older woman in a black pantsuit looked up from the counter.

"Hello, there. I'm Maggie. Are you looking for anything special today?"

"We are shopping for an engagement ring."

The woman's smile widened. "Congratulations. Do you have anything specific in mind?"

Brooks swung his arm along my shoulder and pulled me to his side. "Something that screams she's taken." He winked, and I wanted to punch him in the stomach. "It took me six years to wear her down, so I want everyone to know she finally said yes."

The saleswoman swooned and pressed a hand to her

heart. I had to admit, he was very convincing. For a minute, I had to remind myself that it was only for show.

She led us over to a case with sparkling rings.

We looked through the glass. There were so many shapes and colors that I didn't even know where to begin.

"See anything that catches your eye?" she asked.

Brooks didn't have the kind of money that Baz had. I didn't want to break his bank account on something that would be temporary,

I leaned closer, trying not to get swept away in the moment. "I don't need anything elaborate or over the top, a simple diamond will do."

His jaw ticked. "Let's see that one." He pointed to the simple, solitary diamond in a silver band. The jeweler pulled the tray out and handed Brooks the ring.

"Try it on," he encouraged. Something about seeing him holding the diamond ring made my stomach flutter.

I slid it onto my trembling finger and stared at it. It was simple and elegant, and it fit perfectly.

"It's shiny," his tone was gentle as my thumb grazed over the band.

I nodded while swallowing the lump in my throat. I couldn't let myself get caught up in the moment. Couldn't let myself wish that things could be different. I always wondered what it would be like to wear his ring, and let's say this wasn't what I had pictured.

My vision blurred as I stared at something that was supposed to mean everything but meant absolutely nothing. My chest felt tight, and I wondered if my heart could survive this.

I glanced up at him, wondering if he knew how much this moment hurt me.

"What do you think of the ring?" he asked, holding my hand out and angling it under the light.

"It's pretty."

He raised an eyebrow. "Pretty?"

"Yeah. It's more than I was expecting."

The ring was so much more than pretty; it reminded me of everything I ever wanted but was too scared to fight for.

Brooks looked over at the woman behind the counter. "She's real excited to marry me. Can't you tell?"

I shot him a glare, but he smirked.

"She's probably just overwhelmed," the woman said, trying to reassure him. "I'll give you two kids a few minutes alone."

Once she was gone, he dropped my hand and turned to me. "Really, Harlow? Pretty? That's the best you could come up with?"

"Brooks." My cheeks heated. I didn't know what to say. This seemed like a weird joke.

"What?" he asked, feigning innocence as he leaned against the counter. "We're supposed to make it believable, remember?"

Right. Fake. Temporary. Doesn't matter.

"I'm just nervous."

"There is no reason to be nervous. Just pick a ring. Any ring. The sooner you do, the sooner we can get out of here."

God help me. I wanted to strangle him.

"How are you not freaking out like me?"

"Because it's only a ring."

For him, maybe, but not for me.

He blew out a sigh and placed his hands on his hips. "Seriously, though. I think this once suits you."

The band was delicate, but the severity of what it stood for made it seem heavier than it should have. I stared at the beautiful diamond, twisting it around my finger. This is the exact ring I would want if it were real. The only problem was that it wasn't, and pretending would be harder than I thought. There was nothing harder than faking a relationship with the man I never stopped loving.

"Does it fit okay?" I looked up to find Brooks staring at me.

"It fits fine."

His eyes flicked to me before dropping to the ring. My chest tightened with guilt. I knew what marriage meant to him. We used to talk about the future and how we would build a life together.

This was heartbreaking.

He cleared his throat. "Is that the one you want?"

I nodded, trying to blink away the sting in my eyes. "I love it, but should we at least look at a few more first?"

He stared down at the ring, like he was having a hard time looking away. "We can if you want, but I think that one looks perfect."

I forced a smile. "I agree. Let's go with this one."

He narrowed his eyes, as if he could tell something was off. "What's wrong? You look like you're on the verge of crying."

So many things. For a fleeting moment, I wanted to tell him that I couldn't go through with it. Pretending would be too hard, but this was the only option.

I wanted my mother's house. I wanted to be free of my father's control.

My mind raced, and the diamond mocked me, reminding me of all I could have had if I had stayed.

"Are you sure you want to do this?" I asked, twisting the silver band around my finger.

"What? Have the reception in the church basement or get married?"

I glared at him. "You know what I mean. People are going to find out. They are going to have questions. This isn't a game. This is my life."

I was unraveling. I needed to get a grip.

He set his hands on my shoulders as if he were trying to steady me. "It's my life, too."

I swallowed. "You're right. I'm just freaking out."

This was just a temporary fix. I knew that when I agreed to it. I just didn't think I would feel like this.

He sighed. "Look, Harlow, half the people in this town already thought we'd end up together one day. I wouldn't worry about people believing it. I think you are overthinking."

Maybe I was, but what other choice did I have? I had to follow through with this, no matter how hard it would be.

The saleswoman came back over. "Well, would you look at that? That ring looks like it was meant to be on your finger."

Normally, I would say she was full of shit and only wanted her commission, but the ring was perfect. Like it always belonged on my finger.

I looked up at him. His expression was soft. A moment passed between us, and I wondered if he was feeling the same tangled-up feelings that I was. It felt like I was caught between our past and our new reality. Lines were getting blurred, at least for me.

"We'll take it." He grabbed his wallet and pulled it out of his back pocket. The saleslady beamed and started talking about sizing and stone clarity, but all I could focus on was not falling apart.

She completed the transaction and boxed up the ring. "Congratulations, again."

She smiled while handing me the black bag. "I recognize true love when I see it, and you both have it in spades. I hope you have a long, happy life together."

I smiled and clasped the handles a little too tightly. I had to remind myself that the ring meant nothing. I had to forget this was the same boy I fell in love with when I was twenty-one years old.

The one who told me I deserved the world.

I knew I agreed to this. I was aware of what I signed up for, but that didn't lessen the knot in my stomach.

CHAPTER THIRTEEN
BROOKS

She was taking forever.

I bounced my leg while scrolling through the sports highlights on my phone, trying not to check the time again. Whenever I did, I would get more agitated.

We were meeting our friends at the pub tonight, so I was imagining all the things that could go wrong. We had to put on a show and let the whole town think that we were back together.

Molly had texted Harlow earlier that Finn's parents were watching Emma and wanted us to meet them out. Then, of course, Tuck and Hayes invited themselves when they found out.

They'd been texting me nonstop since our family dinner. I knew they suspected something, so I told them the truth.

I was surprised at how supportive they were, but then again, they were my brothers. I trusted them with my life.

I looked up from my phone when I heard the bedroom door creak open. Harlow stepped out wearing a black dress that was so short I was afraid if she sneezed, the dress would go all Marilyn Monroe on her and there wouldn't be much left to the imagination.

I was tempted to have all her designer clothes boxed up and sent back to the city.

My gaze lingered as I scanned down her body and then back up to her face. "Your dress shows too much leg."

"Really?" She breezed past me, finishing pushing her hoop earring through her earlobe. "I didn't think it showed enough."

"Harlow." I gave her a warning glare. "We are supposed to be engaged. That dress says, 'I'm single and ready to make your dick tingle.'"

She froze mid-step and gave me a look that made my balls shrivel up in my sac. "What exactly are you implying?"

I stood up. "I'm not implying anything. That dress, or lack of one, is nothing more than a piece of fabric pretending to be clothing."

Her eyes narrowed. "It's simply a dress. I don't care what you think. I will dress how I want."

I rubbed a hand over my face. The woman was going to get me in a damn fight tonight. "We are supposed to be convincing the whole town we're in love, not giving them a damn peep show."

She folded her arms across her chest. That little movement caused the dress to ride higher up her legs.

I cursed under my breath when she stepped closer. "You better watch it. And what do you care what I wear, anyway? This is all fake, remember?"

"Trust me, I remember," I grumbled. "That doesn't mean I'm okay with you walking around, giving men the green light to hit on you."

"Wait." She tilted her head. A smirk spread across her lips. "Are you jealous?"

"Don't be absurd. I just don't want the men in town to get a peek. If this is going to work, we don't need any unwanted eyes or attention on you."

I was so full of shit, and something told me she knew it, too.

Harlow stepped closer. I could smell her soft vanilla-scented perfume. "Would you be more comfortable if I put on a sweater and jeans?"

I'd feel better if she dressed like a nun.

I shrugged. "I won't stop you if you do."

She smiled like she knew exactly what I was thinking.

She brushed her hands along her hips. "You're ridiculous. It's not like I'm planning on dancing on top of the bar and doing body shots."

"The night is still young, princess."

"If you really want people to think we're in love, leave your grumpy attitude at the door."

She picked up her purse and gave Diesel a pat on the head as she stepped onto the porch.

I wanted to argue with her, but she wasn't wrong. The truth was, she looked stunning—too pretty for her own good. My attitude wasn't solely about the dress. It was a reminder of where we stood. So, no matter how badly I physically wanted her, I couldn't act on it.

Once upon a time, I could, but not anymore.

"Don't forget, you're wearing my ring on your finger. Keep that in mind when guys start flirting with you."

"Please." She rolled her eyes. "No one is going to flirt with me. You have possessive fiancé written all over you."

I hated it when she was right.

THE PUB WAS ALREADY PACKED by the time we got there. Thankfully, Tuck arrived early and secured us a booth in the back. This was the first time we'd been out in public since people found out about our engagement. I could already feel the weight of everyone's eyes on us.

Harlow walked in front of me as we weaved our way through the bar. A few guys stopped and stared. I couldn't blame them. It was hard not to.

Especially in that damn dress, which was probably illegal in some states.

I kept my glare in place and aimed it at anyone who I thought might try to approach her. It was taking everything in me to keep my hands to myself and not pull her into my chest, so everyone would know she was mine.

"Hey." Molly waved her hands in the air as we got closer.

Molly pulled Harlow into her arms as soon as she sat down. I nodded to Finn as he leaned back, drinking his beer.

The girls were whispering and laughing. I found myself relaxing for a little bit.

"Where is Hayes?" I asked Tuck, who was staring at his phone.

"Over at the pool table." He used his half-drunk beer bottle to point to our younger brother, who was smack in the middle of a group of pretty girls, showing off as usual.

Hayes was the life of the party. He'd always been like that. He thrived on attention, and judging by how the girls were giggling at his antics, I'd say he was getting plenty of it tonight.

I shook my head and turned to my buddy Finn. "The man has no shame."

"None," he said, as we watched my brother lean a little

too far over the table, trying to help some poor unsuspecting girl shoot the ball into the pocket.

"He's always liked playing it up for the crowd," I said, resting my arms on the cool wood table.

"He's putting on quite a show tonight. Gotta respect his determination." We both watched him dramatically line up a shot behind one of the girls. He was pretending to help, but Finn and I both knew what he was up to.

I shook my head. "He's trying too hard."

"He's been trying hard since middle school. The only difference now is he no longer wears his Hollister cologne." We both laughed.

I've known Finn my entire life. We grew up on the same street. Rode our bikes to school every day together. He taught me how to water ski, and I would let him copy my math homework.

When our family's construction business took off, we moved closer to the lake in an upscale neighborhood. My dad built my mom a bigger house in a quiet cul-de-sac. He'd come over for sleepovers in high school. We would sneak out of the basement window once my folks went to bed. Together we were trouble, but he was one of those friends you could trust with your life.

He was also married to Harlow's best friend, which made things complicated, and that was putting it mildly. He looked over where the girls were laughing a little loudly.

"You going to be nice tonight?" I asked, bumping his shoulder.

"My wife threatened me if I wasn't, so I'll try my best."

I laughed, but to be fair, he was there when everything blew up. He saw the worst of it, so I cut him some slack.

I laid my hand along the back of the seat. "Just be cordial, it shouldn't be that hard. If I can do it, so can you."

He tilted his head. "I am cordial."

"No, you look like you would rather eat nails than talk to her."

"I'm just in a sour mood." He grabbed a beer out of the bucket. "One of my guys quit, so I think I hit my limit today on how many hours my old ass can handle shoveling dirt and hauling trees around."

"You're only thirty," I pointed out.

"I feel ancient," he grumbled. "You wait. Two more months and you can join me in the thirty-and-older club."

"I'll be fine."

He squinted his eyes. "I don't know, dude, I saw the way you were stretching your back when you walked in."

I wanted to deny it, but the truth was that I'd been feeling a little off lately. I was pretty sure I pulled a muscle in my back while tearing up the warped floorboards of Harlow's house. We stopped by earlier today to meet with the plumber. I wanted to make sure they pumped all the water out. I only intended to drop off a few dehumidifiers, but I ended up doing a little more physical labor than I planned on. My back was sore, and I noticed my knees weren't bouncing back like they used to. Working in construction my entire life has caused a lot of wear and tear on my body. Thankfully, with my new role in the company, I would be spending more time in the office and less time hauling around heavy lumber.

I leaned over and tapped Harlow on the shoulder. "What do you want to drink?"

She paused her conversation with Molly. "I'll have a vodka with club soda, please."

Finn and I climbed out of the booth and went to the

packed bar to get our girls their drinks. As soon as we were alone, he started in.

"What's going on with you and Harlow?"

I frowned. "What do you mean?"

"Don't play dumb."

I pulled my wallet out and handed the bartender some cash. "I'm only playing the part of the attentive fiancé."

Finn and Molly were the only ones besides my brothers who knew it was fake, but they still didn't know the whole truth.

He leaned forward. "It looks like more than just an act to me."

"Maybe I'm really good at playing my part."

He rolled his eyes. "You're more worked up than usual. You're supposed to be having fun instead of glaring at every guy who looks her way."

My head was starting to hurt. "I am having fun, and I'm not glaring."

He laughed and held his hands up. "Okay, sure, and I'm Lebron James."

I leaned my elbow on the bar and glanced over to check on the girls. "It's all an act. Don't read too much into it."

Have I been tempted to touch her? Hell, yes. But I've reminded myself daily that this was nothing more than an arrangement, even though a growing part of me wished it were real.

"You're a terrible liar. And let's talk about that ring on her finger. That doesn't look fake to me."

I shifted uncomfortably. The weight of his stare was making it hard to stand still. "Good, then we're doing a fine job of convincing people it's real."

"You are such a moron sometimes. You're fake-engaged

to Harlow Bennett, of all people. That ring is not just for show."

"She picked it out."

His eyebrows shot up. "You took her ring shopping and let her pick out her ring?"

I grabbed the drinks off the bar. "Yeah, what's the big deal?"

He rubbed his jaw. "Are you serious? You're walking around town with her on your arm, pretending to be head over heels in love with a girl you claim to hate, all so she can get her house. What's in this for you?"

I looked around the bar, making sure no one else was listening. "I have my reasons. Trust me, okay?"

Finn raised an eyebrow. "Does this have anything to do with the investment banker you're talking with?"

Finn knew that I was looking to expand my business and invest in some new equipment so I could compete on bigger jobs. I didn't even deny it. We both knew how the game was played. I'd put too much work into bringing Dawson Construction to the next level. I would not let something as stupid as my relationship status get in the way.

My hand tightened around Harlow's drink. "I need the deal locked in."

He whistled. "Wow. I get it, man, I do, but it feels like you're playing with fire. I'm worried this whole thing will blow up in your face."

I ignored his piece of advice. I spent the last ten years busting my ass and proving to my dad that I could take over for him. Tuck didn't want anything to do with construction and was happy being the town hero. Hayes was too young and lacked experience. So, that left me. If marrying Harlow gave the investor the picture he wanted to see, I would play along and secure the deal.

I started pushing away from the bar. "I'm not an idiot. I know what I'm walking into."

He pulled on my elbow, stopping me. "I know you're trying to do what's best for the business. I don't want you to get too comfortable. Tread carefully. Things could get even messier than they are now. If things go south, your business will not be the only one to suffer."

I sighed while balancing the drinks in my hand. "This isn't solely about the investors. Marty isn't doing so great."

His eyes squinted. "How bad?"

I lowered my voice while trying to keep it loud enough for him to hear me over the noise. "The doctors said he has a year, if he's lucky. He's always loved Harlow and thought she was the one for me. I want to give him something to look forward to."

Finn clucked his tongue. "Damn, that's heavy, dude."

I nodded. "It is."

He stared at me for a minute. "I had no idea Marty was that bad. I respect what you're trying to do, but please be careful. This isn't just about Marty and the investor."

I patted him on the shoulder. "Thanks for your wisdom, brother. I know what I'm doing."

I started to walk back to the table when he pulled on my arm again. "So what happens when this is all over? When the investors are happy and Marty is well, you know..."

I didn't give him an answer because I didn't have one.

CHAPTER FOURTEEN
HARLOW

"Okay, now that we are alone, tell me what the hell is going on with you two." Molly said, closing the bathroom door and sliding the lock in place.

I spun around and grabbed one of the paper towels from the dispenser. "You already what's going on. Brooks and I are engaged."

She grinned. "I thought you were 'fake' engaged."

I rolled my eyes. "Nothing has changed between us. It's all for show."

She stepped up next to me and propped her hip against the sink. "So, are you saying that you feel absolutely nothing for him?"

I sighed, knowing I wouldn't get out of this conversation without giving her something.

"My feelings for Brooks are complicated. You know that."

You would think, after all these years, I would be over him and that he would somehow manage to forgive me. But I've come to the conclusion that there was too much anger and resentment on his end.

She stared at my reflection in the mirror. "I think it's kind of romantic that he stood up to your dad for you."

I scoffed. "He did it because he can't help himself."

Her eyes softened. "No. He did it because he still cares about you."

I wish she would stop putting ideas in my head. The last thing I needed was to get my hopes up.

"It doesn't mean anything."

She crossed her arms and tilted her head to the side, like I was in some type of denial. "Come on, Harlow. You're not stupid. When is the last time someone went to bat for you like he did?"

"He has his own reasons for doing this."

Her eyebrows shot up. "I don't care what other reasons he has. He could have helped you find a rental. He could have told you to call someone else, but he didn't. Why do you think that is?"

"I don't know. Maybe he felt pressured, or sorry for me because I had nowhere else to go," I said, even though my logic was weak.

Molly scoffed. "Brooks Dawson doesn't do anything he doesn't want to do. You know that."

She was impossible. Even if there was some truth to her words, it wouldn't change anything.

"Molly, I'm trying to be realistic about this. You and I both know I never stopped loving him. If I could go back in time and fix my mistakes, I would in a heartbeat, but he doesn't love me like that anymore."

"Okay, fine, believe whatever you want to believe. But I can assure you on everything I own that you are wrong."

I stepped toward the door, thankful that she wasn't going to push any further. "Can we get back out there now before your husband comes looking for us? I'm already on his bad side."

She looped her arm through mine. "I think he's softening up toward you."

I laughed and gave her a side-eye. "Now, who is the one who is full of shit?"

I swung the bathroom door open as Molly fell into step beside me. We pushed our way through the crowd just as "Man I Feel Like a Woman" by Shania Twain started playing.

Molly nudged me with her elbow. "I love this song. Want to dance?"

I glanced down at the dress that I spent all day fussing over. When I picked it out, my only thought was getting Brooks to notice me. Dancing had never crossed my mind. Now, I wish I had worn something longer.

"Sure."

The dance floor was small, so there wasn't a lot of room to move around, but everyone seemed to be enjoying themselves. Molly and I found a spot and allowed our hips to move to the beat of the music. I closed my eyes for a second, feeling the hem of my dress ride up my leg. I had to keep fighting the urge to tug it down.

There was a guy off to the side who caught my eye. He raised his glass and smiled, but I pulled my gaze away, not wanting to give him the wrong idea.

"It looks like you have an admirer." Molly grinned. I should have known she would pick up on it. She didn't miss a thing.

"He's just being friendly," I said, looking over her shoulder. To my horror, the guy started walking my way. He had a confident swagger as he cut through the crowd. He was cute, but I wasn't interested. My life already had enough drama.

"Hello, there," he said, his voice loud enough to carry over the music. "Mind if I join you?"

Before I could answer, Molly cut in. "She doesn't mind at all. I actually need to check in with my husband. Do you think you could keep her company for a minute?"

The man looked happy to be of service. "Of course."

I shot her a glare, but she just winked back at me as she walked away. I was going to kill her.

This woman was not the sweet, shy Molly I grew up with. This new version of her was the exact opposite of how she used to be. Since she's been with Finn, she's changed. She was more confident and assertive, more like I used to be.

"I'm Danny." He held his hand out, leaving me no choice but to take it.

"Harlow." I glanced over at the table, where I could feel Brooks watching me. His jaw clenched, and his eyes narrowed into slits.

"Can I buy you a drink?" Danny asked, completely clueless about my lack of interest.

"I'm fine, thank you, though."

He started to inch closer, so I took that as my cue to back away. "It was nice meeting you, but I should get back to my table."

"Why are you leaving so soon? You got somebody waiting for you?"

"As a matter of fact, she does, Danny," said the deep voice from behind me.

I turned to see Brooks standing there. His expression remained calm, but his eyes practically dared the man to take one step closer.

Danny hesitated, glancing between the two of us. He raised his hand in mock surrender. "Sorry, boss. I didn't know she was with you."

Brooks swung a hand along my waist, pulling me against his chest. "Danny, I'd like you to meet my fiancée, Harlow."

He looked at my left finger and started to squirm. "I had no idea, boss. Congratulations." He started backing away like he couldn't get out of here fast enough. "Sorry for the misunderstanding."

Brooks lifted my hand and ran his thumb over my ring. "Did you miss this rock on her finger?"

The poor guy looked one second away from wetting himself.

"Yeah, it's pretty dark in here." He looked around as if searching for an excuse to leave.

"Ahh, that explains it."

Danny swallowed nervously. "Congrats on the engagement. I need to go make a call."

He gave us a slight nod and slinked away into the crowd.

I spun around when he disappeared. "You didn't need to scare him off. I was handling it."

He crossed his arms. "It didn't look like it to me."

"He was just being friendly."

His eyes squinted under the low lighting. "He can go be friendly somewhere else."

Every inch of him was coiled tight.

I stared at him. "Are you jealous?"

"No," he said way too quickly. His jaw tightened, and I couldn't help but grin.

I trailed my fingers up his shirt, teasing the edge of his collar. "You are."

He frowned at my hand, and somehow that made me feel less annoyed.

"Harlow, don't."

"Don't what?" I teased, stepping closer. My conversation with Molly now played on repeat in my brain. Maybe she was on to something, or maybe it was the vodka.

"Don't get any ideas in your head." His eyes flicked to my mouth.

For a guy who was pretending not to care, he sure was doing a terrible job at convincing me he didn't feel anything.

I tilted my face up to his. "You really think I don't see how your jaw clenches every time another man looks at me?"

He didn't answer me right away, but with the way his gaze burned into mine, I knew I had my answer. He didn't need to say anything; the confirmation was written all over his face.

He shook his head. "You're being ridiculous."

"No, you are." I pushed on his chest. Not hard, but enough for him to get the point. If he wanted to glower like a caveman, he could at least do it from across the room. "This is fake, remember? You don't get to act like the jealous boyfriend."

He hauled me in by the wrist. "Fiancé."

"Fake Fiancé," I corrected. He's been sending me mixed signals all night. I was ready to lose my mind.

He closed the space between us and towered over me. "I figured you needed a reminder because you didn't seem to mind the attention when he was flirting with you."

He was the one who kept reminding me that this was only pretend. He was the one who asked me to come out tonight, and now he had the audacity to act jealous because some random stranger talked to me.

I rested my hand on his chest. "What does it matter? This is all for show, remember?"

The song changed to something slower. People started to walk off, but Brooks didn't move. His hand slid along my back, anchoring me to him. "Just because this is fake doesn't mean you can go messing around when you are supposed to be mine."

"Wait... what?" I tilted my head up to meet his gaze. "I barely said two words to the guy. I was about to leave when you came storming over, acting like a guard dog."

He gripped my waist. "You were going to let him touch you."

I yanked my wrist free. "I most certainly wasn't."

I barely said a word to the guy.

His jaw ticked. "Looked like it to me."

A short, humorous laugh escaped me. Not because it was funny, but because this entire situation was absurd. "I agreed to this arrangement, but I must have missed the part where you try to dictate what I do and who I talk to."

"That's not what I am doing."

"Then what are you doing?"

He exhaled sharply and rubbed a hand over his jaw. I followed his gaze, and sure enough, our friends and his brothers were watching. They weren't even trying to pretend that they weren't. They were outright staring and smiling.

"Let them think we just had our first lovers' quarrel."

I tilted my head up slightly, catching the sharp line of his jaw. "That wasn't really our first, though, was it?"

He glided his hand up to my face and leaned in.

"Probably won't be our last, either." Then his lips were on mine.

This was such an alpha move by him. I should have resisted. Instead, I opened wider and melted into him. We were supposed to put on a show and play our parts, but this felt like something else.

His thumb brushed my cheek, like it had every right to be there. My fingers gripped the front of his shirt as if it was the only way for me to stay upright. I kissed him back like I needed this connection as much as he did.

Brooks moved his hands into my hair and tilted my head. He was going to take what he wanted, and everyone was going to watch. There would be no more questions after this about who I belonged to.

His soft lips were eager as they moved across my jaw and down my neck. I wound my arms along his shoulders and pressed my body against his.

This was the type of kiss that thundered in your ears and turned you inside out.

He let out a low chuckle. "You were always sensitive there," he said, sinking his teeth into my bottom lip.

This was not an act. I don't care what he said. This moment wasn't about anything other than us. But I couldn't push him to admit that because then he would stop kissing me, and that was the very last thing I wanted.

Someone bumped into us from behind, startling us both. Our lips parted, yet his hand remained in my hair. My heart was in my throat as he stared back at me. "Just so we are clear, that was just for show."

He was such a liar. No matter how convincing he tried to sound, his face betrayed him. But he would rather swallow broken glass than admit how he truly felt.

"Are you sure about that?"

His gaze darted to my mouth. Yeah, that gave me all the confirmation I needed.

As if catching himself, he stepped back. "Harlow, don't go looking for trouble. You know what that kiss was about."

I swallowed hard. He was retreating. Pretending that the moment meant nothing. I could still taste him on my lips. Feel the warmth of his hands on my skin. Did he seriously plan to pretend the kiss meant nothing?

I forced my expression into something neutral. If he wanted to pretend, I'd let him.

"Well, then I guess the show is over." I turned and slipped through the crowd.

My chest tightened with every step I took away from him. The music grew louder. People were laughing and dancing without a care in the world. It felt like my heart had been cracked wide open.

It seemed foolish to hope, to think that there might still be something left between us after all this time. Maybe that was the case, but he had no intention of acting on it.

Knowing that didn't make it hurt any less, either.

CHAPTER FIFTEEN
BROOKS

The office was quiet except for the click of my computer keyboard and the occasional squeak of my chair. I rubbed the back of my neck, reviewing the numbers for an estimate I was working on.

The bid was due yesterday, but the numbers didn't make sense, and the labor hours were off. I was tempted to call the client and ask for an extension. I had to make sure everything was solid because I really wanted to land the project.

Right as I was double-checking the numbers for the cost of lumber, my office door swung open. I didn't need to look up; Hayes was the only one in the building who ignored the concept of knocking.

"Are you still working on that proposal?" he asked, leaning casually against the doorframe.

Couldn't he see that I was trying to get some damn work done?

I glanced up. "Your numbers were off."

He stepped inside, dropped his ass in the chair, and tossed his boots up on my desk. He crossed an ankle over his knee. I could see the soles of his boots were caked in mud. "My numbers were fine. They decided to add extra fixtures and more square footage."

I rubbed my jaw and scanned the spreadsheet in front of me. "Still wrong and their timeline needs to be adjusted, too."

He leaned back in his chair. "Do you want to be the bad guy and tell Mrs. Collins that her sunroom and kitchen remodel is going to take longer, and cost more than we originally quoted her?"

I glared at his feet. "Nope. You are. Now get your dirty boots off my desk."

Hayes smirked and kept his feet rooted in place. "You're getting a little uptight in your old age. Probably why I see a couple of gray hairs already."

I leaned forward and knocked his feet off. "You keep talking like that, and you'll be limping your way out of here."

"Relax, old man. You've got that big dinner tonight. You need to save all that charm for Clark Investments."

I sighed and dropped my pen on my desk. Richard Clark was the potential investor I'd been talking with for months. All our equipment was outdated, and I needed to purchase some state-of-the-art machinery if I had a chance to land the biggest project Marcellus Falls had ever seen.

Clark expressed interest in partnering with us. He had enough cash to lend me the money I needed, but Richard Clark was older than my grandfather. He preferred family-oriented business owners. He had very traditional values, focused on stability and reliability.

I'd been dodging his questions about my personal life, coming up with every excuse under the sun.

I might have lied and told him I was in a serious

relationship. He asked me a few times to bring my significant other to our dinners. I lied and came up with bullshit stories.

The old man wasn't stupid, and I was running out of excuses. Thank God Harlow came back into town when she did and agreed to this deal.

"Don't worry about the dinner tonight. I have everything under control."

"Oh, I'm not worried about the dinner. I'm more worried about you. After seeing you and Harlow on the dance floor last night and how you almost lost it when Danny talked to her, I'm starting to wonder if there is more going on than you've been telling us."

I shot him a warning look. "I didn't almost lose it. Whatever you think you saw was all for show."

I was such a liar and regretted that asshole move the second I kissed her. I wasn't the type of guy who claimed his territory and kissed a girl in front of everyone to prove a point.

But Harlow Bennet wasn't just anybody.

He coughed to cover up his laugh. "Dude, we both know you weren't thinking of Clark Investments when you had your tongue down her throat."

My younger brother had a way of getting under my skin.

"You need to get a life."

"Right, and what about scaring poor Danny away? The guy is petrified to come near you. The crew has a bet going on about how long it will take for him to quit."

"He's not going to quit," I said, picking up my pen and pretending to review the estimate again. Today was shaping up to be a shitty day, and it was only nine a.m.

After a few minutes, he was still there, smirking.

I pushed back in my chair. "Don't you have work to do?"

He laughed, not even trying to hide it this time. "Nah, this is more entertaining."

"Hayes," I warned. "Knock it off."

He rubbed his chin. "You know. You've been grumpy ever since she showed up in town."

"Can you please get out of my office?"

He slapped his knee. "Damn, you are a wreck over this girl. If you want to keep pretending that you feel nothing for her, then you're going to be in for a rude awakening when you realize the only person you're lying to is yourself."

"Get. Out."

He laughed, stood up, and headed toward the door. "Just be careful. I know this is for the business, but it's also Harlow."

I forced a casual shrug because he wasn't wrong. "I'm doing this for Marty, too."

Hayes' grin faded. "So, you're doing this for grandpa?"

I leaned back in my chair. "I want to make Marty happy, and we need this expansion if we want to compete in the market."

My dad and grandpa built this business from almost nothing. They trusted me to take over, and letting them down wasn't an option.

"There are other ways to make Marty happy. We can try to find another investor. You don't need to do this."

I stared at him, trying to figure out if I should be annoyed or grateful for his advice.

"I'm doing what I feel is best."

He nodded and turned to leave. "Good luck tonight. Let me know how it goes."

After he was gone, I stared at the estimate in my hands. Hayes wasn't wrong.

My grumpiness wasn't solely about the investors and Marty. It was about Harlow, too.

No matter how much I tried to deny it, she was under my skin, and that scared the hell out of me because I liked having her there.

CHAPTER SIXTEEN
BROOKS

Harlow was late—fifteen minutes, to be exact. I picked up my drink and sipped just enough to take the edge off. I needed to be sharp tonight. I needed to convince Richard Clark to invest in my business and believe that I was a man madly in love with his fiancée.

Which wouldn't be a complete lie, but we'll keep that between us.

I checked my watch and rolled my shoulders back, trying to shake the nerves and remind myself this was simply a dinner.

She'd been in the bathroom for the past hour while I paced my living room like a caged animal.

"You can come out any minute now," I yelled toward the bathroom door. "Dinner is in thirty minutes, not next week."

When the door swung open, every rational thought left my head.

She looked stunning. No, stunning wasn't even the right word. Harlow was the kind of beautiful that knocked the wind out of you. Her dark hair was curled in loose waves, spilling over her shoulders. Her black dress was sleek and form-fitting without being flashy. The neckline was modest, with a slight dip hinting at what was underneath. She turned to the side, glancing down at her dress, which was the epitome of class and elegance. I almost forgot how to breathe.

"Is this okay? I found it in one of the shops in town."

I should be talking. There should be words coming out of my mouth. Instead, I stared like an idiot.

"Do you not like it?" she asked when I still hadn't said anything.

"You look fine."

She snorted. "That's the best you can come up with?"

I clenched my jaw and looked away, refusing to let her see how badly she affected me.

"Fine, you look nice," I said, trying to sound normal.

She stepped closer. Her perfume wrapped around me, messing with my already frayed nerves.

She patted my chest like I was some grumpy cat that she found adorable. "Thank you. You clean up pretty good yourself."

I was wearing a crisp black suit with a gray and black striped tie. I hated the damn thing, but with the way her eyes dragged over me, slow and appreciative, I was glad I chose it.

I took one last sip of my drink. I needed to get my head on straight. I needed to focus, which would be easier if she wasn't so close, looking like something I couldn't touch.

She looked beautiful. She had always been. That wasn't the problem. The problem was, I was close to crossing a line. I shouldn't be thinking about crossing.

My focus should be on impressing the investor tonight, not pressing her against the nearest wall.

She smoothed a hand along her narrow waist. "You look nervous."

I set my glass down on the table. "I'm not nervous. I'm annoyed because we're running late. No thanks to you."

Her lips twisted. "You realize you're going to have to be nice to me tonight, right?"

"Trust me. I'll be as nice as you want, as long as you stick to the script."

She stepped closer, swaying her hips on purpose. "Relax, fiancé, everything is going to be fine, but you will need to stop looking at me like you want to strangle me."

"If it looks like I want to strangle you, it's because I do."

She laughed, completely unfazed at how easily she was making me come unglued. The little troublemaker leaned in and smoothed a hand along my chest in a way that was completely inappropriate. "Try not to be so uptight tonight."

I caught her wrist as it started to move up along my shoulder. "What do you think you're doing?"

She smirked. "I'm trying to help you loosen up."

"Harlow, I don't need you to make tonight any harder than it already is."

Her smirk widened. "Oh, but I enjoy making things 'hard' for you."

I narrowed my eyes. The girl was playing with fire. She was going to be the death of me. She'd always been a weakness. I didn't think that would ever change.

Tonight was going to be an absolute nightmare.

I pulled on the lapel of my suit coat and extended my hand. "Ready?"

She smiled up at me, tucking a loose strand of hair behind her ear. Her fingers casually trailed the delicate curve of her neck, making my mouth go dry. "Give me one second."

Harlow walked over to the mirror. Her eyes met mine, as if she knew exactly what I was thinking.

In case you were wondering, I wanted to tear that dress from her body and watch it hit the floor. I wanted to bury myself inside her and forget about this stupid dinner.

"You're staring."

I clutched my key fob in the palm of my hand like it was the only thing keeping me from making a bad decision. "I'm staring because I want to get this over with. The sooner, the better."

She rolled her lips together like she knew she had the upper hand. "Whatever you say, babe."

She grabbed her clutch and followed me out the door. Unfortunately, it was the front door, not my bedroom door, which was the one I wanted it to be.

I ADJUSTED the cuff of my suit jacket, letting out a nervous exhale as I scanned the restaurant.

I needed tonight to go perfectly. I'd spent the last six months working on this deal and convincing him that my company was worth investing in. While the numbers were good, he valued family more.

I spotted Richard Clark and his wife, Carol, sitting at a dimly lit table. Both were impeccably dressed and chatting with a server.

Tonight, could make or break my company's future.

Harlow looped her arm through mine as we crossed the room.

"You need to relax," she whispered. "You look like you're about to face a firing squad."

"Feels that way."

She squeezed my arm as we approached the table.

"Mr. and Mrs. Clark, thank you for taking the time to meet with us."

We shook hands, and I stepped aside. "This is my fiancée, Harlow Bennett."

"It's a pleasure to meet you both." She extended her hand across the table.

"The pleasure is all mine, dear." He chuckled, and I hated that I was so nervous. "I was starting to think Brooks made you up?"

There was a smile on her face as she glanced at me. "No one was more surprised than me when he asked me to marry him, but Brooks likes to take his time. If he commits to something, whether business or personal, he wants to make sure it's going to last."

I nodded in agreement, thankful she was such a natural at this. "That's always been my approach," I said smoothly, even though it felt like I was sweating bullets.

We took our seats, and I loosened my tie as we sat down.

"So, tell us about yourself, Harlow." Richard rested his chin in his hand. "We want to hear everything."

She picked up her water, swirling the ice around in her glass. "Brooks and I dated years ago when we were younger, but life happened, and we had to go our separate ways." She smiled lightly and paused like she was trying to figure out what to say next. "We recently reconnected, and well, I'll spare you all the little details, but here we are."

Carol's eyes lit up. "How romantic."

Harlow shrugged while I sat there wondering how she

could make such a simple sentence sound like the best love story they ever heard.

I sat there, half-listening and trying not to show how mesmerized I was that she was pulling this off so smoothly. Harlow answered every question perfectly and laughed at the right moments. She complimented Richard on his taste of red wine and managed to get Carol talking about her passion for traveling.

I watched it all unfold with a mixture of relief and something else. I knew she would be good at this, but she was doing better than I imagined.

Carol tilted her head to the side. "You two make such a lovely couple."

Harlow blushed. "Thank you. I can't wait to start making beautiful babies with him. I'm an only child, so I'm looking forward to filling the house with noise. There is nothing more special than family."

I choked on my wine and quickly brought my napkin up to my mouth.

Richard's laughter boomed across the table. "You might want to go easy on him. He looks like he's scared to death just thinking about it."

Harlow patted my back as my cough finally died down. "Oh, we've already talked about it. Isn't that right, honey?"

I played along. "I can't wait to get started."

Harlow was a natural, and I had a feeling that by the end of the night, the Clarks wouldn't be the only ones enamored with her.

"Do you have children?" she asked, keeping her attention on them.

Carol beamed. "Two boys and one girl. Actually, our eldest recently had a baby. We are officially grandparents."

Harlow gasped, clutching a hand to her heart. "Congratulations. Please tell me you have a picture."

Carol reached for her phone. "You bet I do."

She made them feel like they were the most important people in the room, and they were eating it up. I'd spent months trying to win Richard over, and ten minutes with Harlow, and she had him wrapped around her finger.

Harlow cooed over the baby pictures. "She is precious. I hope to have a girl someday, but I know Brooks would like a boy."

Mrs. Clark laughed. "Trust me, boys are ten times easier than girls, at least in my experience."

Harlow ordered a second glass of wine and placed her hand on my thigh. "I know Brooks is going to be a great dad, no matter what we have. I can already picture him running to the store at two a.m. for diapers."

I inclined my head, giving her a *what the fuck* look. She was starting to spiral a bit, and I was trying to keep my cool. This little show was going way off script, and I needed her to press the brakes. She caught my eye and shot me an innocent smile that said *you're welcome*.

The way I looked at it, I had two choices. I could either panic and make it obvious that this was all for show or follow her lead and roll with it.

Clark watched our exchange. "I have to admit, I was skeptical about the timing of all this. It made me wonder if you were just trying to secure the investment."

My back stiffened, but Harlow, thank God, didn't miss a beat. "I don't blame you. If you knew our history, though, you would understand. We were trying to keep things low-key until we were one-hundred percent certain this time around."

I wrapped my arm around her shoulder and played

along. "To be clear, I'm not that clever, but I get it. I would be skeptical too if I were in your shoes."

I didn't know if he was buying it, but he seemed to be holding on to every word.

"And while we are being completely honest, he does have an ulterior motive for wanting to secure this investment." My hand tightened on her shoulder. What the fuck was she doing? I wiped the sweat forming on my eyebrow as she continued. "He wants nothing more than to give me and his future children a good life. Being a good provider has always been important to him."

I reached for my water, nearly knocking the glass over. I was a jittery, nervous wreck. I had no idea how she was keeping a straight face.

When I caught sight of Richard's expression, I relaxed slightly. He was nodding along, buying it all—hook, line, and sinker.

"It's always good to see a man who is serious about his future."

I bit the inside of my cheek, thoroughly impressed with the woman, and was reminded of all the reasons why I fell in love with her in the first place.

Harlow was always charming and impossible to ignore. I could tell by Clark's expression that she had his full attention. In fact, I wasn't sure he even remembered I was sitting at the table. The conversation kept flowing, and whenever I tried to steer it toward business, Harlow would guide it back to something personal.

She had them engaged and laughing the entire time.

"Oh, I just love her." Carol patted Harlow's hand.

I rubbed a hand over my jaw. Maybe I could secure this deal after all.

I sat back, letting my arm brush against the back of her

chair. Harlow knew what she was doing. She was raised around people like Richard Clark. Maybe that was why she was such a natural.

When her gaze met mine. I watched her lips curve into a sly smile. I felt my pulse trip over itself. For a split second, I forgot about our arrangement, her house, and that this was supposed to be nothing more than a business deal. God help me, I wasn't sure how much longer I could keep pretending. Not if she kept looking at me like that.

Richard checked his watch. "This has been an enjoyable evening, but it's getting past my bedtime."

He shook my hand in a firm grip. "You've got a great girl here. Don't let her get away again."

"I'm not planning to. Unless she figures out she can do better." I winked, and dropped my gaze to her engagement ring.

Something was happening, shifting, and I knew she could feel it too.

After we paid the bill, we said our goodbyes and promised to touch base soon. When we parted ways at the door, I allowed Harlow to walk in front of me. I shoved my hands in my pockets as if it would stop me from doing something stupid like reaching for her.

This was the first time I allowed myself to feel something other than resentment. Tonight made me remember how easy it was to be with her, and I wondered how it would have been if I had fought harder for us.

When we reached my truck, I opened the door for her to hop in. She looked up, those big green eyes locked on mine. My fingers flexed around the handle. I was tempted to kiss her. Hell, I was tempted to do more than kiss her.

Tonight felt like a turning point, and I had no idea if I was ready for it.

CHAPTER SEVENTEEN
BROOKS

I peeled out of the parking lot and clamped my hand around the steering wheel. The sound of my tires rolling along the pavement was the only thing filling the silence between us.

My head was spinning from that dinner.

Her smile and her laughter and the way she charmed the Clarks was fresh in my mind.

She made me look good. She was convincing. She made it seem like I'd be the ideal husband. Surprisingly, I wasn't even pissed about it.

That part was messing with my head.

For the first time in five years, that anger I'd been holding on to wasn't as sharp tonight. Instead, something else was creeping in.

Gratitude.

I swallowed and pushed down on the gas as if I could somehow outrun my feelings.

"That went well, don't you think?"

I nodded in agreement. "It did, although you laid it on pretty thick tonight."

There was a smirk playing at the corner of her lips. "I think what you're trying to say is thank you."

I grinned, despite myself. "You did good tonight."

She crossed her legs and turned to me. "If I didn't know any better, I'd say that was a compliment."

I huffed out a low laugh. "Don't get used to it."

"I told you I could handle it."

"You did better than I expected. Thank you."

When I glanced over, there was no smirk or smile this time. She simply stared, and it made me uneasy.

"Did you really just say thank you?"

I rubbed the back of my neck. "I did."

I shifted in my seat as I rolled to the stoplight. The cab of my truck suddenly felt two sizes too small.

She glanced at me out of the corner of her eye, nervously fiddling with the hem of her dress. I could tell she had something on her mind. Her lips parted like she wanted to say something, but wasn't sure how.

I didn't want to push, but the silence was eating away at me. "Everything okay over there? You're being awfully quiet."

She chewed on her bottom lip as if she wasn't sure how to deal with me any more than I knew how to deal with her. "You're being nice to me."

She made it sound like it was a foreign concept. The guilt made my skin itch.

"Try not to make a big deal out of it, okay?"

A soft laugh escaped her. "That's kind of hard to do."

She wasn't wrong. Since I first came up with the brilliant idea to marry her, I've used my anger to hold this charade together. Keeping her at arm's length was the safest option, but I wasn't sure how much longer I'd be able to keep up the act.

Especially after tonight.

The light turned green, so I stepped on the gas and tried to ignore how she looked at me.

"You surprised me tonight, Brooks."

I arched an eyebrow. "How so?"

She folded her hands tightly in her lap. "Maybe you'll go back to being grumpy in the morning, but right now, it feels like you don't actually hate me."

I should have shut this conversation down. Found something else to talk about. Maybe remind her that this was nothing more than an arrangement, but I couldn't seem to find the words.

"Say something," she pleaded.

I sighed, running a hand over my jaw. "I told you before, I don't hate you, Harlow."

She blinked, like she couldn't believe I just admitted that. "I would understand if you did."

"I don't. I never could. It was easier to pretend that I did."

Harlow had no idea how broken I was after she left. No matter how much she tried to make up for it, the pain was buried too deep inside me to fully move beyond it.

She sat beside me, tapping her feet on the floormat. I wasn't sure if she even realized she was doing it.

I heard her sniff quietly. "You probably won't believe me when I say this, but the truth is, you were always there in the back of my mind. Being apart didn't make me love you any less; it only made it hurt more."

I exhaled slowly. "You can't say things like that."

"Why not? It's the truth. I'm tired of pretending that I don't feel anything when I feel everything."

I kept my eyes on the road while trying to steady my

heart. "I don't know how to do this with you, Harlow. You made me feel like I wasn't worth fighting for."

"I know. It's been my biggest regret."

I pulled the truck over to the side of the road and threw it into park so I could face her.

I shouldn't have stopped. I should have kept driving. I should have remembered all the reasons why we shouldn't be having this conversation.

Instead, my thumb reached out to trace the corner of her cheek. Harlow's skin was soft and familiar. I trailed my hand down to her jaw, tightening slightly and forcing her face toward mine.

Her breathing picked up, and it was hard to miss how her pupils dilated. "Brooks. Why are you looking at me like you want to kiss me?" she asked, sliding her hand up my arm.

This wasn't what I planned, but right now I didn't give a damn. I was already hanging on by a thread.

My grip on her jaw tightened. "What if I do?"

She didn't answer me; she simply moved as close as possible with the console between us. "Then maybe you should stop thinking so hard and do it."

I gripped the back of her head with one hand and lifted her across the seat with the other until there wasn't a single inch of space between us. I was done second-guessing. Done being afraid. No more fighting this.

I smashed my mouth against hers. These feelings have been bottled up for too long to keep fighting them.

She tightened her fingers in my hair and rocked her hips into mine like she needed more. The space was cramped, but we were both too starved for it to care.

She gasped into my mouth while I ran my hands along her sides like a man who had gotten a second chance and had no intention of wasting it. My tongue swept against hers, urging her on. The taste of her lips, the scent of her skin, and the way she moaned were driving me insane.

My hands continued to roam, like I was relearning her curves all over again. I wanted to feel every inch of her.

I dragged my lips from her mouth, tracing a path with my tongue along her jaw to that sensitive spot behind her ear. She let out a sharp hiss, and I smiled in satisfaction at how well she responded to me.

"Tell me to stop." I pleaded.

"No."

Before I could get another word out, her mouth was on mine again. We kissed for what felt like hours. We were both breathing so hard that the windows started to fog up.

Her palms skimmed over my shoulders. I reached my hand to the side of the seat to recline it back. There was no space between us. No hesitation. It was only her—just us. I groaned against her mouth. Harlow moved her fingers down my chest and untucked my dress shirt. The feeling of her nails grazing along my skin made my entire body shudder with need.

I'd been with other women since she left, but they were never her. Not even close.

Harlow made a soft, needy sound in the back of her throat. Every little moan that slipped out lit a fire inside me. All the years of loving her and missing her came rushing back. My hands framed her face as her tongue met mine, stroke for stroke.

We kissed in the dark like we were trying to make up for lost time. I could have kissed her forever. She was in my arms again, and nothing else mattered.

A car sped by, so I pulled back, needing a second to catch my breath. I held her face in a tight grip. She was a mess with wild hair and flushed cheeks, yet she was the kind of pretty that made time slow down. Her eyelids were heavy, her lips were swollen, and the ache in my pants was unbearable.

"Sorry, I shouldn't have done that," I rasped, sliding my hands along her shoulders. "Anyone could see us."

She smiled, soft and sweet, as she squeezed the bulge in my pants. "I don't care."

I jerked back. "What the hell are you doing?"

"I want to make you feel good."

I drew in a sharp breath. "Harlow, we are not doing this right now."

"Why not? I can feel how hard you are for me?"

That was true, but we had already crossed too many lines tonight.

"Sweetheart," I warned, but she didn't listen. I should have pushed her away. But when her fingers traveled to my zipper, slow and deliberate, every nerve in my body was on high alert.

This was dangerous and foolish, but I was a red-blooded male who was turned on like there was no tomorrow.

I gritted my teeth and forced myself to meet her eyes. "You don't have to do this."

The second I said the words, my dick hardened in defiance.

She shifted closer, bringing her mouth to my cheek. "I want to do this, so stop trying to talk me out of it."

I didn't think there was anything she would ask for that I wouldn't give her right now.

"This is reckless. I'm trying to be a gentleman here."

Her fingers traced a lazy pattern along my inner thigh. "You used to like reckless."

"That was a long time ago."

Why was she pushing me so hard? I only had so much control, and what little I had left was about to snap.

Her lips continued to tease the edge of my jaw. "You have no idea how much sleep I've lost because I can't stop thinking about what it would feel like to be back in your bed again."

Jesus.

"I don't know what was in that wine tonight, but you have no idea what you are saying. You will regret these words in the morning."

She only had two glasses of Merlot, so I had no idea what was spurring her on like this.

"I would never regret you." Her fingers fumbled with the button of my pants.

"Why are you doing this?"

"Because I'm afraid that come morning, you will go back to hating me again. If this is my one chance, I'm going for it."

She was making it so damn hard to deny her.

"Harlow…" I began, but she covered my mouth with her hand.

"Please, Brooks. I know what I'm doing. I know what I want, and it's you. It's always been you."

Without waiting another second, Harlow pulled my zipper down and reached inside. I hissed in a breath, nearly jumped out of my seat when her delicate fingers wrapped around me. She gave my length a good tug before circling her thumb along my head.

The woman knew what she was doing. She knew the type of control she had over me. Every little brush of her fingers was setting me off. I dropped my head back and shut my eyes. The feeling was too much.

Harlow tucked a strand of hair behind her ear and pulled me out all the way. Her hand squeezed hard, and the cutest little smirk I'd ever seen broke out across her face. I was tempted to kiss it off her, but when she tugged me harder, I put my hand on the back of her head and pushed down.

She laughed. The vibration wasn't helping. "Relax and let me make you feel good."

"You know I don't like being told what to do."

"You can boss me around when we get home."

You can boss me around when we get home.

I liked the sound of that. Not just the bossing around, but the word "home" coming from her lips.

When Harlow's lips licked their way up and down my shaft, I'd never been more thankful for living in the middle of nowhere before in my life.

"Fuck." I hissed in a breath when I hit the back of her throat. I lifted my hips while she worked her mouth and hands over my cock. My balls felt heavy when she took me deeper.

I gripped the steering wheel when she started making little noises. She was sexy as hell. Whatever restraint I had earlier was gone. I never stood a damn chance against her. "You're better at this than I remember."

Harlow didn't respond; she just kept sucking and tugging on my shaft like she had all the time in the world.

My hips jerked forward. "I'm not going to last."

She released me with a pop and stared up at me. "That's fine, as long as you save some for later."

Then she went back and swallowed me even deeper. Watching her head bob up and down and trying to keep my orgasm from spilling out of me was a losing battle.

Harlow moaned as her eager mouth continued to suck

me into the back of her throat, like she was savoring every single taste.

The woman had some type of magical tongue. She was making me see stars when there wasn't one in the sky.

I gripped the back of her hair, forcing her gaze on mine. "I'm going to make a mess."

Her lips curled into a smile. "I don't care."

She leaned forward and swept her tongue along my tip. I couldn't believe this was happening. We weren't just crossing a line, we were bulldozing right through it. I felt myself thickening in her palm. Her mouth was wet and perfect. I should have been worried about what would happen next, but my only thought was about how good this felt. We had been dancing around each other since she came back into town. She wasn't a random girl I was bringing home for a hookup. This was Harlow.

"Stop fighting this and give me what I want," she pleaded, swallowing me deeper.

I couldn't think. She felt too good.

I sensed myself veering toward the cliff.

"What do you want?" I panted out between breaths. This wasn't supposed to happen, but now that the switch had been flipped, I didn't want to turn it off.

"I want you to come down my throat."

My head fell back, and my eyelids fluttered closed. This wasn't solely about need. It was about all the years we lost and that fire that still burned between us.

My balls drew up, and I came hard. Harder than I'd come in a long time.

"Harlow," I managed to say as she continued to swallow every last drop. "That feels so good, baby."

Once she finished, she sat up and grinned. Her lips were

swollen, and she had a dazed, almost dreamy look in her eyes."That was incredible."

I grinned back, finally finding the strength to sit up. I stared up at the roof of my truck, feeling caught up in the aftermath of what we just did. We were both breathing hard. The world outside the truck was forgotten. I brushed the hair back from her cheek and kissed her forehead. "Yeah, it was."

A bright smile broke out on her face. "I always liked making you feel good."

I groaned against her mouth. "You went beyond that, baby. You wrecked me."

CHAPTER EIGHTEEN
HARLOW

Brooks pulled away from the curb. The inside of his truck was quiet, but there was so much noise in my head that I welcomed the silence.

I snuck a glance at him, gripping the steering wheel with both hands. His eyes were locked on the road, doing everything in his power not to look at me.

I leaned my head back against the seat. "You regret what happened, don't you?"

He shifted his weight and draped his hand over the console like he didn't know what to do with himself. "I'm pissed at myself for losing control. It feels like I took advantage of you."

I couldn't help but snort. "I'm the one who shoved my hand down your pants."

He shook his head with a half-smile on his lips. "You definitely caught me off guard."

My cheeks flushed. "I guess I got caught up in the moment."

Brooks tilted his head, just enough to look into my eyes. "And now?"

I held his gaze, trying to show him there was no regret on my end. "Now, I'm wondering why I waited so long to make the first move."

A low growl rumbled in his throat. "You keep saying stuff like that, and you'll find yourself in my bed tonight instead of the guestroom."

I shrugged. "Fine by me."

I caught the twitch in his jaw as he stared at me from the corner of his eye. "You need to stop talking like that. You have no idea what you're doing to me."

My smile was smug as I stared down at the bulge in his pants. "Oh, I have a pretty good idea."

"You're dangerous."

"So are you."

That made him laugh.

By the time we pulled up to the house, I should have been exhausted, but sleep was the last thing on my mind. "Are we going to talk about what happened tonight?"

He turned to face me fully. "I don't know what you want me to say."

"Why don't you tell me what you're thinking?"

He swallowed and curled his fingers in his lap. "I'm torn, Harlow. I've spent the last five years being angry at you because you left. You didn't choose me." He exhaled sharply. "But as time went on, I wasn't just mad at you. I was angry with myself. I let myself believe that our love was enough. That nothing could touch us."

I blinked hard against the sting in my eyes. "I'm sorry I broke us."

"I know. That's what makes it worse."

Silence stretched between us. I wasn't expecting to have this conversation tonight, but I needed him to see that I wasn't that same young, naive girl who left him. I needed to prove that I wasn't running this time.

"Brooks, I don't want to ignore what happened tonight and pretend that it didn't mean anything." He took slow, steady breaths while staring straight ahead. I saw him slowly begin to rebuild the wall between us, but I wouldn't let him shut me out again. "You don't need to say anything. I only need you to know that I meant every word I said tonight. Every touch meant something to me. I know we are supposed to be pretending, but this feels very real to me."

I sensed he wanted to fight it. Push me away and bury everything that happened. It didn't matter because for the first time since I returned to Marcellus Falls, I saw the boy I used to love. The one who made me feel like this place could be my forever home.

I reached over, lacing my fingers with his. He couldn't take his eyes off our clasped hands. The inner struggle on his face was hard to miss. A part of him still cared, but the other wasn't sure if he could trust me again.

Then, without a word, he let go, pushed the door open, and stepped out of the truck. He walked toward the house, and my heart sank into the pit of my stomach, but then suddenly, his feet halted, and he turned around. He strode over to my side of the truck and opened the door.

When he reached for my hand, I didn't even ask where we were going.

His grip was tight as we stepped inside the house. Diesel ran out to go to the bathroom. Once he was done, he grabbed my hand again and led me through the dark house. We didn't stop until we reached his bedroom. He shut the door before the dog could come in, and in one swift motion, he was crowding me against the wall.

My breath hitched. "What are we doing?"

His eyes searched mine, like he was looking for an answer to a question that he didn't know how to ask.

"Tell me again that you won't regret this in the morning."

I cupped his face as my eyes locked on his. "I could never regret you."

Before I could draw in my next breath, his lips were on mine, like he couldn't kiss me fast enough. My mouth moved against his, desperate and greedy. His hand moved to the back of my head, holding me tight and anchoring me to him.

His hand drifted to my face as he broke the kiss. "We don't have to do anything tonight. We've probably already gone too far."

Instead of answering him, I took his hand and led him to the bed.

"Brooks, please stop questioning it. We both want this to happen."

His hands slid down my side, gripping my hip like he was trying to keep me from disappearing again. "You drive me crazy."

I lifted my chin up, searching for his lips. "And you love it."

He groaned against my mouth. "You are right. I do. I love it too fucking much."

His hand slipped from my side to my lower back. He splayed his fingers out, pulling me closer. "You really want to cross this line?"

"I've done it before with you."

His thumb traced my bottom lip. "Do you have any idea how badly I want you?"

"I think I do, but I'd rather have you show me."

His hand drifted down my arms before he lifted me up and laid me on the mattress.

There was so much desire in his eyes that I wanted to melt.

I leaned up on my elbows and watched him struggle to remove his belt. He watched my expression while pushing his pants and boxers down his legs. I thought I was prepared for this, but I was wrong. Thick muscles and a six-pack that weren't as defined five years ago had me forgetting how to breathe. I swear, my lungs betrayed me. He had always been toned and muscular, but everything on his body seemed bigger.

And I meant everything.

A slow, lazy smile lifted his lips. "Harlow Bennet. Are you checking me out?"

"I forgot how well-endowed you were."

A laugh rumbled from his chest. "Were you not paying attention when you were giving me road head?"

"I was a little preoccupied."

Brooks put his hands behind his head. "Would you like me to keep standing here so you can keep staring?"

My eyes flickered from his eyes to his mouth and back up again.

"No. I would rather have you inside me instead."

He came toward me at a slow, deliberate pace, and planted one knee on the bed. The mattress dipped underneath his weight, but I couldn't move. He was so close I could see the flecks of gold in his eyes. His hand came up, and he brushed a strand of hair behind my ear. His knuckles were warm against my skin, but it wasn't just about the touch, it was about the emotion behind it. He leaned in slowly, like he was trying to memorize every little detail. His one hand slid to the back of my neck so that he could angle my face toward his. The kiss was soft and slow this time, like neither one of us had plans to stop.

My legs wrapped around him and I felt a low growl from his chest. His mouth trailed down my jaw, then to my neck. My entire body ached with need. Not just physically, but because I needed this connection to him. His teeth grazed along my shoulder, and he reached under my dress. I helped him shove the material up and over my head.

"God, I missed this," he said, pressing kisses across my collarbone.

I looked up as he undid the clasp of my bra and slid it down slowly.

His eyes were on mine, as if asking for permission. "Touch me, Brooks."

He dragged his hand to my breast and scraped his thumb across my nipple. "I'm going to erase his touch. I want him gone."

His tongue traced along my jaw and then down between my breasts. He pulled a nipple into his mouth, and I moaned when his teeth bit down. "I wish you were always mine. No one else's."

I rocked my hips into his. "I've always been yours."

Even when we were apart and I swore I was over him.

The tip of his erection slid up and down my center. "Do we need to use anything?"

I let out a moan as he kissed along my throat. "We've had enough years between us, we don't need anything else."

I've been on the pill for years to help regulate my periods, and I trusted him.

"Are you sure?"

"Brooks," I pleaded. "I am sure. Now stop talking. Don't make me beg."

His fingers moved to my clit. He added just the right amount of pressure. "Patience, baby." He slid his finger in and out of my opening before adding another one. "You are so wet and responsive."

I ran my hands along his biceps, loving how his muscles rippled under my touch. "That's because you're really good at this."

He laughed and braced himself above me. "And going forward, I'll be the only one doing this."

My fingers snaked up and gripped the back of his hair. "It's been a while for me, so I need you to go slow."

His gaze narrowed, as if trying to figure out what I meant. I hope he didn't ask because I wasn't ready to confess the truth.

Brooks pinned my arms above my head and laced our fingers together. "Tell me if it hurts too much."

I rolled my eyes. "Don't go getting cocky on me now."

"You used to love it when I was cocky." He exhaled against my jaw. I tried to bend my legs together to relieve some of the pressure, but he pushed them open. "Keep them open so I can see all of you."

My heart thumped wildly in my chest as he ran his fingers through my neatly trimmed pubic hair. "I love that you never shaved yourself bare."

I laughed. "What do you have against being fully waxed?"

"Not my thing. Never has been. I like knowing that you're all woman."

He ran his tip along my opening and slowly pushed himself inside. It was only an inch, possibly two, but I was already struggling to breathe. Brooks leaned forward, capturing my mouth with his as he seated himself all the way in.

"You feel so good," he said through gritted teeth.

I felt him everywhere as he took his time, allowing me to adjust to his size. He pushed deeper, taking more than before.

"Am I hurting you?"

It was painful, but not too bad. "It's worth it. Don't stop."

"I don't plan on it."

He drew his hips back and slammed inside. He was hard and deep, and I was gasping for air.

My eyes slid shut as he continued to push and circle into my warm heat.

"Keep your eyes open," he gritted out.

I moaned as his body took over mine. I was trying to hold on, but I was ready to combust at any second.

Every time he would slam forward, I would cry out. Stroke after stroke sent my heart soaring higher. The headboard thumped against the wall. Every thrust pushed me closer to the edge. Brooks picked up the pace as if he were chasing something that was just within his reach.

My nails cut into his skin as he continued to pound into me. I was gasping for air; the world around me no longer existed. It was just the two of us.

He bent forward, taking a nipple into his mouth and sucked hard. "I love watching you fall apart for me."

"Oh, God," I panted out, feeling my orgasm propel forward. It felt like he was trying to break me into a thousand pieces.

Brooks tossed my leg over his shoulder. The angle was deeper and more intense than I was prepared for. He trailed his mouth along my throat, licking and sucking while I thrashed beneath him. His hips moved faster as he continued to drive me higher and higher to the peak.

"Let go for me, baby," he hissed out and slammed his mouth into mine.

My hips shot forward, and then there was an explosion. The pressure and the release came pouring out of me.

I wanted to help him get there, so I squeezed tight around him and tugged hard on to his hair.

His entire body tensed, so I gripped him harder. His eyebrows pinched together, and he groaned loudly. "Oh, fuck!" He threw his head back and came in hot spurts.

He was warm, and I waited for his movements to slow before I finally let go of his hair.

Once he was finished, he sighed and dropped his face into the crook of my neck.

I wanted to say something, but I didn't know what to say, so I gave myself a minute to catch my breath.

I wanted to ask him what this meant, but I was too chicken shit to ask.

When he finally looked up at me, there was a smile on his face. "This wasn't supposed to happen but I'm not sorry that it did."

My thumb traced his bottom lip. "Me either."

We laid there tangled together, soaking up in the aftermath of what just happened. His arms were around me and my head was on his chest.

I spent years trying to find this type of connection with the man I was supposed to marry, but I never found it. Brooks was the only person who made me feel this way.

As I curled into his side, I was reminded of everything we lost and hoped and prayed with all I had that we could get it back.

CHAPTER NINETEEN
HARLOW

I blinked my eyes open. For a moment, I almost forgot where I was.

I rolled to the side to stretch my arms, and my eyes swept across the room.

There was a book on the nightstand, a flannel draped over the back of the chair, and the same alarm clock he had five years ago.

For a man who worked in construction, Brooks sure did keep a clean house. I'd peeked in this room a few times while roaming the house. It was neat and had character, unlike my apartment in Manhattan, which was more like a furniture store showroom than a home.

This is what a home should feel like, but it wasn't just this house or even the man who lived here. Life in this town was simple. People cared for each other. I never felt that type of connection in New York, maybe because the city moved at a frenetic pace and people were always too busy to slow down. The locals in this community took their time and treated each other like family.

The only thing I missed about living in the city was the

convenience. I loved the diverse cultures, the amazing food, and the shopping on Fifth Avenue. But being back here and waking up in Brooks' bed made me realize I missed this lifestyle more.

I slipped out of bed and grabbed the flannel off the back of the chair. I was in need of a shower and clean clothes, but first, I needed coffee.

When I entered the kitchen, he stood with his back to me, sipping his coffee while staring out the window. There was a fresh breeze, and you could hear the raindrops hitting the roof.

"Morning." I smiled and beelined for the Keurig machine.

Brooks turned, and for a brief second, I started to panic. Would he regret last night? Would he go back to treating me like the enemy? Would he insist on sticking to our rules?

My nervous fingers reached for the coffee cup next to the sink. I sensed him lingering behind me. My pulse picked up as he approached.

"Nice shirt."

I glanced over my shoulder, praying to God I would sound normal because sweet Jesus, he looked delicious. His chest was bare, outlining every muscle on his broad frame. His flimsy athletic shorts sat low on his hips, causing my mouth to go dry. His scruff was thicker today, and his hair was sticking up in places where it shouldn't have been, thanks to my eager fingers last night.

I bit my lip, tempted to drag him back to the bedroom. "Wish I could say the same for you."

He shot me a smirk. "I was being a gentleman and saving my shirt for you."

I rolled my eyes. "Sure, you were."

He surprised me when he wrapped his arm around my

waist, pulling my back to his front. "Are you hungry?" he asked, trailing his finger along my neck. "I can cook something."

I expected awkwardness, not breakfast.

"I could eat," I sputtered when his hand moved up to the underside of my breast. His calloused thumb brushed along my nipple. A small moan slipped out, and he spun me around in his arms to face him.

"So, about last night." He hesitated. "I want to make sure you are okay with what happened."

My eyebrows bent together. "I thought we already went over this."

He rested his forehead against mine. "I'm not just talking about the sex," he said carefully. "You recently got out of a relationship. And things are moving fast. All I'm saying is, we can slow down if you want to."

I studied him. He was really worried. "You still don't get it, do you?"

He frowned. "Get what?"

"I wasn't in a relationship with Baz. What we had wasn't real. It was strictly business. Nothing more."

His jaw flexed. "You were still technically his."

I reached up and slid my fingers into his messy hair. "No, I wasn't, because I've always been yours."

He closed his eyes for a half-second, breathing in deeply like he was trying to control himself.

I slid my hands down his bare chest. "I think deep down, I always knew that I would come back to you."

He opened his eyes. They were dark and smoldering. "You keep talking like that, and I won't be responsible for what happens next."

"Good, because I don't want responsible. I want wild and reckless. I want you, Brooks Dawson, only you."

His mouth met mine in a claiming kiss. I wanted to savor the moment and lose myself in him over and over again. I glided my hands up his chest and wrapped my arms around his neck. I could kiss him all day long until our lips were bruised and swollen, and it still wouldn't be enough.

He pulled back, keeping his hands on my waist. "You are never leaving me again."

My stomach rumbled, and I laughed against his chest. "If you don't feed me soon, I might have to leave and go grab some food."

The edges of his eyes crinkled. "I only offered to cook for you. I never said anything about feeding you."

I smacked his shoulder playfully. "Jerk."

"Have a seat at the counter while I fix us both some breakfast."

Glancing outside, I frowned. "Is it supposed to rain all day?"

It looked like it was coming down pretty steadily.

"It's supposed to clear up this afternoon. Why? Did you have any big plans?"

I watched him move around the kitchen with ease. He seemed lighter today and more relaxed.

I took a sip of my coffee. "I need to head to the lake house."

I wanted to do some cleanup today, but the rain was making me sleepy. I wouldn't mind crawling back under the covers and staying in bed all day.

"I can give you a lift," he said, cracking an egg into the frying pan.

"Are you sure you don't mind?"

"Nope," he said, grabbing the bagels out of the fridge.

I glanced around the kitchen. "Where's Diesel?"

He held the spatula in the air and pointed to the front

door. "He loves the rain. I checked on him a few minutes ago. He was sound asleep on the porch."

"Ahh, okay. I can bring him with me today if you want to get some stuff done."

I had no idea what his plans were, but I didn't want him to feel obligated to babysit me if he had things to do.

He sipped his coffee. "I planned on stopping by to see Marty. Do you want to come?"

I haven't seen Brooks' grandfather in forever. I always liked him.

"Do you think he would be okay with it?"

"I think he would love to see you."

"Then I'll go." I smiled and stole a piece of bacon off the platter. It had been a long time since I'd been this content. I only wished I knew where we stood.

I watched him tend to the eggs on the stove, wondering what would happen now. This playful side to him was throwing me off. Things between us haven't exactly been smooth. It would be stupid to think that last night magically fixed everything.

I shifted on the stool and clutched the mug in my hand. "You always were a breakfast person, unlike me, who could survive on coffee until noon."

He wiped his hands off on the towel. "I remember. That's why I wanted to make sure you ate something."

He set a plate in front of me before grabbing his own.

As we were about to dig in, a loud, wet barking furball rushed into the kitchen. Diesel barreled straight toward me. I yelped as he shook his body, spraying water all over my bare legs.

"Good morning to you, too." I laughed when he started licking my face.

"Well, isn't this cozy?" I turned to see Hayes in the

doorway. He had a mischievous glint in his eyes as he alternated his stare between his brother and me. I lifted my hand and waved.

"And what exactly do we have here?" he drawled, pushing his wet hair off his forehead. "Is that my brother's shirt?"

Kill me now. I knew I should have stayed in bed.

"Don't you ever knock?" Brooks snapped and handed me a towel to dry my legs off.

"That wasn't my question," he said, unzipping his hoodie and folding his arms.

Brooks pinched the bridge of his nose. "It's none of your business."

Hayes let out a slow whistle. "Damn, I was only stopping by for coffee. I didn't realize I was interrupting..."

"Do not finish that sentence." Brooks pointed to him in warning.

Hayes threw his hands up. "For a man who looks like he got lucky last night, you sure are grumpy this morning."

I groaned, shaking my head. "You are the worst, Hayes."

"I know." He winked and sauntered over to the Keurig machine to fix himself a cup of coffee.

"Make yourself at home. Why don't you?" Brooks sat down and scowled at his brother.

He leaned against the counter. "Don't mind me. You two kids can continue doing what you were doing."

Brooks glared at Hayes. "I hope Diesel shits in your shoe."

Hayes pulled up a chair and flopped down beside me. "Wow, that's mean."

"Is it?" Brooks said casually, "Or is it karma?"

I was trying not to laugh, but Hayes could be relentless and loved to poke fun at his brother.

Hayes nudged me in the elbow. "He's being very hostile, are you sure he's not holding you here against your will? Blink twice if you need me to rescue you."

I glanced over at Brooks. "This is your punishment for not locking the door after letting the dog out."

"I shouldn't have to lock my damn door." Brooks picked up his phone to check the time. "Hayes, don't you have stuff to do today?"

Hayes took a long, satisfying sip of his coffee. "Funny you should mention that." He took a treat out of the jar and snuck one to Diesel. "I got a hot date tonight."

Brooks looked at his brother. "Who is the poor, unfortunate woman?"

Hayes raised an eyebrow. "Wouldn't you like to know?"

Brooks shook his head. "It's probably someone he swiped right on."

I picked up my breakfast sandwich. "I hope she knows what she's getting herself into."

"I'll have you both know, I did not meet her on a dating app. Her name is Valerie, and she works the smoothie station at the gym."

"Where are you taking her tonight?" I asked.

"She wants to do some paint and wine thing."

Brooks' coffee mug paused on the way to his mouth. "You hate wine."

He shrugged. "Val is a smoke show. I can suck it up for one night."

I snorted into my coffee. "Does she know it's only going to be one date?"

Hayes looked amused. "Of course not."

Poor Val. Hayes was a charmer and a notorious flirt. Even as a teenager, he was known to be the town heartbreaker. Women got swept away with his pretty boy face and smooth pickup lines. He always had a revolving door of women coming in and out of his life. One of these days, he was going to meet his match, and I hoped I would be around to witness it.

I reached for the cream to add more to my coffee. "I feel bad for the poor girl. She has no idea what she is signing up for."

He threw a hand over his heart. "Are you two ganging up on me now?" He leaned back in his chair, clearly enjoying this. "That's okay. I'm a big boy, I can take it, but enough about me. What's on the agenda today for you two lovebirds?"

"We are going to see Marty," Brooks said, taking a bite of his sandwich.

Hayes nodded. "Good. It will make the old man happy. Are you going to share your good news with him?" he asked, pointing to the engagement ring on my finger.

Brooks picked up his coffee and took a sip. "That's the plan."

"You seem a little bored today. Would you like to join us?" I asked, holding up my plate of food and offering him some.

He snatched up a piece of bacon and popped it into his mouth. "I would love to, but I'm headed to the office for a few hours, and then I need to rest up for my hot date later."

Brooks wiped his mouth with his napkin. "We are going to stop by Harlow's house for a few hours. Do you know when the materials I ordered will be in?"

"They should be here next week." He set his mug down and stood up. "All right, lovebirds, I'm out of here. Try not to have too much fun with Grandpa today."

Brooks stood up and walked his brother toward the door. "Next time, call before dropping by, yeah?"

Hayes looked amused. "So, does this mean you two are an actual couple again?"

Brooks shoved him. "Bye, Hayes. Good luck with your date tonight."

He chuckled, waved over his shoulder, and disappeared outside.

Once he was gone, I glanced at Brooks, who was rubbing his temples.

"You know he's never going to shut up about this, right?"

"Unfortunately."

I took another bite of my sandwich and brought my dish to the sink. "I should probably start getting ready."

Brooks watched me for a moment. Then, without warning, he leaned over, pressed the sweetest kiss on my forehead, and walked away.

My mind raced, trying to piece together all that had happened in the last twenty-four hours. We'd crossed so many boundaries, more than either of us intended to.

I always wondered what it would be like to have him in my life again. The intimacy we shared last night was better than I imagined. My heart knew he was it for me. He would always be the one for me. I had a sinking suspicion that he needed more time to accept me back into his heart, but after last night, I finally had hope.

CHAPTER TWENTY
BROOKS

Pulling into the parking lot of Sunnybrook Assisted Living, I killed the engine and glanced at Harlow.

"This is not what I expected." She leaned forward in her seat and pushed her sunglasses on top of her head.

I laughed. "They have a farmers' market every weekend. It's an ongoing joke with Marty, he thinks I only come for the pies."

"How is he doing?"

"Slowing down, but personality-wise, he's as spunky as ever."

She's only been back for a couple of weeks, and I was already getting used to having her around. Marty, on the other hand, had probably been waiting for this moment forever.

"Ready?" I asked, grabbing the umbrella from the back in case it started raining again, and stepped out of my truck.

She nodded while watching the two old ladies bickering over who had the best hand-knitted blankets.

We stepped up to the courtyard, which had been

transformed into a bustling market. The folding tables were covered with baked goods, crafts, a few CBD oils, and homemade pot gummies.

"Oh, my God. That lady has a cannabis stand."

"Yep, and Ms. Romano sells out fast, so if you're looking for any oils or creams, you better hurry over there."

She laughed. "Is it always like this?"

We weaved through the crowd as a man in a wheelchair whizzed past us, holding a big jar of raspberry jam.

"These residents can get a little wild. Last month, a fight broke out during bingo. Mr. Spears accused Pastor Daniel of cheating."

She snorted. "Who won?"

"I think it was Pastor Daniel. He used to be a marine. Pretty sure he could kick my ass if he wanted to."

We made our way through all the baked goods and knitwear until we reached the end of the sidewalk. Marty's stand was on the corner. His table was stacked with wooden frames, wall shelves, and miscellaneous engraved items.

When he looked up and saw the beautiful woman at my side, his entire face lit up.

"Well, I'll be damned." He shoved his glasses up the bridge of his nose. "Harlow Bennett. Get over here and give an old man a hug, will ya?"

She laughed as he tossed the newspaper aside. He wrapped her in a tight hug. "Hey, Marty, you haven't changed a bit."

He held her out at arm's length. His eyes filled with warmth. He was clearly happy to see her. "You look the same, only prettier."

Harlow blushed. My grandfather was on a roll. "You're looking great, Marty."

He puffed his chest out. "I know, right? Not too shabby for an old guy, huh?"

I shook my head and clasped him on the shoulder. "How are you doing, Grandpa?"

He knocked my hand away and scowled beneath his white mustache. "I told you not to call me that in public."

Harlow inspected the table and picked up one of the wooden frames. "Did you make all these?"

"Damn right, I did. You want that one, sweetie, you can have it."

Harlow ran her fingers over the frame. "Thank you, but I insist on paying you." He waved his hands in the air. "You will do no such thing. You are about to become family. Think of it as an engagement present."

I leaned back on my heels. I should have known we couldn't surprise him. "Who told you?"

"I have connections everywhere." He grabbed Harlow's hand to see the ring better. "You really thought you could keep that kind of scoop under wraps? This town isn't that big. News travels fast. Especially good news." He winked. My grandfather was clearly happy about the news. It made me feel slightly guilty for lying to him, but then I remembered that was the plan.

"We were hoping to surprise you, that's all." Harlow beamed up at me.

"So, what in the world made you decide to come back and marry my idiot grandson? I thought you had more sense than that."

I groaned. "We talked about this, remember? You promised to be on your best behavior."

Marty squinted his eyes. "You talked, and I pretended to listen."

Harlow smiled warmly. "Glad to see you haven't lost your sense of humor."

"That's what keeps me young." He settled back in his chair. "So, tell me about the wedding."

I threw an arm around her shoulder. "We haven't set a date yet."

"Why the hell not?"

I scrubbed a hand down my face. "We are working on it, okay? And when we settle on something. You'll be the first to know."

"Make sure you do. I've had some of the ladies in the cafeteria asking me when the wedding is. They are all fighting over who I'll take as my date. Unless you can give me a plus two or three?"

Guess we knew where Hayes got his rep from. I shook my head as he and Harlow got caught up.

While they talked, I took a few minutes to study him. His sense of humor was still intact, but his energy level wasn't there today. He's always been a tough old man who insisted on doing everything himself, especially when he shouldn't.

I watched him sink into his chair and noticed he seemed more tired than usual. His skin was pale, and the lines on his weathered face were more pronounced. I also noticed his hands were shaking more than the last time. It was hard to believe this was the same man who taught me how to build a shed in the backyard, work with my hands, and be a man.

He looked up when he caught me staring. "What?"

I crossed my arms. "You seem tired."

"And you look like a man who doesn't know how to use a damn razor."

Instead of coming up with a snappy retort, I changed

the subject, sensing he wasn't in the mood to talk about his illness. Harlow, being Harlow, picked up on it. I could see the question and curiosity in her eyes. I gave her a subtle shake of my head, telling her I would explain later.

My grandfather didn't like talking about anything too serious. He didn't want people fussing over him. I let him guide the conversation away from what was really going on with him. Even when he tried his best to act like everything was okay, I could tell he was fighting like hell to keep his energy up.

We sat and talked for the next thirty minutes. A handful of customers stopped by Marty's stand, so Harlow and I excused ourselves to browse the market.

"Are you going to tell me what's going on with him?" she asked, picking up a scented candle and bringing it to her nose.

I shoved my hands in my pockets and looked up at the gray sky. It looked like the rain would start back up again soon. "I'll tell you about it later."

After grabbing a coffee and a box of cinnamon rolls, we stepped up to Betty Sherman's table. She and my grandfather went at it on a daily basis. The rumor going around was that she used to be a con artist, swindling old men out of their money. Marty never trusted her.

Harlow picked up a knitted scarf. "This is so pretty. How much is this?"

Betty beamed. "Well, you're in luck, sweetheart. That piece is on sale for twenty-five dollars."

I scoffed. "Betty, I've seen you sell those for ten."

Hell, she even tried to give me one for free one time.

She shrugged. "Supply and demand, kid. Your girl here has good taste."

Harlow reached into her purse, but I beat her to it. I handed Betty thirty bucks. "Keep the change."

"You are such a sweet boy." She stuffed the money into her fanny pouch with a satisfied grin.

Marty came over and sidled up next to Harlow. "You're not over here scamming my future granddaughter, now are you, Betty?"

"Oh, Marty, don't be ridiculous. I only had to charge a little bit extra because of inflation. My yarn costs me almost a whole dollar more."

Marty pulled on his suspenders. "Inflation, my foot. You've been swindling people since Gerald Ford was president."

Betty gave him a smile that didn't even come close to looking sweet. Then she pulled out a wad of bills and started fanning her face with them. "That scarf took me hours to make. You don't expect me to give my stuff away for free, do you?"

"Your stuff is garbage. I wouldn't pay more than five bucks."

She huffed. "You have horrible taste. Don't you ever wonder why no one wants the ugly crap you try to sell?"

"All right, you two." I settled my hand on Marty's shoulder and started steering him away from Betty's table. "I think we should start moving on down the line. There is an apple pie calling my name."

Marty wagged his wrinkled finger at Betty one last time. "I'm watching you."

As we walked away, Harlow dropped her scarf around her neck. "That was entertaining."

Marty grinned. "Stick with me, darlin'. This place is better than Netflix. Why don't we head inside? I need to take my meds."

Marty's voice sounded tired despite the brave front he was putting on.

We made our way down the hall, past bulletin boards filled with the week's events. I opened Marty's door, letting him shuffle in first, then stepped to the side for Harlow.

Marty's space was simple. It had a bed, two small recliners, a TV that only seemed to play game shows and the news, and a small kitchenette. The walls were covered in photos.

Harlow hesitated for a second before settling into the chair next to my grandfather. I stood by the window with my hands shoved in my pockets.

He took his meds and kicked the stand out on the recliner to get comfortable.

He sighed and looked between the two of us. "It took you both long enough."

I looked at Harlow and smirked. "I had to make sure she wasn't going to run off this time."

She smiled but there was nothing sweet about it. "And I needed to give you enough time to grow a brain."

He grabbed the blanket off the back and laid it along his legs. He grinned up at Harlow. "I always liked you, you know."

Harlow laughed. "I always liked you, too."

Marty faced her. "I'm just glad you decided to come back before I ended up in the grave."

"Hey," I said. "Let's not go there, okay?"

My grandpa leaned his head against the recliner. I saw Harlow watch him. I could tell she was just noticing how thin and weak he was.

He closed his eyes briefly. "You never want to talk about it, Brooks. You want to keep pretending that I'm not sick.

My time on this earth is coming to an end, and no amount of avoiding it is going to change that."

She turned to me, eyes narrowing slightly. "What is he talking about?"

Grandpa cracked an eye open. "You haven't told her?"

I rubbed a hand over my jaw, feeling like a total ass. "I was planning on it."

Harlow's gaze bounced between us. "Tell me what?"

He sighed. "I have cancer."

I clenched my jaw and swallowed down the lump in my throat. I hated that word. Hearing it always hit me hard.

Harlow's back stiffened. Her eyes filled with worry. You could tell she was trying to hide how much that news upset her. "What kind of cancer?"

"Lung cancer," he answered before I could.

She blinked rapidly. "How bad is it?"

"Stage four." His voice was softer now.

Her lips parted as she sat there staring at him. "I am so sorry. I had no idea."

"Because I didn't want you to find out like this," I told her, shooting my grandpa a glare.

For the first time since we got here, there were no jokes or teasing—just cold, hard truths.

He ran a hand over his knee. "I hope I live long enough to see the two of you get married."

I looked away, but I could feel her staring at me from the corner of my eye. Harlow was smart as a whip. She was no doubt connecting the dots. Did she realize that was one of the reasons why I asked her to marry me?

She knew how much I looked up to him. It was no secret that I would do anything to make him happy. Even making sure we got engaged before he died.

"Are they doing anything to treat the cancer?" she asked, adjusting the blanket over his body.

He gripped the arms of his chair. "The treatments are rough. Worse than I thought they would be. Being hooked up to those machines only makes me feel worse."

I forced a breath through my nose. "Why didn't you tell me you weren't feeling good?"

He leaned forward. "Because I know you don't want to hear it, and I don't want my family worrying about me. I'm fighting, doing the best I can. I don't want to be treated any differently."

Harlow leaned over and rested her hand on his arm. "You need to keep fighting. You have a wedding to go to."

His eyes were misty as he stared at her. "I'm going to do my best to be there."

Harlow swallowed tightly; I could tell she was fighting back emotion. "You better be there, because we are saving you a front row seat."

The affection between them was as clear as day. He held her hand like he didn't want to let go. "You remind me of my wife."

She smiled. "That's quite the compliment. I heard so much about her. I wish I had the chance to meet her."

My grandma passed away when I was ten. I don't remember much about her other than she was just as stubborn as he was.

I sat back and watched them. The way she leaned in and made him laugh, and the way he looked at her like she was already family. Something stirred in my chest.

I needed the wedding to happen before he died.

Not just for him, but for me, too.

She was it for me. She always had been.

My only problem would be convincing her to stay this time.

CHAPTER TWENTY-ONE
HARLOW

The rain was coming down hard as we pulled up to my house. Brooks grabbed my hand, and we bolted for the porch.

The wind picked up, howling so loudly that you could almost feel the windows rattle. *God, please don't let a tree fall on the house.* That was the last thing I needed.

I kicked the door closed behind us and shook the raindrops off my shirt.

The house smelled a little musty from being under construction, but somehow it still felt like home.

Brooks ran upstairs to grab a few towels.

"Here," he said, handing me one.

"Thanks." I started drying off my arms, hoping my body would warm up soon. It was one of those wet, gray days when the cold seeped into your bones. It would have been perfect if the fireplace was lit. A little bit of warmth would do me good right now.

Brooks rummaged through the cabinets. "Do you have anything besides pretzels and popcorn?"

I wrinkled my nose. "No. I only bought a few snacks for

when we were here working. I didn't plan on getting stuck here."

We were going to stop and grab a bite to eat on our way back, but when we saw how quickly the weather was changing, we decided to drive straight to the lake house because it was closer.

He glanced at the phone. "We are under a weather alert until midnight."

I kicked my socks and shoes off. "I should probably take a hot shower."

The house still lacked some finished walls and flooring, but at least the plumbing was fixed.

He looked out the window, where he could see the storm-fueled waves lap up over the dock. The water looked like it was ready to boil. "I've got a bag in my truck with a change of clothes. Why don't you hop in the shower first?"

I bounded upstairs and quickly peeled off my wet, heavy clothes. I had a few things in the closet, so I grabbed a sweatshirt and a pair of yoga pants.

As I bent over, searching for a pair of underwear, the floorboard creaked, and I turned to see Brooks standing in the doorway.

"Did you find what you were looking for?" I pointed to the black bag clutched tightly in his hands.

His brown eyes dragged over me as if he hadn't just seen me a few minutes ago. "Yeah."

It was then that I realized that I was standing in front of him, completely naked. My arms instinctively flew to my chest in an attempt to cover myself. His eyes moved over every inch of me. Goose bumps broke out along my skin that had nothing to do with the cold, wet weather outside.

I should have been embarrassed, but I wasn't. Not with the way he was looking at me.

He dropped his bag on the floor and moved forward.

"Sorry." I swallowed thickly. "I was about to hop in the shower."

His steps were slow and deliberate. "You have nothing to be sorry for," he said, slipping his hand along my waist and pulling me to his chest. I could feel every muscle, every beat of his heart against mine.

I threaded my fingers through his damp hair. "I think you need your eyes checked because I am a wet mess right now."

His hands cupped my cheeks, holding me still. I whimpered when he dipped his head and brushed his mouth along the shell of my ear. "I am about to get you even wetter."

I barely had time to react before his mouth was on mine. Whatever insecurities I had about him seeing me without clothes on faded away. Nothing beyond these walls existed. Brooks had a way of shutting off my brain, so all I focused on was him.

My body sagged against his as the kiss turned harder.

He moaned and moved his hand to my hair, keeping me right where he wanted me. This man was the only thing in the world that ever made sense to me. I loved him since I first laid eyes on him. The past few weeks have been nothing but a dream. I didn't deserve him. I never have.

His hand slid down my body, stopping at my core. "I could watch you like this forever."

A noise came from my throat as he pushed a finger inside. "Brooks."

I felt him harden against my belly. "You have no idea how perfect you look right now."

I gasped when he shoved another finger through my folds. My hips bucked forward as he dug deeper. His pace was slow and steady, but it still worked me into a frenzy. "Nothing compares to seeing you like this."

He dropped to his knees and planted his face right at my opening.

"Oh, God." I panted out and gripped my fingers into his shoulders. I rocked myself into him. I couldn't think. I couldn't talk. All I could do was pull his face into me. The storm outside was completely forgotten.

I was going to come from the flicks of his tongue and the touch of his hands alone.

My breathing picked up when he pressed his thumb to my clit and started sliding his tongue back and forth. I was sensitive everywhere. The pressure was almost too much.

"You're almost there, aren't you?" His grin was cocky, but I was too caught up in the sensations he was bringing me to say anything back.

My legs started to shake against his mouth when he latched on harder. I was seconds away from coming undone.

"You're even more beautiful when you lose control," he said, dragging his tongue along my skin. He increased the pressure, and I clenched around him. "That's it, baby, give me every last drop." My entire body shook as he continued to draw every ounce of pleasure I had until there was nothing left to give.

I sagged against the wall, needing a minute to catch my breath. Brooks stood, a smile breaking out across his face.

I couldn't believe this beautiful man was mine again.

He grabbed me by the waist and pressed a kiss to my lips. I tasted myself on his tongue. I should have been grossed out, but this was us, messy, raw, and imperfect.

When he pulled back, our gazes held. I trailed my

fingers through his damp hair. "Do you want to shower with me?"

His lips tilted up into a boyish grin. "I thought you would never ask."

He grabbed my hand, leading me toward the shower, when we heard a car approaching the driveway.

He stilled. "Are you expecting someone?"

I shook my head and walked to the small window to peek outside.

My stomach dropped when I spotted the familiar figure approaching the house.

"It's Baz," I whispered.

I knew it would only be a matter of time before he showed up. The confrontation was bound to happen sooner or later, but I was hoping it would be much later. Like never.

"What the hell is he doing here?" Brooks' face hardened, and I scrambled to gather my clothes.

I huffed and threw my shirt over my shoulders, not bothering with a bra, and slid the leggings up my bare legs. I started moving toward the stairs, but Brooks stopped me.

"Don't." He clenched his jaw. "I've got this."

His angry steps pounded through the house. There was a knot of dread settling in my stomach. This was a powder keg waiting to explode.

I reached the landing at the same moment he stepped inside the house.

"Baz, what are you doing here?"

His polo shirt was soaked, and his jaw tightened as soon as he saw me. "Hello, Harlow. Surprised to see me?"

"I wasn't expecting you, but I guess I shouldn't be surprised," I said, gripping the railing for support.

Brooks positioned himself between me and our unwelcome visitor. "How the hell did you get in here?"

Baz looked between us. "Her dad gave me a key," he said, as if that explained everything.

"That doesn't give you the right to use it and just show up here unannounced," Brooks snarled.

His beady little eyes gave me a slow once-over, lingering long enough to make my skin prickle. "Why? Am I interrupting something?"

Brooks crossed his arms. "As a matter of fact, Bart, you were."

I closed my eyes briefly and prayed for God to take mercy on my soul and get Brooks to shut up. Provoking Baz wasn't going to help this situation.

"My name is Baz, not Bart," he said through clenched teeth.

I pulled on Brooks' arm, silently pleading with him to take it down a notch. "Baz, why don't you tell me why you're here."

He wiped some of the water dripping off his arm. "I think it's time you and I had a little chat, don't you?"

I'd spent the last few weeks pretending that I didn't know he would track me down. Now that he was here, he wasn't leaving until he got answers.

"I guess I owe you a conversation." The wedding might not have been about us, but he was the one left standing at the altar.

He watched me closely. "Do you have anything else you want to say to me?"

I twisted my hands in front of me, resisting the urge to tuck them behind my back so he wouldn't see the diamond on my finger. Judging by the frown on his face, he already knew. There was no way my father kept that news to himself.

"I'm sorry for disappearing without a call or a text."

He tilted his head to the side. "You're sorry?"

"Yes."

He stepped into the living room, his eyes sweeping over the bare floors, patched walls, and paint cans scattered around. "If you were having second thoughts, you should have said something. We could have worked something out."

He was probably right, but it wouldn't have changed anything. I wasn't going through with it, no matter how much pressure he and my father put on me.

"You wouldn't have listened to me. You would have tried to convince me to stay."

"How do you know? You never gave me the chance."

He was wrong, I did know. He would have said all the right things, reminded me of how much the merger benefited our families. He would have made it sound reasonable and logical. He would have made me feel small for even questioning it.

"I felt suffocated. I needed to get away and clear my head."

He looked down at my outfit, clearly not thrilled with my messy, unkept look.

"You disappeared. Left me standing there, fielding questions from our friends and family that I couldn't possibly answer. You have been here for weeks, and I haven't gotten a single fucking phone call! Weeks, Harlow!"

"Watch it," Brooks said, crossing his arms and reminding us both that he was standing right there.

"You stay out of this," he snapped.

"Baz," I said softly, hoping to bring the tension down in

the room. "I didn't mean for things to turn out this way, but I knew if I expressed my concerns, you still would have pressured me to follow through with the plan."

He inclined his head to the side. "Is that supposed to be an apology?"

Brooks chuckled beside me, and I shot him a death glare. "After what you and her father put her through, I'd say it's more of an explanation than you deserve."

Baz flicked his gaze to Brooks, his eyes scanning him from head to toe. He was aware of our history. I never hid that from him. He always knew what Brooks was to me and never liked the idea that another man owned my heart. Not that he wanted it for himself. He simply didn't like anyone or anything standing in his way.

His frustration was obvious with how he shoved his hand through his hair. "Your father is furious. We had an agreement."

"I realize that, but I did us both a favor. We weren't marrying for the right reasons."

He looked away like he didn't want to admit that I was right. "And yet you still said yes when I asked you."

I hung my head because he had a point. But knowing it and accepting it were two different things. When I woke up that morning, it finally dawned on me what my future would look like, so I ran.

Straight down the church steps, where hundreds of guests were waiting inside.

"I did say yes, but then I realized I was being exploited, and I didn't want to be a pawn in whatever sick, twisted game our fathers were playing. I wanted more for myself."

"Harlow, don't stand here and play the victim card. You knew the rules when you agreed to the terms."

He tried to step closer, but Brooks stopped him. "I don't think so, pal."

My ex shoved his hands in his pockets and rocked back on his heels. "This is fast, even for you, Harlow."

I winced because, yeah, that last one got me. "I didn't plan this. It just happened."

He scoffed. "That's all you have to say?"

I rubbed my temples. This was an absolute nightmare, and I was standing right in the middle of it.

"I didn't leave you standing at the altar so I could run straight back to him. That's not what happened. I ran from the church because it felt wrong and I couldn't go through with it."

He dragged a hand down his face. "You should have been an adult and talked to me. We could have figured something else out. Marrying me wasn't supposed to feel like a death sentence."

"I felt trapped."

"Do you think I was thrilled about this arrangement? I didn't ask for this either, but I was willing to suck it up, because I needed that marriage to happen."

I blinked. "Wow. I'm flattered."

He sighed. "I'm not trying to be an ass, but I did my part. I lived up to my end of the deal."

"Do you hear yourself? This was nothing more than a business deal."

He rolled his eyes. "All you had to do was smile for the cameras and make me look good, and you would have been set for life."

I exhaled sharply. "I haven't busted my ass to make a name for myself in the business world, just to settle and be a piece of arm candy."

Baz would never understand my reasons because the

plan worked for him. He never cared about the cost to me. I was merely the tape that held it all together.

"So, what you're saying is you busted your ass, walked away from millions to live in bumfuck nowhere and play house in the woods?"

Brooks tensed beside me. "Watch your mouth."

"My family's reputation took a hit. You embarrassed me, and for what? Because you got cold feet? We had everything lined up. It was the perfect partnership. You could have had it all. Instead, you decided to blow it up."

"I get that you're mad, but I don't want that life."

His face darkened. "You needed it enough when you agreed to marry me."

I thought I needed it until I looked at myself in the mirror while wearing that dress. I felt more like a prisoner on a perp walk than a bride ready to walk down the aisle.

"My priorities have changed."

Baz let out a dry laugh, shaking his head. "Please. You're just trading one arrangement for another. You want the house, and being married is the only way you're going to get it."

My breath caught, and Brooks tensed beside me. "You're right. I do want my mother's house, but that's not the whole story. Brooks isn't some replacement or means to an end. I loved him long before you and I made that arrangement."

"You are making a huge mistake. I hope the house is worth it."

I shook my head. "No. I made a mistake five years ago that nearly cost me my happiness. I will not make that same mistake again."

He grabbed the house key out of his pocket and threw it on the table. "Good luck to you, Harlow, because when this little charade blows up in your face, don't come crawling back to me."

"That will never happen."

"No one makes a fool out of me and gets away with it."

Brooks' hand touched my back in silent support. "Stop threatening and trying to scare her. She is my fiancée and, quite frankly, I'm done listening to this shit. You were nothing more than a choice she made for all the wrong reasons."

His hand tightened around the door. "You have no idea who you're dealing with. I have the power to destroy you. All it would take is one phone call, and I could make your little hometown construction business collapse."

Brooks didn't flinch. Not even a blink. "I dare you to try."

Baz let out a humorous laugh. "It's hilarious that you think you can go up against me?"

Brooks tilted his head to the side. "I know your type. You threaten and intimidate to get your way. You think by throwing money around that people will bend to your will. News flash, buddy, I don't bend for anybody."

Baz placed his hands on his hips. "This is your last chance, Harlow. Come home with me now, and we can smooth this whole thing over. You can tell them you had a breakdown and needed rest. I can have a statement prepared by morning."

I couldn't believe he thought that was even a possibility.

Brooks moved closer to me. "There is no chance of that happening. My ring is on her finger. She has made it perfectly clear what she wants, and it's not you."

Baz kept his face blank, but I could tell the lack of control of the situation was killing him. He was used to getting what he wanted, and he knew he wasn't going to win this one.

"Whatever. I'm done here." He brushed a piece of imaginary lint off his chest. "By the way, you might want to change the locks in case someone tries to break in again."

The door clicked behind him, and I let out a slow exhale.

Was that a warning or a threat? Whatever it was, it didn't sit right with me.

Brooks came over and wrapped his arms around me. "Are you okay?"

I lifted my head and nodded. "I think so."

That had gone worse than I expected. I should be thrilled that we got that conversation over with. But something told me that wasn't the last we'd seen of Baz Zimmerman. I would be calling a locksmith tomorrow to change the locks. I didn't feel like I was in physical danger, but he wasn't the type to let things go. I wasn't taking any chances.

CHAPTER TWENTY-TWO
BROOKS

The lake was calm, as if the storm had never happened last night. The dock was damp under my hands as I sat there, watching the sunrise and trying to settle the mess in my head.

Last night had been a wake-up call. Seeing that man she had left me for, sent me back five years. I lay awake, long after he left, staring at the ceiling fan, trying to make sense of how she could have agreed to go through with it in the first place.

No matter how hard I tried, I couldn't seem to unravel my thoughts.

I heard her light and cautious footsteps approach. She eased her body next to mine, quiet and careful.

"I woke up to an empty bed," she said, resting her head against my arm.

I took a sip of my coffee. "Sorry, you were still sleeping, and I needed some fresh air."

She didn't press me for more. Just stared out at the water like me. I glanced at her. Her hair was pulled back in a ponytail, and her long legs swung back and forth. She was wearing another one of my flannels.

"What are you thinking about?" she asked, grabbing the coffee cup out of my hands and taking a sip.

I clenched my jaw. "I can't believe you almost married him."

She tensed. "I know."

I turned to face her. "I don't think you do. You left me for that piece of scum."

"But I came back."

I looked away from her. All I could see were the two of them together. It made my blood boil. For five years, he got to hold, kiss, and be with her. Five years that I didn't.

"I know that, but seeing him still bugged me. There is no logical reason to be jealous of him, but I am, and what pisses me off is that I don't know how to make it stop."

She reached for my hand, lacing our fingers together. "Trust me, you have no reason to be jealous, but is this really what this is about?"

Silence stretched between us. How did I explain it to her in a way where I didn't sound like an irrational asshole? "I don't know how to deal with these feelings. I know this sounds completely absurd, but I've only wanted you to be mine. Just mine. And yet, all I can think about is that you let him touch you."

She smiled. "No. I didn't."

I blinked. "Excuse me?"

Her fingers were cold, but her grip was tight. "I never slept with him. We had an agreement. He could have my hand in marriage, but not my body."

I couldn't believe the words coming from her mouth.

"He agreed to that?"

In my head, I knew it was nothing more than an

arranged marriage, but I always assumed she would cross that line with him. I never imagined that she wouldn't.

She nodded slowly. "He wasn't thrilled, but it was either that or nothing."

"So, let me get this straight. You were never intimate with him?"

"No."

I swore under my breath, dragging a hand through my hair. This was not what I expected. None of this made sense.

"Was there anyone else?"

The question came out before I could stop it. I held my breath, not sure which one was worse, her sleeping with him or someone I never knew about.

"No. There was never anyone else. My focus was on my career." She hesitated. "And trying to get over you."

"Harlow, I don't even know what to say."

Her confession knocked the wind out of me. She had never been with him. There had never been anyone else. Yet, we still lost so many years together. I felt guilty as fuck because I couldn't say the same.

I dated a few girls over the years, but nothing ever became of it. They were never Harlow.

"You don't have to say anything. I just want you to believe me."

I turned and dropped my forehead to hers. "I know you would never lie about that. I'm just surprised." I searched her eyes, needing to be honest with her. I pushed some hair back from her face. "I need to figure things out. I need to know that I can trust you to stay this time. I don't want to wake up tomorrow and have you tell me that you changed your mind."

I wasn't trying to hurt her, but I couldn't ignore the doubt growing in my chest.

"Does that mean you don't want to go through with the wedding?"

I struggled with what to say and how to say it.

"Honestly. I'm questioning if it's smart to go through with it. Things are unstable and messy right now."

What would happen once she got the house? When I secured the deal? Would she run again when things got tough? Were we setting ourselves up for more heartbreak?

"No, they are not. I am where I want to be. I'm not going to change my mind again. Not today. Not tomorrow or the day after. I finally got you back. I'm not leaving you again."

I looked back out at the water. "I want to believe you."

"Brooks, I can't continue to go on like this. I don't know what else I can do to convince you that I'm here to stay. I'm starting to question if you refuse to believe me, or if you simply just can't get over the past. If that's the case, then we are both fooling ourselves into believing this will work."

I stayed silent because I didn't know how to answer that.

Her fingers curled around mine. "We can't keep looking backward. You can't keep punishing me for the choices I made when I didn't even know what the hell I was doing."

I ran a hand over my jaw, trying to get my thoughts in order. I hated that I was allowing him to get inside my head, but I didn't know how to stop waiting for the other shoe to drop. "I know you're trying. I just need a little patience here."

She pulled her hand away. "I don't know how many times I can say it until it finally sinks in. I want to move forward with you. I want us to try again. Not because of the house or convenience. It's because I don't want to live a life without you in it. I know I can do it, but I don't want to. However, I can't keep trying to prove it to you if you keep waiting for me to leave."

She wasn't going easy on me. I could feel the fight in her voice. She was asking me to trust her. To meet her halfway.

"I don't know how to stop being afraid," I told her honestly.

She brought her hand up to my cheek, forcing me to meet her eyes. "Then let me help you."

"How?"

"By wanting this as much as I do."

I stared at her for a beat. Her eyes were clear and honest. There was no doubt in my mind that she meant every word. Maybe she was right. I've spent the last few weeks questioning everything. Perhaps it was time I started believing in her again. In us.

The wind whipped her hair around, so I tucked it back behind her ear. "I'll try."

Her lips parted slightly, like she wasn't expecting me to give in so easily. "Thank you."

Then, before she could say anything else, she leaned in and kissed me. It was sweet, soft, and everything else. It was as if she were trying to make up for all the years we'd wasted. I held her tight as if my life depended on it. In fact, I was pretty sure it did.

CHAPTER TWENTY-THREE
HARLOW

The roar of the motorcycle filled my ears as Brooks and I made our way along the winding roads. I tightened my grip around his waist, holding on for dear life as the warm air whipped against my face.

I always loved riding on the back of this bike. It'd been years, yet I was surprised at how natural it felt to hold on to him like this.

We didn't talk. I didn't ask where we were going, because we had traveled this road so many times, I already knew.

The second he pulled down the dirt path, my breath caught in my lungs.

The same willow tree stood tall along the shore of the lake. The dock we spent many hours on was still there, looking worn and weathered.

I slid off the bike; my hands trembled as I removed my helmet.

Brooks swung his legs over the bike and set the kickstand down.

He grabbed something from the saddlebag, and my

heart almost tripped over itself when I saw the picnic basket and blanket in his hands.

"You planned a picnic for us?"

He shrugged, trying to play it off. "I figured it was a nice day out. We don't have too many of those left, so I thought it would be nice to spend the afternoon outdoors."

He could have taken us anywhere, but he chose this spot. A place that mattered to both of us.

I wrapped my arms around my middle and stood a few feet back, taking it all in. Brooks spread the blanket out under the tree. The same spot where we spent so many hours talking about the future. This was where we shared our first kiss and spent countless hours staring at the stars in the sky.

I knelt beside him as he unpacked the fruit, cheese, and crackers and placed them on a little cutting board.

"You remembered?" I asked, kicking my white sneakers off and pulling the bottle of wine from the basket. I held it up and stared at the label. It was from the same winery where we went on our last date before I left to go back to school.

He stretched his jean-clad legs out on the blanket and tilted his head to the sky. "Of course I did. You drank the entire bottle and cried about how bad you were going to miss me."

I laughed, covering my face. "I was a mess."

He reached inside the basket and pulled out a corkscrew. "You were a cute mess."

I looked out at the water. "Have you been here since I left?"

I don't know why I asked. Why it was so important?

He sat back, bent his knee, and rested his arm casually around it. "I used to come here a lot. I thought maybe if I sat here long enough, I'd find some peace and stop being so damn angry."

I took a small sip of my wine. "Did it help?"

He shook his head. "No. Not one bit."

My chest squeezed. "I'm sorry."

He ran a hand along the back of his neck. "It's okay."

I wanted to reach out and touch him. Show him how much I meant it. He said he believed me, but I still felt the need to convince him. My conversation with Molly from a few weeks ago popped into my mind. I'd been toying with the idea of starting something on my own. Given how comfortable I'd become with the thought of living here, I'd found myself thinking about it more than ever.

I pulled on my white crop top when I felt it riding up my back. "There is something I've been thinking about, but I've been waiting for the right moment to share it with you."

He took a bite of his strawberry. "I'm listening."

"I decided to put down some roots here and possibly start my own business," I blurted out.

His gaze snapped to mine. "Pardon?"

"I don't want to spend the rest of my life chained to a desk and bust my ass for someone who doesn't appreciate me. I want to do something meaningful. Something that makes me happy."

He studied me for a minute. "What would you do?"

My fingers toyed with the edge of the blanket. "I thought about opening a nursery and specializing in landscape design."

A look of understanding settled on his features. "Your mom?"

My eyes watered because, of course, he would connect the dots. "Do you think it's stupid?"

He reached for my hand. "No, baby. I don't think it's

stupid. I'm just surprised, in a good way," he stressed. "Between Finn and me, we could send a lot of business your way."

My eyes drifted across the lake to where my house sat on the opposite shore. It wasn't visible because we were so far away, but I knew it was there. "What if I fail? I don't know the first thing about running a business."

His gaze followed mine. "You will not fail. I remember how pretty the flower beds were in front of the lake house. Anyone can plant flowers and shrubs, but you knew how to lay them out and combine all the different kinds of plants."

Tears stung my eyes. Sometimes it felt like he believed in me more than I believed in myself. "You really think I could do it?"

"Without a doubt in my mind. It's a great idea. You're a natural. I'm proud of you."

A single tear slipped down my cheek. "Damn it," I said, swiping at my cheeks. "I wasn't planning on crying today."

He chuckled, reached into the basket, and pulled out a napkin. "And I didn't plan on this conversation when I was packing the cheese and crackers."

I chuckled lightly while dabbing under my eyes. "I'm still trying to wrap my head around the idea myself."

There was something about this moment, with the smell of fresh cut grass, the birds chirping in the distance, and the sound of the water rippling against the shoreline, that made me feel lighter. We talked and brainstormed on ways I could draw customers in and all the things I would do. The more we talked, the less it felt like a whimsical idea.

He stood up and stretched. "Wanna go for a swim with me?" he asked, crinkling up his napkin and throwing it in the bag.

"It's almost September. The lake is freezing."

"Come on." He grabbed my hand to pull me up. The muscles on his back flexed as he walked. I tried not to stare, but the man's body was a work of art. I loved how time had sculpted his body, but he was still the same guy inside.

"Brooks." I pulled on his arm, stopping him as we got closer to the water. "I don't think jumping in the lake and freezing our asses off before we have to hop on your motorcycle is a good idea."

He smirked at me as if I had just issued him a challenge. "I can warm you up before we head back."

I shook my head with a laugh. "Not happening."

He backed me up under the willow tree. His grin turned lazy and familiar. "Do you remember this tree?"

I narrowed my eyes. "You know I do."

It was where he first kissed me.

He leaned in, brushing a strand of hair from my face. "I convinced you to take a chance on me then. Now, I'm asking you to trust me. I have blankets in the back and a dry hoodie for you to wear."

I looked out at the sky. The sun was slipping below the horizon. "My answer is still no."

"You sure?" His hand went to the back of my neck. "You told me you wanted to be wild and reckless."

His mouth teased mine, slowly coaxing my lips open. I pushed on his chest. "I meant in a warm bed, not in a cold lake where hypothermia might set in."

His laugh rumbled against my lips. "You just said less than five minutes ago that you wanted to plant some roots here. If you want to fit in, you need to live like a local."

"And jumping into the lake fully clothed qualifies me as a local?"

He smiled and shook his head. "Nope, but skinny dipping does."

I sputtered out a laugh. "Now, I know you are crazy."

He smirked like he was up to something. "The lake looks perfect. You can't tell me you're not tempted."

I raised my brows. "What part of it will be dark soon, and I have no desire to ride my wet butt on the back of your motorcycle, do you not understand?"

He rolled his eyes. "Where is the girl who stripped in front of me when she was twenty-one years old and made me jump in the lake with her?"

"She grew up and realized that you can't skinny dip on public property without the cops getting called."

His shoulders shook with laughter. "It's a good thing I know the sheriff now."

"I still think I should stand here on the grass, fully clothed, and keep a lookout for you."

He braced one hand on the tree and the other along my hip. "I think you need a little motivation."

I pushed on his chest as if that would somehow save me. "You really think kissing me is going to get you what you want?"

He tilted his head and brought his mouth to mine. "I don't know, you tell me?" His lips were slow and gentle as he applied the right amount of pressure to my mouth. He knew exactly what he was doing. And the worst part was, we both knew he could talk me into anything.

His hand slid under the hem of my white crop top. I moaned when his calloused fingers teased along the curve of my back. "Still don't think I can talk you into it?"

I grinned against his mouth. It tasted like wine and strawberries. "Nope, but feel free to keep trying."

His fingers went to my back, grabbed the hem of my shirt, and whipped it over my head. I was too dizzy from the kiss to fight him. "Do you still need convincing?"

"I think you need to try harder," I said, letting out a breathless sigh. I was ready for him to strip my clothes completely off and do whatever the hell he wanted.

"Oh, sweetheart, you have no idea how hard I can go."

My laugh turned into a squeal as he bent down and threw me over his shoulder like I weighed nothing.

"Brooks Dawson, you put me down right now." I was laughing so hard as he moved toward the water.

"You will thank me later."

And then he threw my ass in the lake.

I shrieked loud enough that you could probably hear it from the next town over. I sputtered as the cold water swallowed me whole.

I resurfaced and pushed my wet hair out of my eyes just in time to see him yank his clothes off, toss them on the grass, and dive in.

The water rippled around us, and when his head popped up, he looked pretty pleased with himself.

I splashed water at him as he swam closer. "Don't you dare come near me?" I tried to scowl, but I was too busy laughing.

"Refreshing, isn't it?" He ignored me and pulled me toward him.

"You're lucky I love you."

My eyes widened the second I realized what I said.

"Oh, trust me. I know." His fingers brushed over my waist. "And I love you too."

I wasn't expecting him to say it back, but I was relieved that he did. I never thought I would hear those words come from his mouth ever again. I was grinning and thankful that he wasn't making it awkward.

I wrapped my arms around his neck without even

thinking. "If you love me, don't ever throw me in this freezing-ass lake again."

He chuckled. "You're kinda cute when you're mad."

We drifted lazily in the water. The sun was beating on my face as I floated on my back. It felt like another lifetime ago when we would come to this very spot. When we were younger, it was about being out of sight, where no one could hear us. It was our own quiet little cove where the rest of the world faded away.

"What are you thinking about?" he asked, pulling me to his chest.

"I was thinking about how far we've come over the last few weeks."

He pushed the wet hair back from my face. "Me too. I want to take advantage of this second chance we've been given and do it right this time."

The water lapped around us. "I know we still have a lot to figure out, and I don't know what things look like long term, but Brooks," I said, pulling him closer, "I don't want to marry you just because it's convenient."

"I don't want that either," he said, surprising me.

"So, what do we do now?"

His hands slid lower, gripping my hips as he pulled me deeper into the lake. "Now, I kiss you."

The kiss started out slow and gentle, but it deepened quickly. I sighed against his mouth and clung to him. The sun began to dip, but I didn't want to rush this kiss. Every sweep of his tongue was a promise. Every caress of his fingers was an unspoken vow. I kissed him back with everything that I had.

His fingers traced a small path down my back as if he were afraid I might disappear.

I had no intention of going anywhere. Not this time.

CHAPTER TWENTY-FOUR
HARLOW

The fresh scent of new paint filled the room as I ran the beige paint roller against the wall. I wanted this house to feel like a home again. I'd been at it for hours. My arms ached, but I couldn't bring myself to stop. It was actually soothing, and a sense of pride came over me as I stepped back to survey my work. This room was almost done. There were only a few spots to touch up, so it seemed like progress.

My phone rang from the windowsill behind me. I put the roller in the tray and dried my hands. The ringing stopped before I could answer.

I checked the screen and groaned when I saw my dad's name. Then it started ringing again. I stared at it for a beat, debating on if I should ignore it or answer. I shook my head, knowing the calls wouldn't stop until he got through to me.

I hit accept and tried to sound as polite as possible. "Hi, Dad."

"Have you completely lost your mind?" he said, skipping over any type of greeting.

I leaned against the windowsill. "I'm fine, thanks for asking."

I should have gone with my gut and let the call go to voicemail.

"Baz told me he drove almost five hours in the middle of a storm to talk to you, and you sent him away. You were supposed to come back here and do damage control."

I closed my eyes; the paint fumes were starting to mix with the headache I felt coming on. "I already told you; I'm not coming back."

There was a long pause, long enough for me to think maybe he would hang up. No such luck.

"Do I need to remind you who you are dealing with here?"

I pressed my fingers to my forehead. "I've made my decision. You and the Zimmermans need to accept it."

He sighed again. "I don't understand where this nonsense is coming from. I have opened doors and given you opportunities that most people would kill for."

I jabbed a finger through my hair. "I never asked for any of it. You wanted those things, not me."

"I warned you before what would happen. Don't think for one second that I won't follow through with it."

My jaw clenched. "Stop threatening me."

"If you don't come back by the end of this week, your little vacation will be over."

My hand trembled as I held the phone up to my ear. "Then I guess we have a problem, because I'm not coming back."

"I am not going to stand by while you throw your life away and everything I've worked for. It's time for you to do the right thing, like you did before."

My hand was shaking so badly, I could barely hold the

phone. "I need you to listen to me very carefully. I am staying put, and I'm going to marry Brooks, whether you like it or not."

I could hear his heavy breathing on the other end. He was about to explode. "Think again. I will ruin that man's reputation so fast, he won't be able to get a job fixing the siding on a garden shed."

A cold sweat broke out along the back of my neck. "You leave him alone."

"You might want to reconsider because you won't like how this ends."

This was his way of intimidating me. He couldn't bully me into coming home, so he was using the only tool he had left.

The same one he used before. The difference was that I wasn't giving in this time.

I pressed my lips into a thin line, trying to hold it all together. "I'm not afraid of you anymore."

"You should be."

My heart raced so damn hard; I could feel my pulse in my ears. "If you so much as touch him or try to make good on any of those threats, you will regret it."

And then, without waiting for another word, I ended the call.

I dropped the phone on the couch and exhaled a long, drawn-out breath through my nose.

It was time he realized I wasn't the same girl who let him decide everything for me. I was done selling my soul to make him look good.

My phone buzzed again. I picked it up and was ready to chuck it across the room when I saw the caller ID. It was Brooks' grandfather, Marty.

"Hello."

"Harlow, I'm sorry to bother you." Marty's frail voice at the end of the line made my stomach clench.

"Is everything okay?"

"I'm not feeling so great. The boys are all on a fishing trip today, and I can't get a hold of my daughter-in-law."

I moved to the mudroom to find my shoes. "Tell me what's going on."

"I've been throwing up since this morning and feel unsteady on my feet."

My pulse quickened. "Where are you now?"

"In my room." He sounded like he was having trouble breathing.

I grabbed my keys off the hook by the door. "Can you call for a nurse?"

"They will want to bring me to the hospital, and I don't want to go."

I shook my head. He was so stubborn.

"I'm on my way. Stay put."

I ended the call and locked up the house before running out the door.

The ride into town passed by in a blur. My thoughts bounced between worry and regret. I'd been so busy, wrapped up in my own mess, that I hadn't spent as much time thinking about him and his health.

Marty was sick, and there was nothing I could do other than be there for him.

When I pulled up to the assisted living facility, I rushed inside and headed straight for his room.

I found him sitting on the edge of the bed. His face was as pale as the white sheets beneath him.

"Hey." I kneeled in front of him and put the back of my hand on his forehead. He was hot. Definitely had a fever. "Tell me what's going on."

He coughed, and I could see every ounce of strength draining from him. "The meds make me feel horrible. I don't want people fussing over me, but I can't keep anything down."

My heart squeezed at how frail he looked. "We are going to the hospital right now."

"No."

I pinned him with a look. "Yes. It's not up for discussion."

He coughed again. "You sound just like them."

"Will you be okay in my car, or do I need to call an ambulance?'

"I'm not riding in a damn ambulance."

"My car it is," I said, helping him stand up. He grumbled the entire way to the hospital.

I found a spot near the ER and helped him out of the passenger seat. The paperwork took thirty minutes to complete.

I brought the clipboard to the receptionist and then joined Marty on one of the hard plastic chairs.

"I hate this place," he muttered, eyeing all the sick people waiting to get called back.

"I think everyone feels the same way," I said, checking my phone again.

I tried calling Brooks, but he hadn't picked up yet.

After waiting for almost two hours for a room to open up, we finally got him settled into a hospital bed. His eyes were closed as a bag of fluids dripped into his IV. I sat beside him, gripping his hand.

A doctor came in and explained that he was dehydrated, a common side effect of his cancer treatments. They gave him some medicine to help relieve some of his symptoms. I could already see some of the color returning to his cheeks.

I reached for my phone, ready to call Brooks again, when the door burst open. He was the first one to step into the room. His face flooded with relief when he saw me. His dad and brothers were right behind him.

In two long strides, he was at my side. "Is he okay?"

I nodded as his dad, Tuck, and Hayes rounded the bed. "He was dehydrated. They are giving him something to help with his symptoms."

He blew out a sigh of relief. "Thank God."

Marty cracked an eye open and groaned. "Look who finally decided to show up."

Keith leaned over and rested his hand on the bedrail. "We were on the water. Our phones had no cell service."

"Must be nice," he grumbled.

"You scared the hell out of us," Tuck said, stepping forward.

Marty sighed. "I just needed a bag of fluids. Don't make a big deal about it."

Hayes snorted and leaned over to pat his arm. "Sorry to leave you hanging, old man."

I walked over to the window to give them all a few minutes alone. The doctor came in, went over everything, and reassured them that he could go home tomorrow as long as he continued to show signs of improvement.

After the doctor left, Marty sighed and adjusted his head on the pillow. "Now that I'm fine, you can all go home and stop hovering over me like a bunch of mother hens."

"What if we want to stay a little longer?" Hayes asked with a grin.

Marty grunted and stared down at his hospital gown. "Too bad. I'm tired of looking at all of you. Why don't you go get dinner or something? Maybe cook some of that fish you caught. You did catch a fish, right?"

"Of course we did," Tuck answered, giving him a small pat on the shoulder.

Marty's eyes looked heavy. I could see he was worn out. "Good. Now, go home and cook it, and let me rest."

I kneeled over the bed and kissed his forehead. "Get some sleep."

He glanced at me and patted my hand gently. "It's been a long day. Thanks for coming to get me, sweetheart."

"Always." I gave him a small smile.

He turned to Brooks. "You got yourself a good one."

Brooks looked down at me with affection in his eyes. "I do."

"Don't screw it up." And then he pointed a shaky finger at me. "That goes for you, too. No more leaving town, you hear?"

I rolled my lips together. "I'll be back tomorrow."

Brooks grabbed my hand and led me out of the room. He shut the door and spun around. "I'm glad you were with him."

I sagged into his chest. "Me too. I was so scared."

He kissed the top of my head. "He called you for help."

I nodded, feeling the emotions of the day catch up to me. "I'm just glad it wasn't anything too serious."

He stared down at me. "It could have been worse, but you got him here in time. I don't think I could ever repay you for that."

"I only did what anyone else would do."

He shook his head and pressed his forehead to mine. "No. Not everyone would. You stayed with him. Made sure he was okay. You kept him calm."

"It was good for both of us because I needed the distraction."

His eyebrows pulled together. "From what?"

I looked down the hall and back at him, unsure if now was the right time to tell him about the call I had with my dad. He already had enough on his plate, and I didn't want to pull his attention away from where it needed to be, but I knew he would be more upset if I kept it from him.

"My dad called right before Marty."

He tensed. "What did he want?"

"He said if I don't come back by the end of the week, he is going to ruin you."

He blinked. "He said that to you?"

I rolled my lips together. "He actually said worse, but I'll spare you all the details."

He clenched his jaw. "You think I care what he says? I'm not afraid of your father."

"I don't want to be the reason why you lose everything."

His face softened as he stared down at me. "Harlow, I know how your dad operates."

I pressed my palms to his chest. "Don't underestimate him or his reach."

He cupped my cheek. "Listen to me. We are going to live our life the way we want to. Let him try his best."

He might not have been worried, but my dad wasn't the type to throw idle threats around. He was frustrated that I wasn't falling in line. I wanted to believe that things were different this time around, but his reputation was on the line, and I needed to be prepared.

CHAPTER TWENTY-FIVE
BROOKS

I pulled up to Clark Investments, shifted into park, and threw my head back against the headrest. There was so much on my mind lately: Harlow, her dad, and Marty's health. But today, I had to get my act together and secure the financing for our business expansion.

I pulled on the sleeves of my dress shirt so the cuffs would show out of the arms of my sports coat before heading through the front door. The office was sleek and modern, a far cry from the construction trailers I was used to.

The receptionist peered up from her keyboard and gave me a polite smile. "Hello, how can I help you?"

I straightened my tie and cleared my throat. "Good morning. I'm Brooks Dawson. I have an eleven o'clock meeting with Mr. Clark."

She placed my name in the visitor's logbook and handed me a plastic badge to clip to my jacket. "He is expecting you, Mr. Dawson. You can head down to the conference room." She gestured to the double glass doors at the end of the open office, filled with dozens of occupied cubicles.

I gave her an appreciative nod and walked past all the employees, typing on their computers with their ears covered by headsets. The place was so quiet, you could literally hear a pin drop.

I entered the conference room to find Richard Clark, the man who held all the power of taking my business to the next level, already seated at the long glass table. He was dressed in another sharp suit and sported an all-business look, which was a stark contrast to the relaxed man that Harlow and I had met at the restaurant last week. Today looked like it was going to be all business.

"Thanks for taking the time to meet with me," I said, holding my hand out.

He didn't smile, didn't shake my hand, just frowned, and gestured for me to take a seat. "I almost canceled our meeting."

My stomach dropped. "I'm sorry. Did you find something wrong with the proposal I sent you?"

Harlow double-checked the numbers and made sure everything was accurate. She pored over the spreadsheets, and we corrected errors until the proposal was perfect. I had no idea what the issue could be.

He picked up his phone and held it out for me to see. "William Bennett called me this morning."

I gulped and dropped down into one of the rolling chairs at his table. I should have anticipated Harlow's dad would fuck with me and try to screw up this deal. He did warn us, so it was foolish of me not to take the threat seriously.

"He said you were trying to pull a fast one on me. That the engagement to his daughter was all bullshit." His eyes were sharp and critical. "I don't do business with liars, Brooks."

I inhaled a deep breath and pressed the palms of my hands against my thighs. "I don't even know where to start."

I could barely look at him and wasn't sure what to say, but I knew I was done lying.

He leaned forward. "Why don't you try telling me the truth for a change?"

I adjusted the collar of my shirt, nervous that everything I worked for was coming unraveled. The investment would cover the costs for the new equipment I needed to position myself to place a competitive bid for the new hotel project.

Lakeside Resort would be the biggest development project that our little touristy town had ever seen. Winning this bid would not only be a game changer for me personally, but it would position Dawson Construction as one of the area's top construction firms in the state. It would be my chance to prove myself, level up, and secure larger deals. And it would bring in more jobs and bigger exposure. Now it was all dangling over a cliff because William Bennet wanted revenge.

"First, I'd like to apologize. He never should have dragged you into this, and I wish I could say he was one hundred percent wrong, but there is some truth to what he said." My hands were shaking as I folded them in my lap. "The engagement started under false pretenses. I was trying to help Harlow get out from under his thumb. William Bennett is a manipulative and controlling man. He is the reason why she and I broke up all those years ago. He was trying to force her into an arranged marriage. I wanted to help her. So, when her father showed up and demanded that she go back, I stepped in without thinking and told him we were already engaged." I leaned forward so I could look him in the eye. "I am sorry that I lied to you, but I wanted the deal so badly that I was willing to do whatever was necessary. That's not the kind of man I am, and you deserve better."

He didn't speak, simply stared, so I continued. "I know it looks bad, and while this might have started on a lie, that's not the case anymore. Over the last few weeks, Harlow and I have reconnected. What we have is one hundred percent real. I know the bell can't be unrung, but I still owe you a sincere apology."

He leaned back in his chair and folded his arms across his chest. "You went to those extremes just to land the deal?"

I nodded slowly. "Yes. My father and grandfather entrusted me to take over Dawson Construction. This business isn't just a paycheck for me, it's my family's legacy. I wanted them to see the business thrive and make them proud. So, yeah, I wanted this project more than I wanted anything, but I don't want to sell myself out to get it, and that's exactly what I did, and I'm not proud of that." I swallowed hard and glanced away. "I'm ashamed that I lied, and that's something I will regret for a long damn time."

His eyes narrowed slightly. "What's her father after?"

Control. Power. Greed.

"He wants to punish her. He's angry that she screwed up his deal. He threatened to take her home away and fired her from her job because she dared to make a choice that he didn't agree with. And now he's doing everything he can to make my life miserable."

He leaned forward and steepled his fingers under his chin. "That's one hell of a mess you got yourself tangled in."

I laughed lightly. "Yeah, it sure is."

"I still don't like that you tried to pull a fast one over me." He glanced down at the manila folder on the table. "And while the numbers are spot-on, I don't attach my business to people I can't trust. I worked too hard to build my company's reputation."

I swallowed hard because that made sense, and I couldn't blame him. "I understand." I stood up and pushed my chair back. "Thank you for hearing me out and giving me a chance to explain."

I was walking toward the door with my tail tucked between my legs when he stopped me.

"Brooks, wait." I turned around, surprised to see him standing, too. "I wasn't finished. Sit back down."

I blinked, confused, but followed him back over to the table.

He motioned for me to take a seat, so I did. "I've seen what power and greed can do to people. And I've seen people stand up for what's right and show up for those they care about."

I stared at him, unsure where this conversation was going.

"I've been in this game long enough to know when someone is scrambling to cover their tracks and feed me a line of bullshit, but I've also seen people with their heart on their sleeve and hold sincerity in their eyes."

I blinked. "Thank you."

I expected him to throw me out of his office, not to go easy on me.

He smirked when he noticed my confused expression. "I admire a man who has the balls to own up to his mistakes.

I'm not going to pretend that I'm happy about what you did, but I'm willing to give you another shot."

My shoulders dropped, and I felt all the air rush from my lungs. "You're giving me a second chance?"

He flipped open the folder and picked up his black pen. "I am, and you better not let me down."

I laughed and ran a nervous hand through my hair. "I don't mean to sound ungrateful, but why?"

He lifted his head and met my eyes. "Any man who is willing to stand between a woman and a father like hers is a man who has his priorities straight."

I swallowed hard. "I'm all in."

He smiled. "I can tell."

He extended his hand. "You got yourself a deal."

I rose to my feet and offered him my hand, and this time he took it. "Thank you, sir. I can't tell you how much this means to me. I promise you won't regret it."

"You better hope I don't." We both laughed. He slid the folder he'd been looking at across the table. "I had my legal team finalize the numbers. You'll find everything is as we discussed. All you need to do is sign, and we are officially in business."

My nervous fingers flipped open the folder. I quickly scanned the paperwork. Everything looked exactly as I had hoped.

I picked up the pen and signed my name. The weight in my chest lifted as I leaned back and smiled for the first time since I stepped into this office.

Clark reached forward, flipped the paperwork around, and closed the folder. "Congratulations."

I did my best to maintain my composure, despite the excitement I felt. "Thanks for seeing past my faults and for the opportunity. It means the world to me. I promise to do everything right this time."

His smile was warm. I was filled with disbelief and awe at how compassionate this man was. "Tell Harlow she deserves better than the way her father treats her."

I shook his hand one last time and left the office feeling relieved. The second I slid into my truck, I picked up the phone to text her. Before I could click on her contact, Hayes was calling.

"Hey," I answered, still riding the emotional roller coaster from securing the deal. "I've got some good news. We got the green light. The deal is happening," I said, leaving out all the other details. I'd fill him in later.

"Congratulations," he said, but there was something off in his tone. "I hate to rain on your parade, but we have a small problem."

I stared through the windshield. "What kind of problem?"

"There was a mix-up with the flooring for Harlow's house. They delivered the wrong one. Now we're looking at a delay."

I pinched the bridge of my nose. "How long?"

"Could be a week. Could be a month. They don't have an exact timeline for when they can get the correct material in."

I swore under my breath. "Great. This was the last thing she needed to deal with."

"Unfortunately, that's not all. Her piece of shit ex filed a grievance with the town about the work permit. Said she wasn't technically the owner, so our permits are invalid."

My jaw clenched. "You've got to be fucking kidding me."

It was clear that her dad and the Baz-hole were in this together, plotting to make our lives as difficult as possible.

"Wish I was." He sighed into the phone. "The town called this morning. We have to stop the project until we can straighten the ownership thing out."

I slammed my eyes shut. "That sack of garbage has nothing better to do than to sabotage every part of her life."

"Yeah, well, that sack of garbage isn't just screwing with her. He is trying to fuck us over as well."

Of course, he was. He was doing exactly as he said he would. They both were. Just when I thought things were finally going my way, they had to come along and stir up trouble.

"There is more," Hayes said. "Baz has been sniffing around town, trying to dig up dirt on you two. He's telling people your engagement isn't real. That you're only pretending to be engaged so she could get the house."

I felt something dark and painful twist in my chest.

"I'll deal with him when I get back."

This was their way of trying to stay in control. Neither of them had any intention of letting her walk away without paying a price.

"How exactly do you plan on handling it?"

I didn't answer right away, but deep down, I already knew what I had to do. I'd been trying to take things slow and give myself time to figure things out, but marrying her would stop all this bullshit, real quick.

"Let me think about it, okay?" I looked at my GPS. "I have about two hours on the thruway. I'll call the supplier myself and see if I can put some pressure on them. I'll stop by the town building when I get back."

"I'm sorry to stress you out after the good day you've had."

"Don't worry about it. Keep an eye on things until I get back. I'll get everything sorted out."

"You got it. Drive safe."

I hung up and drummed my fingers against the steering wheel.

I would be dammed if I let those two men ruin my business and continue to bully her until they got what they wanted. I wasn't stupid. I knew they weren't going to let up until they did everything they could to make sure we didn't find an ounce of peace.

However, that didn't mean I had to stand back and let it happen. I would do whatever I had to do, even if that meant I had to marry her tomorrow. As my mind searched for another solution, it became clear that was the only one.

CHAPTER TWENTY-SIX
HARLOW

I was hungry and anxious by the time Brooks' truck pulled in the driveway. Despite the multiple texts I'd sent, he kept me in the dark about how his meeting went with Mr. Clark.

The man was maddening at times, but I figured if he was taking me to dinner, then that was a good sign, right?

When he stepped out of his truck, I thought my brain would short-circuit.

The sleeves were rolled up on his black button-down, showing off his strong forearms. His dark jeans looked like they were custom-made just for him. I couldn't help but do a not-so-subtle scan from head to toe. When he started walking toward me, I forced myself to play it cool, despite the heat creeping up the back of my neck at the sight of him.

He met me at the bottom of the steps; his hand rested on the railing.

"Ready for our date?" He grinned.

I leaned against the post. "Are you going to tell me if we are celebrating or not?"

He shook his head. "If I told you, it wouldn't be a surprise."

I huffed, not liking this little suspense game he was playing. "You know I hate surprises, right?"

He chuckled. "Trust me."

I tried, really, I did, but not knowing the outcome of the meeting was killing me.

Brooks didn't say where we were going. He kept his hand on the steering wheel, tapping his thumb to a country song playing on the radio.

"How far of a drive to this mystery place?"

"Not far."

I played with the hem of my dress. "That's not an answer."

"It's the best one you are going to get."

As we drove toward town, I felt my nerves settle a bit. I cracked the window open enough to let the soft breeze into the truck.

We passed most of my favorite shops and restaurants, and I was about to ask him another question when we took a left at the firehouse, driving in the direction of the Marcellus Falls Country Club. "I'm not dressed for the club," I said, looking down at my outfit. The private club was the fanciest place in town. We were members there when I was growing up, and we always wore our best clothes when we went.

"Good," Brooks said, taking a right and driving up a winding road. "Because we aren't going to the club tonight."

I glanced out the window as we drove further up the road. I leaned forward, peering through the windshield as we reached the top of the hill. Rows of grape vines were on either side of us.

We passed a big green and gold sign that read, "Welcome to the Amber Inn Winery."

"Is this place new?" I asked, turning in my seat to face him.

Brooks found a spot in front of the building. "It is, and I hope you like it."

"I'm sure I will. What kind of food do they have?"

"Mostly small plates and wood-fired pizzas, but there is a dining room with a more formal menu."

"I'm good with pizza," I said as he helped me out of my seat.

He grabbed my hand and laced our fingers together. "You can have whatever you want because we are celebrating tonight."

I looked up at him and stopped walking. "You got the deal?"

A smile tugged at the corner of his lips. "Yup."

I turned in his arms and threw my hands around his neck. "Brooks, that's incredible. I am so proud of you."

He brushed a piece of hair back from my face. "We signed the paperwork this morning."

I blinked and smacked his chest. "I can't believe you left me in the dark all day."

He laughed. "I couldn't have done it without you."

A warm feeling spread through my chest. "Well, in that case, maybe I'll order everything on the menu."

He ran a hand over his jaw. "There is another reason why I brought you here."

"What's that?" I asked, blinking up at him.

He rubbed his thumb along my engagement ring. "I talked to the event coordinator today. We are meeting her to go over the catering options."

My eyebrows bent together. "So, we're not here for pizza and wine tasting?"

His Adam's apple bobbed as he swallowed. "I figured it was time we started planning."

Now I understood why he seemed so distracted today. I chewed on the inside of my cheek, giving myself a minute to think this over. We agreed to get married. I knew that, but somewhere along the way, this turned into more than a simple arrangement.

As I stared out at the sprawling vineyard, the reality of what we were doing settled in.

"Are you okay with this plan?" He scanned my face like he wasn't sure I was okay with this sudden change.

I swallowed hard, trying to get a handle on my emotions. I wasn't sure how to explain what I was feeling without him taking it the wrong way. "Yes, I just wasn't expecting this to happen tonight."

He watched me closely. "You're not thinking about backing out on me, are you?"

I looked away toward the water. It had a gorgeous view of the lake. "No. I'm just surprised."

He shoved his hands in his pockets. "I don't want you to feel rushed, but some things have happened recently, and I think we need to get married sooner rather than later."

"Does this have something to do with your meeting today, or did something else happen?"

I watched him closely, trying to read between the lines. Trying to figure out if this was something he wanted or felt pressured to do.

He reached for my hand, lacing our fingers together. "Harlow, you are my first, last, and only true love. I've always wanted to marry you. In fact, I should have married you years ago. I know this is a surprise, and I certainly wasn't planning on this today, but after everything that's happened, I'm convinced we need to get married as soon as possible."

I blinked. "What are you talking about, Brooks?"

"Your dad called Clark before our meeting and told him that our engagement was all an act and that we were trying to scam him. He tried to tank the deal."

"Wait, what?" I stood there with my mouth hanging open. Not in shock, because he had warned me, but I was mostly angry and disappointed. It shouldn't hurt this bad, but I wanted to believe that he wouldn't cross that line. It was naive of me to think that I could handle any threat he threw our way.

He squeezed my hand tightly. "I will tell you everything later, but Clark knows the truth about us now."

I stared at him wide-eyed. "He knows we lied, and he still gave you the deal?"

He played with the sleeve of my dress. "He did."

I stared at the gravel under my feet, focusing on not letting my tears slip out. "I'm so sorry that you got caught up in this mess. While I'm happy that you secured the investment, I am livid with my father. I don't know how, but I will find a way to stop this."

I was so angry with him. He's done nothing but push me and threaten me. I would not let him ruin what little I had left.

He lifted my chin to face him. "Look, it doesn't take a genius to connect the dots here. Your father and Baz are doing everything they can to fuck with us. Hayes called when I was leaving the meeting. Baz has been all over town, snooping for information and spreading rumors about you and me. He filed a grievance with the permits, which means we have to stop the construction until it's resolved."

"I don't even know what to say. I'll call Molly, maybe she can help us untangle this."

"If she can find a way around it, great. But, Harlow, I want to protect you and build a life with you, that's all I ever wanted. If putting a ring on your finger gives you an extra layer of protection, then I'm doing that. Not just because I have to, because I've never wanted anything more."

I looked around the vineyard. It wasn't lavish and over the top, like the flashy Long Island country club my dad picked out to show the world how important he was. This was simple and beautiful. This was exactly the type of place I would want to marry him.

However, there was something about this whole situation that made me realize the clock was ticking. This felt rushed, like we were being bullied into doing something, and it made me doubt everything. This should have been a happy moment, so why couldn't I keep my thoughts from spiraling?

He placed a hand gently on my face, as if he could sense my inner panic. "I know everything is happening fast here. And yes, it would be great to do this at our own pace, but I don't want to risk waiting. We both know the truth and have way too much riding on this, and I can only imagine all the fuckery those two idiots could bring into our lives if we don't marry soon."

I wiped a tear as it slipped down my cheek. "I'm sorry. I'm not trying to take away from this moment, but it feels like we are scrambling. I know we originally agreed to get married, but things have changed between us. I love you and want to marry you. I just don't want this to feel like a competition, like we're trying to beat my dad to the finish line."

"I don't want that either." His thumb stroked the moisture away. "But I also want to make sure you get that house. I know how much it means to you. I don't want anyone to take that away from you. I don't want you to worry about Baz or your father. Most importantly, I want to build a life with you because I'm in love with you."

Things felt tangled, messy, and complicated, but as I looked at the only man I had ever loved, it also felt like we'd been given a second chance, and I would be a fool to waste it.

I rested my hand on his chest. "I want to make sure you know that I want to marry you because I love you, not because someone is closing in on us and we feel forced."

He wrapped his arms around my shoulders and pulled me into his chest. "Just because we have to move up the wedding doesn't mean we have to let them take the moment away from us. It's still ours. Let's not let them ruin this for us, okay?"

I closed my eyes briefly, allowing myself to believe that this wasn't about the house or holding on to a deal. That was about us finding our way back to each other.

I nodded, leaning into his touch. "Okay."

CHAPTER TWENTY-SEVEN
BROOKS

I pushed the safety glasses against my face as I cut through another piece of wood. The smell of sawdust filled my nose as the early morning sun beat down on my back. I wasn't supposed to be working on the house, thanks to her ex causing a hissy fit and making bogus claims about the permits, but I wasn't going to let some rich assholes stop me. Harlow wanted her house back. She deserved it, and she was going to get it.

I wiped the sweat off my brow and stepped back. Finn's beat-up old truck rolled to a stop in the driveway. He climbed out and slammed the door with his boot. "Why the hell am I still doing manual labor in my thirties?"

I flipped my glasses to rest on the brim of my hat and started to help him unload the shrubs from the truck bed. "You're the boss now. Don't you have a crew who can deliver for you?"

"Yeah, but seeing that the work permits were tangled up in red tape, I didn't want to get my guys involved."

I set the arborvitae down next to the fence. "I appreciate it, man. I'm sorry to drag you out so early."

He pulled a brown tarp back over a few bags of mulch. "Molly told me that her dad tried to sink the deal."

Of course she did. Those two told each other everything.

I wiped a bead of sweat off my forehead. "Yeah, that was one hell of a meeting."

He leaned against the truck and kicked a rock down the driveway. "So, what's the deal with you two? Are you still playing house, or is it something else now?"

I walked over and leaned on the tailgate. "We crossed that line a long time ago. This is as real as it gets."

"That's what I figured." He took a sip from his travel mug, looking amused. "I also heard you were moving up the wedding date."

I laughed and shook my head. "Yeah, no sense in dragging it out. We have too much riding on this."

Finn folded his arms and watched me carefully. "Molly said she plans to put down some roots and start a business here."

"She is." I couldn't stop the grin from spreading across my face thinking about it.

He nodded, but I could tell he still had concerns. "I hope for your sake she doesn't screw it up this time."

"She's trying, Finn. We both are," I said, adjusting my cap to block the sun from my eyes. "It feels different this time."

He shook his head. "I can't believe I'm saying this, but I'm rooting for you two."

I laughed because I knew how hard that was for him to admit. "Thanks, man."

He clapped me on the back. "Just don't ask me to hand deliver anymore shrubs. My ass is getting too old for this."

"Hey," I called out as he approached his truck. "Do you wanna grab a beer after work later?"

"You buying?"

"Yeah, I think you earned it today."

He opened the driver's side door and grinned. "I'll meet you at the pub at five thirty."

The stones bounced off the metal of his truck as he peeled out of the driveway.

I understood where his concern was coming from, but it was a relief that he was finally coming around. Not just for me but for Harlow, too.

I turned around to face the house and exhaled. Harlow didn't know that I had ordered the shrubs. They were a little something extra to help make this house feel more like a home again.

I went back to work feeling lighter than I had in a long time. My life finally felt like it was headed in the right direction for a change. Maybe Harlow and I would get it right this time, after all.

IT WAS A WEDNESDAY NIGHT, so thankfully, the pub wasn't too busy. Finn and I found Tuck and Hayes in their usual spot at a high-top by the window, they each had a cold beer in their hands.

"How's it going, loverboy?" Hayes called out and slid a stool my way. "What took you guys so long?"

"I had to stop at the hardware store and pick up a couple bags of sand. The soil in front of Harlow's front porch wasn't very well drained."

"Tell me again why you are working without an active

permit and risking getting fined by the town?" Tuck asked as I slid onto my seat.

I picked up a cold beer from the bucket. "Because she wants it done, and I'm not letting that asshole slow us down."

Finn wiped off some of the condensation from his beer. "Molly has been making some calls, trying to find a loophole around the permits."

I sighed, running a hand through my hair. "I hope she does. This bullshit is the last thing Harlow needs right now."

My brothers leaned back in their chairs, staring at me in a way that made my skin itch. "What?"

"You guys really are fucking, aren't you?" Hayes asked without a hint of teasing in his tone.

"You better shut your mouth," I snapped.

Hayes' jaw dropped. "Holy shit. You totally are. I mean, I assumed when I stopped by and she was only wearing your shirt, but..."

The vein in my forehead pulsed. "Hayes, I'm warning you. I don't want to fight you, but if you don't shut your mouth, I will kick your ass from here to Schenectady."

He snapped his mouth shut. Smart man.

Tuck leaned forward. "Are you going to tell us what's going on with you two, or are we supposed to keep guessing?"

"We are trying to work things out," I admitted, rolling my beer bottle between my palms.

"What does that mean, exactly?" Hayes asked carefully.

Finn threw an arm around my shoulder and grinned like a goof. "They cleared the air and talked about their feelings."

"And then you fucked?" Hayes asked. I pinned him with a glare while Tuck kicked him in the shin.

"And you wonder why I never call and invite you to do anything," I muttered. Sometimes it seemed like my little brother was a twelve-year-old kid trapped in a grown man's body. Either that or he was just a weirdo.

"Wait a minute." Tuck's gaze alternated between Finn and me. It was sharp and assessing. I called it his cop stare. "He knew before us?"

Hayes let out a dramatic gasp. "Dude, we are your flesh and blood. How could you?"

"Okay, first of all, he only found out today when he dropped the shrubs off. He figured it out just like you two geniuses."

Tuck leaned forward, resting his hands on his legs. "I knew it."

Hayes slapped me on the back. "She's always been it for you, man. If you're happy, then we're happy."

I kicked my legs out. "Yeah, but it's not just about how I feel. There is still so much we have to figure out. It feels like everything is moving a million miles a minute. It would be nice if we could take some time to breathe a little, work on all the things we needed, but time isn't on our side. The wedding has to happen in order for her to obtain the title for the house, and I want Marty to be healthy enough to see us get married."

"Sounds like you are overthinking it," Hayes said, shifting his weight. "She makes you happy. Focus on that."

I ran my thumb over the neck of my bottle. "I am happy, I only wish we didn't have the pressure of the wedding hanging over our heads."

A part of me thought we should wait. Give us some time

to adjust and iron out all the wrinkles, but the other part knew time wasn't on our side.

Tuck leaned back in his chair. "I understand this feels rushed, but you've loved her forever, even when you pretended you didn't. I'm starting to think you're more afraid of it working out than not working."

I shot him a look. "You think so, huh?"

He scratched the side of his cheek. "I don't think, I know. You don't want to ruin something that's starting to feel real again."

I chuckled. "Since when did you become so poetic?"

He shrugged. "I might have read a few of Mom's romance books that she kept hidden in the bathroom when I was on the toilet."

I shook my head while they all chuckled.

My back was facing the door, but when Finn glanced over my shoulder, I noticed his grin fade from his mouth.

"Ah, fuck."

I turned around to see who walked in, and there he was. Mr. Trust Fund Snob himself. He looked like he just stepped off the golf course in his yellow polo and khaki pants.

My fingers tightened around my beer. He should have been long gone by now, but I guess he was still poking around.

He made a beeline straight to the bar. "I'd like a Macallan, neat."

Ryan glanced at me and back at him. "Sorry, we're all out."

I coughed into my hand to cover my laugh.

He pulled out his wallet and took out a hundred-dollar bill. "Then I'll have whatever top-shelf whiskey you have."

"Sorry," Ryan said, polishing off a glass. "I'm not serving you."

Baz slapped his hand on the counter. "Why the hell not?"

A few heads turned. He was drawing attention.

Ryan smirked. "Because I don't serve assholes."

The beer I'd been drinking came spraying from my nose and mouth. Finn ducked his chin into his shirt to quiet his laugh while my brothers sat silently watching.

"You can't refuse me service," he snapped, acting as if his rights were somehow being violated.

Ryan seemed unfazed as he turned to stack the glasses. "I can and I just did."

Baz straightened his shoulders, like he was gearing up to protest. "I want to speak to the manager."

Ryan threw a white dish towel over his shoulder. "You're looking at him."

Finn laughed into his beer.

"I have every right to be here."

Ryan leaned across the counter. His eyes met mine briefly. "No, you don't. You've been sniffing your dirty nose around town, stirring up trouble."

As if he could sense me, Baz turned and locked eyes with mine. "Really?" he snapped.

I stood up slowly and calmly, even though every muscle in my body was pulled tight. "This is the type of service you get once you start pissing people off. No one wants you here."

"I'm a paying customer. I want a fucking drink!"

"You heard the man, he said no." I shook my head, stepping closer. Finn and my brothers were right at my back. "No one in this town is impressed with you or your money."

"What the fuck do you know about money? You hit nails for a living."

I smirked. "That's not the only thing I'm hittin' lately."

I shouldn't have said it. I knew that, but I hated this man with a passion. He was messing with my business. He wanted my fiancée. He believed he could buy his way into whatever he wanted. I had zero fucks to give when it came to him.

He scoffed. "You think Harlow's going to settle for a woodchuck like you? She left you once. What makes you think she won't do it again? Why don't you do the smart thing and walk away. I'll even make it worth your while. I will write you a check right now. Name your price."

I stared at him for a full five seconds before I laughed in his face. "That's your answer for everything, isn't it? Thinking that throwing money at a problem will make it all go away?"

He rolled his eyes. "Think about all the tools you could buy? Hell, you could even buy yourself a new truck. All you have to do is take the money."

He sounded weak and desperate, as if he knew he was fighting a losing battle, but his pride would never allow him to accept it.

I folded my arms. "I'm not for sale or some problem you can get rid of."

"Are you sure about that? It worked last time."

Rage took over my vision. I heard a few stools tip over, but I was already moving. I was sick and tired of his shit. After everything he'd pulled, messing with the permits, lurking around, and making her life miserable, I was done. This little showdown was five years in the making.

"Don't come into my town and think you can throw a check at me and get your way. She is not going back to your sorry ass. Get that through your thick head."

He bumped his chest into mine. "You would be a fool

not to take me up on my offer. She is not worth it. She will walk again."

"For an Ivy League college boy, you sure are pretty dense. She wants nothing to do with you or William Bennett. So, stop throwing a hissy fit and move along, Bartholomew."

I smirked. He wasn't a fan of his given name, and I couldn't blame him.

His nostrils flared. "You going to turn down my offer for a bitch that doesn't even put out. You are dumber than I thought."

That did it.

I picked him up by the collar and dragged him across the bar. "Say that again. I fucking dare you."

He stumbled back into a table, knocking over a basket of wings. His smirk dropped. "Do you know how much power and influence I have?"

"You don't look like you have a lot of power right now, you little shithead," I spat, standing over him, letting him know this would be a very short fight if he kept pushing my buttons. "Stay away from her!"

He laughed sarcastically. "You think I'm afraid of you?"

I shoved him again, and this time, he pushed me back. I had six inches and thirty pounds of muscle on the guy, but he didn't even flinch. I stepped back and threw my hands out. "If you want to back up your tough talk, go ahead and throw the first punch."

It happened so quickly that I didn't have time to prepare. One minute, I stared him down, and the next, I felt his knuckles connect with my jaw. It wasn't even a good punch, but it still sent me off balance. I didn't think he had it in him.

Before he could even think about taking another swig, I shot my fist up to the bridge of his nose.

He fell back, and suddenly, Ryan was hopping over the bar to break things up. He pulled me back, and Finn appeared at my side.

Ryan stood between us; his chest was heaving.

The entire bar went silent.

"That was your last warning, I said, as he staggered to his feet. "You aren't getting another one. You lost. You know it. I know it. The whole damn town knows it. So, pack up your shit and go back to the city and don't bother coming back."

He wiped at the blood flowing from his nose and came at me like a drunk frat boy with something to prove. I guess he wasn't listening. Don't say I didn't try to warn him.

He took a wide swing and barely touched the side of my head. I was fueled by adrenaline and five years of bad blood. I landed a hot, angry hit to his stomach. He doubled over so I finished him off with a headbutt. It hurt like a bitch, but it hurt him more. He bent to his knees, trying to catch his breath. I was about to give him one last pop before someone grabbed my wrist, stopping me from going after him again.

"Enough!" Ryan held his arm out, keeping his hand on my shoulder. "No fighting in my bar."

I yanked my arm free. "Fine. We'll take it outside then."

"That won't be happening," Tuck said, appearing at my side. "Let's not forget who the sheriff is in this town."

"Brooks." Hayes' voice sounded like a plea as he held on to the back of my shirt. "Please, for once in your life. Listen to Tuck."

I wiped the corner of my mouth where I could feel a

sting and pointed toward the door. "Somebody, get him out of my sight."

Baz staggered to his feet, glaring at me like a man who was more pissed about losing his pride than he was about losing the fight.

His collar was ripped, and his nose was swollen and bloody. "You're going to regret this. You have no idea who you're fucking with."

I rubbed my burning knuckles. "You can throw your name and money around all you want, but it won't change anything. And if you know what's good for you, you won't step foot in this town again, and if you do, I'll do more than kick your ass next time."

Tuck was already dragging him toward the door. "Get your hands off of me," he spat. "You'll be hearing from my lawyer."

"Keep it up and you'll be sleeping in one of my jail cells," Tuck snapped.

I tucked my shirt back in my pants and exhaled. I glanced down at my swollen hand. It was sore, but Baz definitely took the brunt of the blows.

"Well," Hayes said, throwing me a towel. "That escalated quickly."

I rolled my shoulders back as Ryan slid a cold beer in front of me. "Sorry, Ry."

"All good. I've seen worse." He gave me a salute and walked back to serve his customers.

Tuck dragged an empty stool up to the table. "You okay, brother?"

I leaned back, sore and pissed. "I am for now."

I didn't know what tomorrow would bring. There was a good chance he would only stir up more trouble, but tonight, I didn't care; I stood up for her. For us. And I'd do it again in a heartbeat.

CHAPTER TWENTY-EIGHT
BROOKS

It was late, almost nine o'clock by the time I pulled up to the house, so I was surprised to see that the lights were on. After my fight with Baz, I hung back with my brothers while Finn went home to help Molly tuck Emma into bed. I needed to cool off because I knew Harlow would have a million questions. The last thing I wanted to do was walk through the door with bloody knuckles and a bad attitude. I called her on the way home because I didn't want her to worry or get second-hand information.

I peered through the windshield, where she was patiently waiting for me on the porch swing. Her brown hair was pulled back, her legs were tucked beneath her, and she looked like she had been crying.

She stood the second I stepped out of my truck. I wasn't sure what to expect when she started walking toward me. Was she going to hit me or hug me?

My question was answered when she ran into my arms and folded her small frame against my body.

"I'm so sorry."

"Wasn't your fault," I said, wrapping my arms around her and burying my face in her hair.

"You wouldn't have been in a fight if it weren't for me."

I tightened my hold on her. "Do not apologize for him."

She sniffed and curled deeper into my chest. "He isn't going to let this go. This is so unfair to you."

"Stop." I pulled back to look into her eyes. "He threw the first punch. He started it, but I'm going to end it. I will find a way, I promise you that."

She wiped at her eyes. "But he hurt you."

I smirked. "I've been hurt worse in a pillow fight."

She pressed her cheek to my chest and stared at my bruised knuckles. "Are you sure you're okay?"

"I'm a big boy," I said, trying to reassure her. "Once we're legally married, he has no more leverage."

She stepped back. Her eyes swept over me before bringing my swollen hand up to her lips. "You really got him good, huh?"

"I would have liked to have gotten in a few more punches, but yeah, I believe I gave him a lot more than I got."

She shook her head. "Come inside. I'll get you cleaned up. Your hand needs ice, and I want to tell you about my conversation with Molly."

"Harlow, I'm fine."

She scowled, like she didn't believe me, and pulled me through the door. Diesel came running up and dropped a tennis ball at my feet.

Harlow picked up the ball and set it on the kitchen table. "Not now, Diesel."

It was the first time I'd ever seen her make him pout. I guess she wasn't in the mood to play games tonight.

I gave him a quick pat on the head as she pushed me into a kitchen chair. "Let me get you an ice pack."

She started rummaging through the freezer. My hand hurt, but nothing too terrible. I could tell she needed to do something, so I let her fuss over me if it made her feel better.

"I made dinner," she said, applying the ice pack to my knuckles.

I lifted my head in surprise. "You cooked?"

"Sort of." She shrugged and walked over to the sink to grab a wet washcloth.

"What did you make?" I asked, staring at the stove. It smelled like fish. Now, I was nervous. Harlow wasn't known for her culinary skills. She was better at making spreadsheets than supper.

"I picked up some salmon at the store earlier."

My gaze lifted to hers. "You bought salmon?"

She grinned, looking proud of herself. "I did."

I scratched the side of my head. "You know I have fish in the freezer in the garage, right? Free fish that I caught with my own hands."

She rolled her eyes. "It was a last-minute decision, and I didn't want to bother with thawing out frozen fish. I wanted fresh."

I bit my tongue and kept my thoughts to myself. "Can't wait to try it."

She parked a hand on her hip. "Are you mocking me?"

"I would never." I grinned and adjusted the ice pack on my hand. "What are we having with the salmon?"

She narrowed her eyes and then went to the cupboard to grab a few plates. "A tossed salad and rice." She turned and smiled. "Just in case you were wondering, the salmon came in its own baking pan and was already seasoned, so all I had to do was cook it."

I offered her a crooked smile. "So, I don't have to worry about dying tonight?"

She pulled the oven open and pulled the pan out. "From the food, no. But if you keep making fun of my cooking, there is a good chance you won't see the light of day tomorrow."

Harlow and I sat and ate in silence. The fish wasn't that bad. The edges were a little crispy, but I ate every last bite.

"So, what did Molly have to say about the permits?" I asked, leaning back in my chair to give her my full attention.

Her smile was wide. "She spoke with my mom's attorney, who is the trustee of my estate. He has the responsibility to make sure the assets in the trust are properly cared for. He's applying for new permits under the name of the trust."

I took a sip of my water. "I don't know much about the law, but that seems like a solid argument."

She was playing with her fork when she looked up at me. "I also did something else today."

"What's that?"

"I picked up Marty, and we went to look at a few parcels of land. I wanted to see what was out there, so I could start working on some figures for my business plan."

I paused, setting my fork down slowly. "You did?"

"Don't act so surprised."

I could sense the excitement in her tone. I knew she was thinking about it, but I had no idea she was looking at property.

"Did you find anything?"

"Kind of." She nodded slowly. "Marty convinced me to

consider some land over on Pottery Road. He knew of someone who was selling a few acres."

"The Smiths?" I asked.

Chris and John Smith owned a detailing garage. The land was flat but had a beautiful view of the hills visible from the main road. There was enough space to build an office, parking lot, and a greenhouse.

"Yeah." She cleared her throat. "Marty convinced them to give me a good deal. I was hoping you would help me build something."

I leaned back in my chair. "I would be happy to. That land will be perfect for what you need it for. It's peaceful, quiet, and there is enough room for you to do what you need to do."

She was beaming. "I thought the same thing. It's a little over five acres, so there is plenty of room to grow."

I smiled. "Your eyes light up when you're talking about it. I like seeing you like this."

"Thank you, but I'm still afraid people will think I'm crazy."

"I told you before, you're not crazy. You're starting something from scratch. Something totally different than what you're used to. That takes a lot of courage."

She played with her fork. "It feels right. Like it's a blank slate and a fresh start. I just need to figure out the financials of it all."

I reached for her hand across the table. "I think you can handle whatever is thrown your way. You won't have any trouble figuring the rest out."

At first, I thought she would cry, but then she laughed and squeezed my hand. "I needed to hear that. Now, I'm ready to admit that I overcooked the fish."

I stood and walked my plate over to the sink. I rinsed it

off, watching her out of the corner of my eye. "It wasn't bad, but you're going to have to feed me better than that if you want me to build you an office building."

"I'll work on my cooking skills."

"I'm not a fancy guy when it comes to food, so it's a pretty low bar to clear." I winked playfully. "How was Marty today?"

She leaned back and folded her arms. "He wasn't happy that I just showed up and took him out for a drive without asking him first." I laughed because I bet he wasn't. "I had to bribe him with a Big Mac from McDonald's."

I turned the faucet off and wiped my hand on the rag. "How did he seem health-wise?"

"He was having a good day, so I don't think he minded a little change of scenery."

My grandfather loved Harlow as much as his own grandkids, but the man was a creature of habit. He lived by routines. He was a tough old bird and set in his ways. I was surprised she convinced him to leave to begin with.

"Thank you. I'm sure he appreciated the gesture."

She chuckled. "He complained for the first thirty minutes, but once we arrived at the property, a light switched. He seemed more like himself. I stood back and watched him flirt with the secretary and talk shop with the owner. I know these good days are rare, so I let him be himself. When I saw him getting tired, I called it a day and brought him back."

I swallowed hard and looked away. My heart was filled with gratitude and a touch of sadness. Knowing he was sick was one thing, but knowing his days were numbered was something else. I was glad she got to see him like that today.

"I gotta get over there this week and see him."

She nodded. "We had a great day, I even took him to the Amber Inn. He helped me go over the menu, and then we stopped by the stationery store to look at invitations."

The glow of excitement on her face hit me square in the chest. "Don't make this too hard on yourself. It's just my family and our close friends."

She rolled her eyes. "It doesn't matter. I want to send them. We don't exactly have months to plan. We have two weeks," she said as if I was slow to catch on. "The only reason why the timeline isn't stressing me out is because we are keeping it small and simple." She stood to bring her plate over beside mine. "If someone told me a year ago that we would be sitting here in this kitchen, planning our wedding, and talking about starting my own landscape design business here in Marcellus Falls, I would have thought they were crazy, but here we are."

I shook my head. "I still can't believe we're doing this."

She tilted her head to the side. "You're not freaking out on me, are you?"

"Harlow, I've been waiting to marry you my entire life."

"You know," she said softly, "a part of me always knew it was supposed to be you. Maybe that's why I couldn't marry him."

I reached out to tuck a strand of hair behind her ear. "I don't give a damn what that trust says, or about what anyone else thinks. I want to marry you because I love you. You're it for me. I don't care where we live, here, the lake house, an apartment, or a trailer, you are my home."

Her smile was wobbly. "I never thought I would get a second chance with you again. I can't wait to be your wife."

I brought her mouth to mine and kissed her. It was the type of kiss that said we are in this together now, and there is no turning back.

She wrapped her arms around my neck, pulling me closer.

I dragged my lips down to her jaw and sucked on the side of her neck where her pulse raced. "I thank God every day that you came back to me."

Her hands slid under my shirt. My muscles jumped from her touch. "I don't remember you being so religious."

"I'm not, but I should probably change that because the things I plan on doing to you will definitely require a trip to confession."

My mouth crashed to hers again, this time with urgency and need. "What do you plan on doing to me?" she asked, her hands gripping the sides of my hair.

I grabbed hold of her hips and lifted her onto the counter. I settled myself between her thighs. "How about I show you instead?"

She wrapped her legs around me. "I was hoping you would say that, just be careful with your hand."

I slid my hands under her shirt, pulling it up slowly. "Trust me, nothing would make my hand feel better than feeling you come all over it."

"I hope you don't plan on going slow. I need you," she whispered, as my hands skated along her sides.

My thumbs brushed the underside of her breast. "I know exactly what you need because every inch of you belongs to me."

I tugged the rest of her shirt off and threw it on the floor. "God. I want you, Brooks, please."

I pressed my mouth to her nipple and swirled it around the peak. "Say it again. Tell me how much you want me. Say it louder this time. I'll never get tired of hearing it."

She arched into me and gasped when I bit down. "I never wanted or needed anyone like you. Please don't stop."

I sucked and circled, feeling her heart pound against her chest. "You're going to feel me everywhere. You're already shaking for me."

Her hands went to my jeans, fumbling with the button. I helped her slide them down my legs. Our breaths were frantic as we both removed our clothes.

Once her panties were off and she was completely naked, I gripped her thighs and shoved a finger inside. She was already wet and ready. I teased her with my fingers, loving the way she trembled from my touch. "You are the sexiest thing I've ever seen."

Her lips parted with a moan, and her head fell back. "I love the way you touch me."

"I'm going to do more than touch you. I'm going to bring you so much pleasure. You won't be able to think straight."

Then I pushed into her, and she gasped. Her fingers dug into my shoulders, and she threw her head to the side. I loved knowing I was making her so desperate. I continued to drive into her. The heels of her feet dug into my back. Her tits bounced with each push. I increased the pressure, feeling her clench around me. I kept drawing out every ounce of pleasure I could. She moaned and kept her eyes on mine. I continued sliding in and out. I loved this woman more than I could ever explain.

"Brooks." She moaned. "You feel so good. I can't hold on for much longer."

"Then let go," I said, slipping my hand between our bodies and rubbing her clit.

She came apart with my name on her lips. And just like that, all the drama from her ex, all the bickering and doubts over the past few weeks, slipped away. All that mattered was the way her body moved with mine. The way she moaned my name, and the way we seemed to fit like we were made for each other.

I greedily continued to fill her up until I felt the familiar pressure build. She held on, giving me her body and letting me take what I needed. She felt like heaven. I don't think I could ever get enough of her. I slid out and slammed back in, burying myself to the hilt. She squeezed herself around me and I came. I followed her to a place that left me panting and satiated.

Once I was done, I closed my eyes and brought her to my chest.

I kissed her damp hair. "Did you happen to pick up any dessert at the store?"

She laughed. "You're seriously thinking about food right now?"

"I'm starving. All you fed me was a small piece of fish and a scoop of rice."

She smacked my chest. "The only dessert I have for you is called the 'Chef's Surprise,' and it's between my legs. So, I suggest you bring me to bed and enjoy the hell out of it."

"Best dessert ever," I said, and lifted her over my shoulder and stalked to our room. All that mattered, all I needed, was right here in my arms. And I could not wait to build my life with her.

CHAPTER TWENTY-NINE
HARLOW

The scent of fresh roses and gardenias hit my nose the second I stepped inside Bloom & Vines. It was the same flower shop Molly worked at when she spent the summer here with me before our last year of college. It looked exactly the same, with overflowing flower buckets and gardening tools scattered across the counter.

"Look what the cat dragged in," Mona, the owner of the shop, said, looking up with a wink.

"Hey, Mona." I smiled as I crossed the shop.

"You're cutting it a little close, aren't ya?" she teased, brushing a few white curls off her forehead. "Most brides give me at least six months' advance notice. You're giving me fourteen days. This isn't a drive-thru, you know."

I laughed. "If anyone can pull it off, you can."

She was adjusting a bouquet of carnations, and I noticed her hands were a little shakier than I remembered. "Luckily for you, I'm a miracle worker."

"I didn't realize you were still running this place until Molly mentioned it."

She hopped off the stool slowly and pulled me in for a

hug. "I have a few kids who help me out from time to time, but they don't last very long. You know me, I need to keep busy. I don't do well sitting still."

Mona would probably be running this place until the day she died, but she was obviously slowing down. My guess is that everyone was aware of it except her.

"You look good," I said, standing back to meet her eyes.

She swatted my shoulder. "Flattery isn't going to get you a discount, honey."

I snorted. "Never thought it would."

She placed the bouquet under the counter and motioned me to follow her to the back.

"So, do you have any jitters?" she asked as we reached her office. She pulled out several photo albums filled with pictures of wedding arrangements she had created over the years for other brides.

"Not one. I can't wait to get married," I said as I thumbed through the pages. The arrangements were stunning and simple, but nothing was grabbing my attention.

"That's the way it should be. If you're not second-guessing your decision, then you know it's the right one."

"I couldn't agree more."

"All right." She wiped her hands down on her green apron. "You said simple and elegant." She grabbed the album and advanced about ten pages from where I was. "What do you think of this?"

"I love the white roses and green vines," I said, my eyes trailing over to the next page that was filled with wildflowers.

Her gaze followed mine. "You like those, huh?"

"They are gorgeous." I smiled, feeling that those were exactly what I was looking for. My fingers lightly rubbed over the picture of soft petals and the delicate stems. They reminded me of the flowers my mom would plant.

"You've got good taste." She pulled a notebook out of her apron and scribbled something down. "Do you want to pick out boutonnieres for the guys?"

"Sure, I'll check with Brooks and see what he wants."

She looked at me over the top of her glasses. "What about your dad?"

I looked down at the floor. "He won't be there."

She pressed her lips together. "I probably shouldn't say anything, because it's probably nothing."

That usually meant it was something.

I leaned my hip against the counter. "Whatever it is, you can tell me."

She leaned in and lowered her voice even though we were the only people in the shop. "Are you familiar with Bob, from the hardware shop in Seneca Hills?"

Seneca Hills was the next town over. "I can't say that I am. I've been finding everything I need at Hardware Haven. I haven't had a reason to make the drive over there."

She cleared her throat and looked over her shoulder to make sure we were still alone. "Well, he stopped by this morning, as he does every month to pick up flowers for his wife. He mentioned that an older guy from a New York City area code called him asking if he had specific things in stock. Later that night, right before closing, a younger fella came to pick up the order. He said the guy was acting strange and didn't seem to know his way around a hardware store, but he didn't think much of it until he saw him at the pub that night he got into a fight with Brooks."

"Are you serious?"

She nodded. "Honey, I wouldn't joke about this. He

started connecting the dots and realized it was the same night your house was flooded."

My stomach dropped. "Are you saying it was Baz Zimmerman?"

Mona wouldn't say something if she didn't think it was true. There is only one explanation as to why my ex would step foot in a hardware store.

She nodded slowly. "Afraid so. Bob said he was odd, but he likes to keep his nose out of everyone's business, so he didn't say anything. But he knew it wasn't just a coincidence when he saw him at the pub."

I suspected either Baz or my dad, but it never occurred to me that they were working together. Now, it all started to make sense, and I'm not sure which one shocked me more.

"I didn't mean to upset you," she said gently. "I just thought you should know."

I blinked. "No. I'm glad you told me."

I slumped down onto one of the benches and gave myself a minute to let that news sink in. I always assumed that deep down, my dad had a soft spot for me, no matter what. He was my father, after all, but at the end of the day, this only confirmed my place in his life.

Mona came to sit beside me. I didn't want to cry. Not here. Not at all, but the tears came anyway. I stared at the floor while Mona placed her hand on mine.

"I'm sorry, honey. I didn't mean to upset you."

I wiped my eyes. "I don't know why I am so surprised. I think a part of me knew my father was somehow involved."

"He doesn't deserve your tears."

"I know that, so why does it hurt so bad?"

"Because he's your dad. It doesn't matter how ugly his soul is; every little girl wants her daddy's love. You're allowed to grieve the loss of that relationship." She squeezed my hand. "Now it's your turn to show him that your life is your own. He doesn't dictate who you marry. You have one life to live. You live it for you. No one else."

My entire body shook. I was on the verge of crying hard and ugly, but something inside me snapped.

This was the nail in the coffin.

I stood and wiped my cheeks. "I need to go."

They were both about to learn that I wasn't the same girl that they used to manipulate. I was so over their shit.

CHAPTER THIRTY
HARLOW

I don't even remember walking out of the shop. One minute, I was hugging Mona and saying goodbye, and the next, I was packing an overnight bag and heading to Manhattan.

I didn't care that Baz had his hands in this, but my father?

I tried to find one good memory. Just one where I felt like he loved me, but nothing came to mind.

There were no bedtime stories. No surprise visits after school to get ice cream like there were when my mom was alive.

I convinced myself that he cared about me in his own way. He just didn't know how to show it. Now, I finally saw him for what he was.

When I stepped off the elevator, my dad's receptionist, Rosanna, gave me a startled look. She knew who I was. Everyone did. My old office was right down the hall. It had a corner view and a job title that most people could only dream of. But at that moment, I didn't feel like I belonged there. Maybe I never did.

I walked past her desk, not even taking the time to greet her. I saw his office was empty, so I walked right in. The room looked the same as it always had, so I wasn't sure why it felt different.

Floor-to-ceiling windows and a massive mahogany desk with big leather chairs that were overpriced and uncomfortable. A bookshelf with limited edition books that he paid a fortune for but probably never read.

The office was all for show, just like him.

I crossed the room, needing to feel something other than the hurt twisting around in my stomach.

I walked around the perfectly polished desk and slumped in his chair. There was not a single picture of me anywhere. Only award plaques and brag photos of him shaking hands with celebrities and politicians.

I had no idea what possessed me to reach inside the top drawer. Maybe it was hope that I'd been wrong, that I'd find a school picture or one of the many birthday cards I gave him over the year. Something, anything that showed he actually cared.

There was nothing but ledgers, invoices, and business cards, all clipped neatly together. I was about to shove them back inside when something caught my eye. I recognized the logo at the top. It was a receipt for Bob's Hardware store in Seneca Hills, NY.

My hands shook as I unfolded the piece of paper.

Adjustable Pliers, pipe wrench, screwdriver, gloves, bucket, and towels.

There was only one reason why he would have this receipt. Because he was guilty as hell.

I was holding proof that my father was behind what happened to my house.

I could hear commotion outside the office, so I stuffed the receipt in my purse as he entered the room.

"Did you find what you're looking for?"

I looked up to see him standing in the doorway. He had his phone in his hand, typical arrogant expression, looking at me like my visit was nothing more than an inconvenience to him.

I was slowly coming to terms with the fact that that was all I was to him.

I took in a deep breath, trying to get my nerves to settle. "I came to clean out my office and thought I would stop by for a chat."

He narrowed his eyes, but I didn't flinch, which was a miracle considering how anxious I was.

"Really? Because it looks to me like you were going through my things."

Oh, he had no idea. I wanted to call him out on what I found, but something told me to hold on to it. It was the only evidence I had connecting him to this mess, and I would not give up any leverage I had on him.

"Nope. I was looking for a key to the safe. I need to grab a few documents so I can apply for my marriage license."

He placed his coat casually on the hook, like we were about to have a friendly chat about the weather. "So, you're still planning on going through with it, huh? Maybe we should talk about that."

My hands shook as I clutched my purse. "Actually, why don't we talk about all the trouble you and your little sidekick are trying to cause."

He closed the door, deliberately slow, and glanced briefly at his desk. "It's unfortunate that we had to stop the construction on the house, but maybe if you hadn't walked out on your wedding and everything we worked for, then things wouldn't be such a mess."

It didn't go unnoticed that he used the word "we."

"You're not mad about the wedding. You're mad because I embarrassed you and cost you a deal you've been working on for years."

He stalked across the room and stared me down. "Can you blame me?"

"Oh, I'm sorry. Please forgive me for not wanting to be married off into some loveless marriage so that you could close in on another piece of property."

He planted his hands on his desk and glared at me. "I had high hopes for you. I gave you everything you needed to succeed in life. And this is how you pay me back? By walking away from everything I planned for you?"

He didn't care that he hurt me. He didn't care about anyone but himself. I was so done because he apparently didn't care for me at all.

"Dad, I came here to end this once and for all. Years ago, you made sure that Brooks and I never had a chance. You threatened to destroy him and his family if I didn't walk away, and I did because I was scared, but I'm not scared anymore."

He walked over to the window and stared out at the skyline. "I was protecting you."

"No, Dad. You were trying to stay in control. You knew how much I loved him. He was a threat to you and the plans you had for me. I allowed you to hold that over my head for years, but you can't control me anymore. You took five years away from us. You tried to ruin him, and it didn't work."

He was calm and composed as he stepped away from the window. "I did what I had to do."

"No, you tried to destroy him, so I would come running

back. You wanted to remind me that you always win, but you're not winning this time."

His expression hardened. "Just because he's still standing doesn't mean I'm done with him."

"Go ahead. Keep threatening me, but understand this: If you do, I will go public and tell every reporter and news outlet that will listen to me that my engagement to Baz Zimmerman was nothing more than a contract. That you and Senator Zimmerman were working together. I'll make sure to tell them everything."

"Careful, Harlow. Daughter or not, I don't take kindly to threats."

I smiled. "I learned from the best. You raised me to be strong. You just never expected me to turn that strength on you."

He didn't react. Simply stared at me like I was some spoiled teenager who was having a temper tantrum. "Just because you are my daughter, doesn't mean you won't face consequences. If you walk away from me and this life, you walk away from everything that comes with it. The money, the connections, you will lose it all. Everything comes at a price."

"I've already paid the price, Dad." I met his eyes, feeling a dull ache in my chest. One that will probably never heal, but I had to remind myself that what I had waiting for me in Marcellus Falls was so much better than this. "I don't want this life. So, I would appreciate it if you stayed out of mine. If you try to interfere with me or Brooks again, you will regret it."

He tilted his head. "Don't forget who you are talking to. I am still your father."

"No. You had a chance to be my father, and you blew it," I said, trying to keep my voice calm. "I did everything you asked of me. Everything. I showed up at every fundraiser. I smiled for the cameras, dated who you wanted me to. I tried so hard to be the perfect daughter. The one you wanted, but in the end, you only wanted a puppet. Something you could control to get what you wanted."

He leaned against the desk and studied me like I was some project he was trying to figure out.

I looked around his office. It was filled with framed degrees and awards sitting on glass shelves. It was all about him. It was cold and stiff. Even the plants in the corner looked fake. Everything in his life had a place, except I was the one who never fit. It was such a moment of clarity, one that I wished had come five years ago.

"You want to walk away, fine. You go right ahead, but you will regret it."

I shook my head because he still didn't get it. All those years, I tiptoed around him, careful not to make too much noise, got the best grades, all so I could earn his love. Now, I realized I was trying to earn something from him that couldn't be given.

"I don't think I will."

He shook his head. "I thought you were smarter than this, but I see now that I was wrong. You don't have what it takes to make it in my world."

"I do have what it takes. I just want no part of your world. Your world is empty. You want a perfect little robot, but I am a human being. I have feelings, hopes, and dreams. I'm done letting you push me around."

"Push you around? That's rich coming from a girl who is turning on her father."

"All I ever wanted was your love and approval."

"You had my approval when you agreed to marry Bartholomew Zimmerman. I wanted you to marry into a good family. Carry on my family legacy. I did what was necessary."

"Dad, I've spent my entire life pleasing you, trying to satisfy you, but it's time I start choosing myself. If you have any fatherly instincts left in you at all, you'll want me to be happy." I stepped around his desk and met him head-on. "I know I will never be the daughter you envisioned, and I'm done trying. I don't need your approval anymore, but let me say this," I stepped closer, and his eyes narrowed. "If you ever try to interfere with my happiness again, you will find out how far I am willing to go to protect the man I love."

He glanced down at his watch, like he had more important things to deal with. "Is that all?"

"One more thing," I said, ready to be done with this conversation. "I made a few calls. Construction starts back up tomorrow. The town cleared the permits. If you so much as step foot on my property or do anything to interfere again, you will be hearing from my lawyer."

Without saying another word, I turned and walked out the door. I didn't say goodbye because he didn't deserve it.

My footsteps echoed in the long, empty hallway. I paused by the office that once was mine. The small space that held so many dreams and possibilities. Now, I realized it was nothing more than a prison cell of my own making. I turned away, not bothering to take anything.

As I neared the bank of elevators, I almost didn't notice him.

Baz was walking out of a conference room. There was a pretty redhead grinning up at him. There was red lipstick on his neck, and his tie was crooked. He stopped in his tracks when he spotted me and did a double take.

His smile was smug as he leaned against the wall. "Harlow, what are you doing here? Shouldn't you be back in

Marcellus Falls, baking cookies or running a yard sale? Or did you finally come to your senses and come back to beg for my forgiveness?"

I took in a slow and steady breath and gave him a once-over. Expensive suit, polished shoes, and a cocky grin that had no right to be there. "Like that would ever happen, but I'm glad I ran into you, because I have something to say and you're going to listen." I smiled sweetly while adjusting the strap of my purse. "Stop lurking around town and trying to cause trouble for me and my fiancé. Whatever plan you and my father had is over."

He raised an eyebrow. "I have no idea what you're talking about."

I stepped forward, just enough to smell his sharp, expensive cologne. "Don't play dumb. It doesn't suit you."

He scoffed. "You're the one who started it when you embarrassed me."

The girl standing next to him went quiet. She looked like she didn't want to be in the middle of this, so I kept my attention on him. "You embarrassed yourself, Bartholomew."

He hated it anytime someone used his full name, which was precisely why I said it.

He looked annoyed. "You think you can find someone better than me? Good luck to you, sweetheart. Have fun with your little broke builder."

I let out a small, breathy laugh. "Oh, I plan on it, so listen to me very carefully. If you keep showing up, trying to cause problems for us, then the entire world will know that you're not the golden boy you make yourself out to be, and that's the last thing your dad needs right before an election."

He folded his arms, trying to appear more confident

than he was. "Do you seriously think you can threaten me? Have you forgotten who I am?"

"No, I didn't forget." I smiled sweetly as I pressed the button on the elevator. "But like I told my father, I'm done caring."

And with that, he finally shut up.

When the doors finally closed, I sank against the wall and blew out a deep breath. I was ready to leave all this behind and start my new life.

I pulled out my phone and clicked on Molly's name. I typed out a quick text asking her to call me when she got a chance.

And when I stepped outside onto the bustling streets of New York, I felt free as a bird and was ready to go home.

CHAPTER THIRTY-ONE
BROOKS

Bob's hardware store was a short twenty-minute drive, just on the other side of the county line. It was small, and the type of place you only shopped at if you had a reason to go there. My dad and I used to come here when we needed something that the bigger chains didn't carry. Bob was a quiet guy who didn't like getting pulled into other people's messes.

That was why I had to be careful when I walked through the door and started asking questions. I had just left the flower shop. I had only stopped by to pay for the flowers that Harlow ordered. The moment Mona spotted me, she beckoned me over to the counter. Her voice was low as she went into detail with me about the conversation she had with Harlow earlier. By the time she was finished, I was thanking her for letting me know and flying out the door.

Now, I was standing outside the hardware store, trying to keep my temper in check so I didn't come across as a crazy lunatic. The bell jingled as I stepped inside. I spotted Bob crouched low in front of the electrical aisle, balancing a box of outlet covers on his bad knee. He didn't ask why I was there, because he already knew. Instead of beating around the bush, I pulled out my phone and showed him a photo. It was a picture of Baz, all decked out in a tux, with a slimy smile on his face.

Bob took one look at the photo and confirmed everything. It was clear, based on his recollection, that I needed to call my brother.

I wasn't sure what pissed me off more? The fact that Baz would mess up her house, or that she almost married the guy.

I paced outside the hardware store, probably looking like a strung out coke head. I watched the traffic crawl by, waved hello to a few people I recognized, but I was about ready to jump out of my skin by the time Tuck's car rolled down the street.

He pulled up to a parking spot in front of the store, put his cruiser into park, and stepped out.

"What's going on?" he asked, pushing his sunglasses onto his head.

I folded my arms. "According to Bob Henning, Baz was at the store the night Harlow's house was flooded. He was rude and acting weird. He didn't think much of it until he spotted him at the pub the night we got into a fight. Said Baz came in and picked up some supplies right before closing."

"What kind of supplies?" he asked, glancing over at the store and staring through the glass window.

I exhaled through my nose. "The kind of supplies you would need if you wanted to flood someone's house."

I had my suspicion, but this was more like a confirmation.

He squinted his eyes against the sun. "How did you figure that out?"

"Mona," I said, placing my hands on my hips, trying to stop them from shaking. "Bob was in Blooms and Vines this morning. He and Mona got talking. Said everything clicked when he saw him at the pub last week. I showed him a photo on my phone, and he confirmed it was him. There was no hesitation."

Tuck went quiet for a moment and ran a hand down his face. I could see him thinking that over and connecting all the dots. "I'll need to obtain his statement. Does he have a copy of the transaction?"

"I didn't ask," I said, rubbing at the knot in the back of my neck. I had so much nervous energy flowing through my limbs, I was about ready to burst. "Do you think that's enough?"

He adjusted the badge on his waist. "Not sure. I'm going to check. The ID helps, but if he has a copy of the receipt, that's even better. It might still be all circumstantial, though."

"Figures." I kicked a pebble off the curb. "But this is good, right?"

He nodded his head and pulled his phone out. "I gotta call Chief and see what he thinks. I need to get a formal statement from Bob. It definitely helps make the case."

It was a strong lead. I hoped it would be enough.

I paced the sidewalk while I waited for Tuck to finish up his call. I didn't know what would happen next or if this would even lead to any charges, but it was a start. It was the only proof we had that connected him to the house. It still blew my mind how far an entitled asshole would go to get what he wanted.

She never did a damn thing to either of them, yet they

both treated her like she owed them her life. All she wanted was a little peace, and they couldn't even give her that.

I wanted to drive to New York and kick down his door so I could finish what I started, but I understood this had to be handled the right way.

Tuck pocketed his phone and started walking toward the store. "I'm going inside to talk to Bob and see if he is comfortable making a formal statement."

"I'm coming with you," I said, falling into step beside him.

He rolled his eyes as he reached the door. "Let me do all the talking, and don't go all Sherlock Holmes on me."

The corner of my mouth twitched. "I'm not stupid."

"That's up for debate." He gave me a warning look as we reached the entrance. "Remember, I'm going to ask the questions and you're to stay out of it."

I gave him a nod, even though we both knew I would have a hard time keeping my mouth shut. For Harlow's sake, I would have to. It was the least I could do.

CHIEF SCOTT WAS STILL in his office, sipping from a chipped coffee mug while eating a turkey sub from the gas station across the street, when we walked in. His office was sparsely decorated, consisting of a metal desk, a small file cabinet, and a coffee machine that was probably older than me sitting by the window.

"What do you got?" he asked, looking up from his computer monitor.

Tuck and I slid into the two chairs at his desk. "There is a witness who places the victim's ex-fiancé at the hardware store the night the damage occurred. The items he purchased are consistent with what was used to do the damage. So, there is an eyewitness, a paper trail, and a motive."

Chief Scott picked up his glasses and pored over the report without saying a word.

He looked up and scratched his bald head. "So, let me get this straight. We're dealing with Senator Zimmerman's son, who purchased supplies the night his ex-fiancée's house was flooded, and you want me to charge him with trespassing, breaking and entering, and vandalism?"

Tuck tapped his hands on the desk. "Are you good with that?"

Chief leaned back in his chair. "We need to be careful. If we go in too hot, it could blow up in our face."

Tuck leaned forward. "It would be by the book, I swear."

He rolled his pen between his fingers like he was thinking it over. "I need to reach out to my NYPD connections. It may take a few days, and we will have to bring in a bigger agency to take over."

Tuck smiled and nodded. "I'm only looking to bring him in for questioning. We don't need to book him."

He exhaled and rubbed his chin. "This is a big deal, Tuck. Even if we politely ask him to come in and answer a few questions, someone high-profile like this will draw attention. We can't afford to make any mistakes." He looked at me. "You shouldn't even be in this room, Brooks. You understand that going forward, this is an official police matter."

I nodded, letting him know I understood how serious this was. "I'm aware."

"I mean it, Brooks." He narrowed his eyes. "You are

already a liability to this case. This is a small town. We are family friends, but I'm asking you to step back."

He wasn't wrong. I knew it, and I couldn't blame him for saying that. Chief Scott used to be our neighbor. My brothers and I went to school and played ball with his sons. We would get invited to family barbecues and birthday parties, but right now, he was drawing a line, and I needed to respect that.

I folded my hands in my lap and gave him the confirmation he needed. "I give you my word, Chief."

He took a sip of his coffee and folded his arms. "This guy has connections. His father makes phone calls, and people start panicking. If you want to help your girl, you stay out of our way and let us handle him."

"Done."

"Good, because if we bring someone in on that level, we can't give his lawyers anything to latch onto, and you better believe he will have a big-time lawyer."

Oh, I had no doubt. They would probably assume he would get off, too. That's how rich people worked. They bribed, schemed, and threw money at problems to make them go away. That was why I would not do anything to screw this up. I couldn't let my emotions get in the way.

Tuck cleared his throat and spoke up. "I should probably excuse myself and turn this over to someone else due to a conflict of interest."

Chief laughed. "Well, seeing the department has ten employees total, that narrows our options."

The three of us laughed, but the weight of everything was finally catching up to me. This was real. It was happening. He would probably get a slap on the wrist, maybe walk away with a fine, but his precious reputation would be tarnished. I would make sure of that.

At the very least, he would sweat it out. He wasn't the type of guy who answered to anybody.

But as far as the investigation went, I would stay out of it.

I walked out into the waiting room while Tuck and Chief finished up. My head was spinning. All I could think about was Harlow. I just wanted her to move on from all this bullshit.

I glanced down at the text message she sent me earlier today, letting me know she was going back to New York. I had to be honest, for a split second, I thought she was leaving me, until I learned why she was going.

Now, I needed to drive to New York so she wouldn't have to face those two idiots by herself.

CHAPTER THIRTY-TWO
BROOKS

It was almost dark by the time I found myself standing outside Harlow's front door. The building was on the Upper East Side, just a few blocks from Central Park.

I called Molly, to get Harlow's address and we talked about how we're going to handle this. Once we knew when they planned on bringing Baz in for questioning, Molly would call in an anonymous tip to her friend, who worked at the local news station.

That way, if for some reason, Baz was able to weasel his way out of the charges, he wouldn't be able to escape the negative publicity.

Which, for him and his family, would be just as bad.

I pulled on my shirt and tapped my knuckles on her door. Her little steps could be heard on the hardwood floor.

Probably no more than ten seconds had passed, although it felt like hours until the door whipped open. And there she was.

"Brooks." She stood in the doorway, barefoot, in a pair of jeans and a black sweater. Her hair was thrown up on top of her head, and she didn't have an ounce of makeup on her face. Her eyes were red-rimmed, like she'd been crying.

"You drove here?"

I didn't answer her right away. Just crossed the threshold and pulled her into me. She tensed for a second before melting into my chest.

"Tuck and I talked to the owner of the hardware store," I said, breathing into the top of her hair. "He confirmed that Baz was there the night you came back into town. Tuck got his statement."

She stood back slowly and adjusted a strand of hair that came loose from her bun. "Mona told you?"

I leaned against the doorframe. "Yes."

She blinked, not saying anything at first. I thought she would be happy. Her silence was throwing me off.

"Come inside so we can talk." She led me through the small entryway. I inspected the living room as she led me to the couch. The place was modern and clean. It was a little too small for a big guy like me, but otherwise, it looked comfortable. The walls were a warm beige. The furniture was classy and inviting, exactly what I had pictured for her.

She dropped into the worn spot in the corner of her L-shaped sectional and fiddled with her hands. "I have proof that Baz and my dad were behind the flooding of my house."

I suspected that was the case when Bob said the guy who phoned in the order sounded older, but for her sake, I hoped it wasn't.

"That's why you came back here? To confront him?"

She nodded. "That was the plan."

I brushed my thumb across her cheek. "What do you mean, that was the plan?"

She pulled a pillow onto her lap and twisted her fingers around it. "When I got to his office, he wasn't there, so I snooped through his things."

"What did you find?"

She reached over and pulled out a slip of paper that was folded neatly in half.

"I found this in his desk. It's a receipt from the hardware store. The date matches. The supplies match. They both knew exactly what they were doing."

I reached over and handed her a tissue when I saw the tears start to fall. "I'm so sorry, Harlow. You don't deserve this. I promise they will pay. Molly and I already have a plan in place."

"I know, she told me, and I am one hundred percent on board."

I glanced down at the piece of paper. "Are you okay with turning over that receipt to the authorities? It will definitely help."

I knew how hard this was for her. She'd been fighting for her father's love and approval for her entire life. She was doing her best to stay strong and hold herself together, which gutted me more than anything. I could tell she was tired. Tired of being manipulated, tired of trying to fit inside a world that she never felt comfortable in.

And what made it even worse was that it was clear to me she still loved him. I could see it in her eyes and sense it with every shuddering breath that left her lungs.

She leaned back and tucked her knees to her chest. "I was trying to figure out what to do with this information. I thought about holding on to it as leverage to keep them both away, but I worried that it wouldn't be enough and, quite honestly, I'm sick of keeping secrets."

That got my attention. "What do you mean?"

"What I'm about to tell you, I should have said a long time ago." She rested her chin on her knees. "Do you remember the night I left town?"

I stiffened. "Of course, I do." It was one of the worst nights of my life.

"I didn't leave because I was choosing my dad over you." She swallowed and looked away. "I left because my dad gave me a choice. I could either walk away, or he would do everything in his power to ruin you and everyone you cared about."

I was so stunned; you could have knocked me over with a damn feather. "That's why you left me?"

All these years, I assumed she just chose her dad. That she was too loyal, and he was too controlling. I told myself over and over again that she was a coward for not standing up to him. I believed nothing I could ever say or do would be good enough. I never understood why until today. She was protecting me.

She twisted her hands in her lap. "I couldn't let you and your family lose everything because of me. My dad has money and connections. He would have done irreparable damage to your reputation. He threatened to go after your family's business."

That man took years away from us. All those nights I'd laid in bed, hating her. Now that I knew the truth, I hated myself more for not seeing it.

"You should have told me," I said, staring at the woman I spent years trying to get over but never could. "Why did you let me hate you and think the worst?"

"Because I knew you would be angry and go after him."

I looked away. My heart was racing because she was

right, I would have. And maybe it would have cost us everything, but at least I would had know why.

I reached out and brushed my thumb along her ankle. "I get why you did it, but I wish you hadn't made that decision for both of us."

She hung her head. "I know. I'm sorry. I struggled with that decision for a long time. That's why I spent years avoiding Marcellus Falls. It was too hard for me to think about running into you, but the day I ran from the church, I knew I had to go back." Tears filled her eyes. "Are you mad?"

"I am, but not at you. I'm angry at him for tearing us apart. I'm mad that he stole years from us that we will never get back."

"I understand. So, what happens now?"

I glanced at the window. The city of Manhattan buzzed on the other side. I looked down at my watch, knowing I didn't have much time left.

I squeezed her hand gently. "I need to do something, and you need to let me."

She tensed. "Please don't. I just want to put all this behind me and go home."

I smiled at the word "home" coming from her beautiful lips. "I want that too, but you know the kind of man I am. I can't let this slide. He didn't just mess with you, but he tried to ruin me, too."

She sighed and leaned back on the couch, knowing she wasn't going to talk me out of this. "Fine, but please don't get arrested."

I laughed. "I promise not to throw the first punch. How is that?"

"I guess I'll have to trust you." She stood up and started moving across the room. "I'm going to pack a few boxes.

I've already contacted a realtor about listing this place. There is nothing left here for me. I'll be ready to go when you get back."

I stood up, gave her one last kiss, and stepped out onto the streets of New York, determined to reclaim our life and be done with the son of a bitch once and for all.

CHAPTER THIRTY-THREE
BROOKS

William Bennet lived in a penthouse on the Upper East Side. It was only a few short blocks from Harlow's apartment. It seemed the closer I got, the quieter the streets became. I hadn't been in this building in years, but it was the kind of place you never forgot. The outside of the building was nothing special, but the green canvas canopy, brass-plated doors, and the doorman standing outside in his navy-blue uniform screamed money.

I spotted a guy in his mid-forties walking toward the main entrance. He had his earbuds in, so I slipped in behind him. I was close, but not close enough to draw attention. The doorman was talking to a delivery guy, but spotted me when I tried to breeze past him.

I pulled the keycard that Harlow had given me out of my wallet and flashed it to him. "I'm here to see my father-in-law, William Bennett."

He held his hand up. "Wait a minute. You need to be approved."

"I'm good." I picked up my stride as he sprinted toward me, telling me to hold on, but I was already at the elevator.

I swiped the key, thankful that the door opened, but I could still hear him yelling as the doors closed.

I leaned against the wall as it took me to the top floor. I clenched and unclenched my fists, waiting for the doors to open. I was worked up and antsy, not out of fear, but from the fire that had been burning in my chest for the past five years.

I stepped into the long hallway and took a left, walking to the familiar door. I rang the bell, and when he swung the door open, he was already on the phone with the guy at the front desk.

His eyes met mine. "He's already here. Don't worry about it. I'll handle this."

I walked past him, not waiting for an invitation inside.

He hung up and slammed the door. "Who the hell do you think you are barging in here without an appointment?"

I forced myself to stay calm and hoped this would be the last time I'd ever have to see the man again. "I didn't think I needed an appointment to come talk to my future father-in-law."

His jaw clenched just enough for me to notice. "What do you want?" He walked over to the liquor cabinet and poured himself a scotch.

My hands curled into fists. "I want you to stay the hell out of our lives."

His eyes narrowed. "She is my daughter."

"And I'm the man who will make sure you will never hurt her again."

He sat down on an oversized leather chair and leaned back. "All this over a damn house."

"It's not just a house to her," I snapped.

He still didn't get it. I wasn't sure he ever would.

He turned and waved his hand to the glass window, where the skyline spread out before him. It was late, so the entire city was lit up. It was too bad I couldn't enjoy the view.

Do you think I got to where I am today by being soft? Every decision I have ever made came with a sacrifice."

I stared at the man, questioning how someone as cold-hearted and ruthless as he could father a person as amazing as Harlow. I know she wanted to believe that he loved her, but I doubted he was capable of it. He only loved the version of her that was compliant, attended the best schools, wore the right dresses, and married the man who would benefit him and his business. Her life was never about her.

"Oh, trust me, I am very well aware. Harlow told me everything."

He crossed his arms. "You'll have to be more specific."

"You forced her to leave me five years ago. You threatened her by promising to destroy me and my family if she didn't come back to New York City."

He crossed his legs and swirled his liquor around in the glass. "How noble of her to tell you."

"You made me think that I wasn't good enough for her. I believed that she didn't love me."

He took a sip of his drink. "Then I guess my plan worked."

I shook my head and stepped forward. "I spent years hating her because of you."

The muscle in his jaw ticked. "All I have ever done is what's best for her."

I shook my head. "You do what's best for you, William.

No one else. You've allowed her to think that love came with conditions and strings. You made her believe that being with me would come with a cost that she wasn't willing to pay. And once she grew a backbone and walked away, you couldn't handle that."

He rolled his eyes. "That's an interesting interpretation."

"I think it's spot-on."

He straightened his shoulders and adjusted his tie. "I think it would be best if you turn yourself around and walk back out that door before I'm forced to do something you won't like."

I crossed my arms. "Do your worst. I'm not afraid of you."

"You should be, because you are just like my daughter. You have no idea how the real world works."

I laughed because this was so messed up, it wasn't even funny. There was no remorse or regret. He would never admit that he was wrong because he didn't believe he was. He wasn't fit to be a parent. He only cared about trying to shape her into who he wanted her to be. Maybe he was right. I didn't understand how his world worked. I've never been a pawn in a merger. I've never been pushed into a corner like her. He's never tried to understand her. Hell, he barely acknowledged her until she decided to stand on her own two feet and walk away.

I used to think he was just overbearing and controlling, but this went much deeper. And I was so glad she finally woke up and removed herself from this life.

"You tried to force her back into a life that she didn't want. When she didn't bend, you made the decision to break her. That's not doing what's best for her. That's you trying to stay in control. I'm done letting you interfere in our lives."

He glared at me. "Are you done playing hero now? I've got work to do."

I stepped closer but still kept a little distance between us. I didn't trust myself. "I love her," I said, my voice low and fierce. "Always have. I'm going to marry her. I'm going to protect her, and I'm going to make damn sure that you never get inside her head again. I might have been young and naive before, but I'm not stepping aside this time. So, I'm telling you one last time, if you come near her, I won't just show up here with a warning. I'll burn your whole fucked-up world to the ground."

He didn't move a muscle. He simply sat there with his smug expression, believing he still had a chance to win this round. He would never admit defeat, even though he had already lost.

"Good luck to you both." He turned in his chair and picked up his iPad like he was trying to dismiss me. "If she ends up miserable and broke, tell her not to come crawling back to me for help."

I stalked forward, leaned my head over his shoulder, and spoke into his ear. "She may not be rich, but she will never have to beg you for a fucking dime. I will make sure of it."

For the first time, there was no snappy comeback. No smirk or arrogant dress down. Only silence.

"This is your final warning. Your reign over her ends today. Whatever power you think you hold over us is over. You can keep coming at me all you want, but if you so much as breathe in her direction, I won't be so polite next time."

I walked to the door, and with every step I took down

the hallway, I felt the weight I'd been carrying for the past five years fall from my shoulders.

When I stepped outside and took my first breath of fresh air, I made a promise to myself that I would spend the rest of my life trying to undo the damage he did to her heart and state of mind.

It was time to put all this bullshit behind us and start moving forward.

CHAPTER THIRTY-FOUR
HARLOW

I pulled up to the lake house and parked my new Nissan Rogue beside Brooks' truck. Molly and I went car shopping earlier this week because if I was going to live in this town, I couldn't keep begging people for rides.

I stared at the outside of the house. I hadn't expected it to look so different. The construction trucks and building materials were gone. It looked like a brand-new home. Even the sidewalk pavers were new, and there were shrubs and flowers lining the front.

I should have known he was up to something when he told me to stay away from the house and focus on the wedding planning.

My phone buzzed in my purse as I walked up the driveway. It had been ringing nonstop since the media reported the story that Bartholomew Zimmerman was being brought in for questioning as a potential suspect for the vandalism of his ex-fiancée's house. His face had been plastered all over the media, and Senator Zimmerman was running for cover while his campaign was falling off the rails.

As for my father, his reputation was unraveling, one headline at a time. The story was out there for everyone to see. The wealth and power he treasured most were slipping through his fingers faster than sand in an hourglass. The best part of all was that I didn't have to do a single thing. They did it to themselves.

The afternoon sun was hitting the front porch, and I could hear the water from the lake lapping along the shore. A feeling of peace settled over me the second I stepped inside the house. I swung the door fully open and gasped.

The new hardwood floors were the first thing I noticed.

What did he do? I spun around in a circle, taking it all in.

The house was finished. You could smell the fresh paint everywhere, and it wasn't just the walls that got a new look. There were pictures and decorations everywhere I turned.

I was in disbelief as I moved from one room to the next.

Brooks installed bookcases along the fireplace. There was a framed portrait of us along the main wall. He literally thought of everything. I pressed a hand to my heart, allowing the tears to spill over at the sight of my mom's blanket folded over the back of the couch. I totally forgot about that knitted blanket. I had no idea where he found it, but I was too overcome with emotion to think straight.

I looked past the open room into the kitchen. He painted the maple cabinets white. Even the fixtures were new.

The door creaked open, and Brooks stepped inside. I wanted to weep at the sight of him.

"You're early," he said as he wiped his hands off on a towel.

I nodded, feeling dizzy and overwhelmed. I wasn't sure if I would be able to speak. "What did you do?"

He glanced around and back at me. His cheeks were red, as if he was unsure if I would like this surprise. "I was hoping to get a few more things done before you saw it."

"I can't believe you did all this," I whispered. I was at a loss for words.

He stepped closer. "Do you like it?"

I sputtered out a laugh. "Are you serious right now? I'm stunned. How did you manage to get it all done?"

He shrugged his shoulders. "Called in a few favors. Had my guys working around the clock. I wanted this done before our wedding tomorrow. It's my gift to you."

"Brooks." I covered my mouth and hiccupped on a sob. "I don't even know what to say."

He closed the distance between us and pulled me into his arms. He was sweaty and smelled like paint and sawdust, but I didn't care. I rested my forehead against his chest while his hands went to my back. I took a moment to breathe him in and allow myself to sink into the comfort of his arms.

"There's still room for you to add some of your personal touches," he said, swallowing hard and tightening his grip on my back. "I wanted you to walk in here and feel like it was yours. I wanted to surprise you."

I looked up and ran my fingers along his stubbled jaw. "Thank you. This is the best surprise."

"You've been through hell, and I know I don't have the kind of money you're used to, and can't buy you everything, but this was something I could give you."

"I don't want anything, Brooks. You are all I need."

His thumb rubbed small circles along the base of my spine. "I just want you to be happy."

"Well, congratulations. I've never been happier."

He grinned and took my hand. "Come on, it gets better."

Before I could ask where we were going, he led me upstairs. When we reached the top of the landing, it took me a second to realize he was leading me to the master bedroom.

"Go on," he encouraged and slowly opened the door.

There was a king-sized bed where the queen used to be. A soft, blue quilt and throw pillows were neatly arranged on the mattress. He spun around, and I followed him over to the closet.

Flannel shirts and Henleys hung neatly next to my sweaters and dresses. A pair of beige Timberland boots sat on the floor beside my heels.

"What is all this?"

He stepped up to my back. "This is going to be our house."

His words knocked the wind right out of me. I turned around and blinked hard. "What about your house?"

We hadn't talked about it, but I assumed he would want to keep it. I would have been perfectly fine using this as a second property. At the very least, I thought we could use this on the weekends when the weather was nice.

He placed his hands on my hips. "It's just a house. I don't have a sentimental attachment to it like you do here."

He was trying to rationalize and play down how much it meant to him.

"But you built that house."

He exhaled and looked away. "Yeah, I built it for a life I envisioned living. The truth is, when I built that house, I was looking for a distraction, something to pour my energy into. Anything to keep me occupied and take my mind off you. That house wasn't built for us; this house matters. It means something."

His confession shattered something inside me. Because he was standing in front of me, telling me it meant nothing, but it meant everything. He was willing to give something up that he poured his heart and soul into just to make me happy. I was the one who walked away, and he still wanted to build a life with me. I pressed a hand to my mouth, trying to hold it all in, but the tears came anyway.

"Listen to me." He wiped at my cheeks. "I don't need that house. We can sell it, keep it, or do whatever we want with it. We don't need to make that decision today."

When I looked up, I saw a man who would give up everything and fight until his last breath for me. I didn't feel like I deserved him, so when the tears started up again, they came fast and heavy. He didn't wipe them away this time; he pulled me closer and wrapped his protective arms around me.

"I'll never be able to repay you for all you've done for me."

He kissed the top of my head. "You don't owe me a damn thing."

God, this man.

He didn't just renovate my house; he put me back together, piece by piece. He believed in me when I didn't believe in myself. He loved me when I gave up on us. He was giving me a second chance when I didn't deserve one.

I brought my hands up to his face and traced the strong lines of his jaw. I don't think I've ever felt this type of certainty in my life. This is the type of love I'd never be able to find with anyone else. It was the type of love that scared you and settled you at the same time.

I looked around the room again, at all the little details and personal touches I hadn't expected.

It was filled with so much love—more love than I ever imagined feeling. For the first time, I finally understood true happiness.

I might have come back for this house, but I was staying for him, and this was so much better.

This might have started as a temporary solution to a messy problem, but somehow, our fake arrangement became something real.

Now, I didn't just have my house back, but I had his love, too.

And I would never let anyone take that from us again.

EPILOGUE

The DJ played a Luke Bryan song while our friends and family danced, looking like they were having the time of their lives. It was the type of reception I always wanted, full of love, good food, and lots of laughs.

My heels were somewhere under the table, and my veil came off the second we said, "I do."

I couldn't remember a time in my life when I was this happy.

We actually did it

We were married.

I looked across the lawn, feeling so many emotions at once. Today was perfect. It nearly seemed like a dream.

I turned to see Brooks standing at the bar, laughing with a few friends. His hand was wrapped around his beer bottle as Finn slapped him on the back. His jacket was off, his tie was loose, and the sleeves of his dress shirt were rolled up to his elbows.

My husband was hot.

He caught my eye from across the lawn and winked. I

swear, my stomach fluttered every time he looked at me like that.

Would it always be like this? There were so many times when I doubted we would ever get here, moments when it seemed our love would never suffice. People thought we would never work. They thought we were too opposite. We had too much baggage, but we did it. We fought, and here we were.

I was about to grab another glass of champagne when I spotted Molly heading my way. "Marty looks like he's having a good time."

I looked over to see Mona sitting next to him, gesturing with her hands widely and telling him some outrageous story that had him laughing so hard that he had to wipe the tears from his eyes.

"I'm so happy to see him enjoying himself."

Molly grinned. "They seem pretty cozy."

I rolled my eyes. "Leave them alone. He deserves to have a good time. Especially after everything he's been through these past few months."

Looking at him today, you would never have guessed the toll his cancer treatments had taken on him. There were days when he could barely get out of bed. Times when I feared we would lose him any day, but he continued to beat the odds. His days were still numbered, and I didn't even want to think about how we would deal with that loss, but right now, he was here. Determined to live life on his terms.

When I asked him to walk me down the aisle, he told me I granted him his dying wish. We both cried.

Just thinking about it made my eyes sting.

"Are you okay?" Molly's voice was soft, sensing my sadness.

"I'm fine," I said, wiping at my eyes.

I had to remind myself that today was a happy day. I wouldn't think about my father or anything that would make me sad.

Finn made his way across the lawn. His hands were shoved in his pockets, looking as uncomfortable as a man who hated wearing suits could look.

"Hey, Finn." I waved awkwardly and smoothed a hand along my dress.

His mouth stretched into a half smile. "Harlow, there's something I'd like to say to you."

"Not now, Finn." Molly elbowed him in the stomach.

"It's nothing bad, I swear." He held his hands up. "I owe you an apology."

I blinked. "Oh." I wasn't expecting that.

His laugh was uneasy, a reminder that this was difficult for both of us. "I'm sorry for how I treated you when you came back into town."

"It's okay. I would have done the same thing."

He squeezed Molly's shoulders while keeping his gaze on mine. "I was still wrong. Molly told me the reason why you left. I'm sorry that I was so hard on you."

Molly had no idea until I sat her down at breakfast the other day and told her why I stayed away. She was pissed at first, but once I explained that I didn't want to put her in a position to lie or keep a secret from Finn, she took it far better than I expected her to, which was a massive relief.

"Thank you, Finn. You didn't need to apologize, but I appreciate it."

He held his hand out. "Friends?"

I knocked his hand away and hugged him instead. "I'm ready to put the past behind us and start fresh."

"Thank God." Molly sighed deeply and glanced

between us. "Now I don't have to worry about you two strangling each other whenever you're in the same room together."

The three of us laughed. I hadn't realized how much the tension between Finn and me had weighed on everyone around us.

"Molly told me about the plot of land you secured over on Pottery Road. Sounds like you've got a solid business plan."

When I put my apartment in New York on the market, it sold on the first day. The buyers offered me cash, so I used my savings for the down payment and then went to the bank to take out a loan. Dawson Landscape Designs wasn't just a silly little dream anymore, and I had no idea how freeing it would feel to own something that was completely mine until I signed the paperwork.

"Thanks, it feels real now."

"I've got a lot of connections and can send plenty of customers your way when they're looking for design options."

"You would help me?" I stared at him, wondering what was happening. Extending an olive branch and apologizing was one thing, but this was on a whole other level.

He nodded. "If you let me. This is going to be a big change for you. I'll help with whatever you need."

"I appreciate that because I'm going to need it." I laughed.

He nodded. "I'll go get us a drink." He kissed Molly's temple and disappeared into the crowd.

She turned to me with a smirk. "See, he has a heart in there somewhere."

"Whoever would have thought?"

I was still smiling when a warm hand slid around my waist. "Did I just witness a truce between you two?"

I leaned into my husband automatically. "You were watching?"

He grinned. "I always have my eyes on you, wife."

Molly crossed her arms. "He is so full of it. He's just being nosy."

He squeezed my side. "Seriously, did he apologize?"

"Yes."

"Did you at least make him sweat it out a little bit?"

I shrugged. "No, but he did offer to help, so maybe I'll take advantage of that."

He chuckled and pulled me in for a kiss. "Don't go easy on him. Make him pay."

Molly swatted his shoulder. "Hello, remember me? The wife of the man you are plotting against."

Brooks slipped his hands into his pockets. "You live to drive that man crazy. I would think you would be fully on board with that plan."

Molly laughed. "She's my best friend. He's my husband, so my loyalty is divided." She patted my arm. "I'm going to say hello to your in-laws." She gestured to where Brooks' mom was rearranging the cupcakes on the dessert table, and his dad was walking around, taking pictures of everyone.

When she walked away, Brooks brushed a strand of hair behind my ear. "Are you sick of being the center of attention yet?"

I rested my head on his shoulder. "Why? What are you thinking?"

There was a slow curve to his lips like he was up to something. "I was thinking we should sneak out soon."

I glanced around. "I don't know. I think we are required to stay until we at least cut the cake."

He turned me around in his arms and gave me a look that I was all too familiar with. "It's our wedding. We can do whatever the hell we want. I haven't kissed my wife properly since yesterday."

"You just kissed me an hour ago when Tuck gave his best man speech."

"That doesn't count. We were being watched."

I laughed and straightened out his tie. "Poor thing. You've been married less than a day, and you're already feeling deprived?"

His gaze fell to my lips. "It feels like torture."

"I'll tell you what? How about we compromise?"

He raised an eyebrow. "You've got my attention."

"I'm going to dance with Marty. You go take a few pictures with your mom, and then I'll meet you in the bathroom upstairs in fifteen minutes."

He groaned dramatically. "You know my mom. That could take forever."

I shrugged. "That's marriage, babe. It's called compromise. You better get used to it."

He smiled at me in a way that made my knees go weak. "I love you."

I shoved his chest playfully. "I know. Now go smile for the camera. I'll see you in a few minutes."

He watched me walk over to Marty and lead him to the dance floor. It was ridiculous how he still made me feel like a giddy teenager. We were surrounded by all these people, yet all I could think about was finally getting a few minutes alone with him.

Fifteen minutes later, I walked inside the venue and made my way upstairs toward the bathrooms.

"You're late," he said the second I reached the landing.

I rolled my eyes. "I am not."

He slipped his arms around my waist. "You are. By a whole minute."

"Oh, my God. A whole minute," I teased.

"I don't like waiting."

"Well, we better get started then." I pulled on his tie and dragged him into the nearest bathroom.

The second the door closed, our mouths crashed together in a hungry, *I can't believe I just got married* kind of kiss. My back hit the vanity as his hands went to my hips. "You know how needy I am when it comes to you."

I smiled because I did, and I loved it.

His mouth moved to that spot below my ear. "I've been thinking about you in this damn dress since the second I saw you." His voice was rough as he nudged my legs apart. "I don't think you have any idea what you are doing to me."

"Oh, I think I have a pretty good idea." I panted, already tugging at his shirt.

"Of course you do. Hold on to this dress and make sure it stays out of my way."

He kissed me slow and deep, not caring one bit that we were abandoning our family and friends.

I did what I was told and groaned when his fingers slid under the lace of my underwear. "Fuck, Harlow. You are already soaked."

"Jeez, I can't imagine why?" I said, wrapping my legs around him and kissing him deeper.

I barely had time to catch my breath before he slid another finger inside me.

My head dropped forward, and I tried to stifle my moan.

"We are married. You don't have to be quiet."

I tilted my head to the side and glared at him. "Do you want all our guests to hear me?"

He gave me a wicked grin. "It would give them something to remember."

And then he dropped to his knees.

He looked so out of place in his rented suit, spreading my thighs apart, looking like he was about to feast on his favorite meal.

I guess, in a way, he kind of was.

Just as he was about to bury his head under my dress, a sound interrupted us from the other side of the wall.

We both froze.

My eyes were wide. "Did you hear that?"

Then, we heard a muffled moan and the rhythmic thumping of someone's body hitting the wall.

"What in the world?" I gasped, pushing him back. I glanced at the door on the end. I hadn't realized this was a Jack-and-Jill bathroom until now.

Then I heard a chuckle. My mouth flew open, and Brooks put his finger over my lips. There was no mistaking who that sound belonged to.

"That's your brother," I whispered.

"Fucking Hayes," he muttered and dragged a hand down his face.

We both stared at each other. Neither one of us knew what to do.

"He's having sex in the bathroom," I spoke as quietly as I could.

"Fuck, baby, that feels good. Dig those heels deeper in my ass."

Brooks slapped a hand over my mouth while I fought like hell to stifle my laugh. A loud thump shook the wall while the sounds of my brother-in-law having sex echoed throughout the bathroom.

Brooks winced. "I wish I could unhear this."

The thumping grew more urgent, and the moaning got louder.

"You're going to ruin my dress." The woman giggled.

"I'm going to ruin more than your dress." Hayes groaned.

We both stared at each other, blinking. Silently asking, *Now what the hell do we do?* Because sitting here, listening to Hayes go at it with God knows who was making me uncomfortable.

Just when I thought things couldn't get any worse, our door creaked open. "Brooks, are you in here?"

Then, I shit you not, my mother-in-law walked in and stopped mid-step.

Her eyes went to me, perched on the vanity, dress bunched up along my waist, then to her son, who was kneeling on the floor. Messy hair, untucked shirt, and my lipstick all over his neck.

Kill me now.

I don't think I will ever come back from this.

Her eyes swept over us when a climaxing moan came from the other bathroom.

"Please tell me this isn't what I think it is?"

"Uh—" Brooks stood up, and that's when we heard another moan.

Josie blinked and shouted, "Hayes Michael Dawson, you better zip that fly up right now!"

A string of curses followed. And then the sound of two people scrambling.

I hopped off the vanity and straightened my dress while Brooks looked up at the ceiling fan as if that could help him disappear.

"And you two." She pointed.

"We weren't doing anything," Brooks started, but she cut him off.

"Then I suppose your shirt conveniently came untucked and her lipstick just magically landed on your neck." She held up her hand. "Never mind. Don't answer that. I don't want to know."

The adjoining door opened, and Hayes stepped out, red-faced, with wild hair and an unbuttoned dress shirt. A beautiful woman who was not on the guest list appeared next. I had no idea who she was, but she was stunning. Her long auburn hair was a mess, her mascara was smudged, and she looked mortified.

Brooks stepped forward. His body was stiff. "You've got to be kidding me."

"What?" Hayes asked, fumbling with his pants. "We met at the outside bar."

"What the fuck are you doing, Hayes?"

Hayes tugged at his belt. "Apparently, the same thing you are."

"Do you even know her name? Because I do."

Hayes looked between him and the mystery woman. "Who is she?"

The mystery woman stepped out around him. "Brooks?"

Hayes blinked as his gaze darted back and forth between them. "Wait? How do you two know each other?"

Brooks placed his hands on his hips and gave his brother a sharp look. "Hayes, meet Skylar Preston. The new project manager for the Lakeside Resort. She is the one overseeing the construction on our new project."

Hayes's face turned white as a ghost. "Oh, shit," he muttered as my eyes nearly popped out. This was the woman they would be working with for the next eighteen months until the new hotel was finished. This was the deal Dawson Construction had been working on for months? The one that would put his company on the map.

She literally held their future in the palm of her hands, and my brother-in-law just banged her in the bathroom stall.

Hayes had the nerve to shoot her a grin. "Small world, huh?"

It looked like things were about to get interesting here in Marcellus Falls.

The End

Wish I Never Fell For You
Coming Spring 2026

BONUS SCENE

Dear Reader,

I hope you enjoyed Wish I Didn't Want You Back. Brooks and Harlow's story is very special to me. I had so much fun writing them, so I wanted to give you a fun bonus scene about what their life is like now with two kids and a baby on the way. Think, two exhausted parents, two little troublemakers, and a vacation filled with chaos and enough memories to last a lifetime.

All you have to do is click on the link below or scan the QR code with your phone to sign-up for my newsletter.

New to the newsletter? Scan this code:

https://dl.bookfunnel.com/77khwud0el

Already subscribed? Scan this code:
https://dl.bookfunnel.com/mk6weze06n

WANT to stay up to date on my new releases, sales and comings and goings? You can find all my social media links on my website here:

https://geni.us/sjonesauthor

If you want to keep up to date on preorders and new releases, you can follow me on Amazon.

https://geni.us/sjonesauthoramazonpage

THANK YOU

Thank you so much for reading. I know you have many other books to choose from, I am so grateful you took the time to read mine. If you enjoyed it and if you get a chance, I'd be so grateful if you could leave a review.

I can't wait to share more stories with you.

Love,

Sandy
xoxo

ALSO BY S. JONES

THE HARD SERIES

Hard to Love (Chase & Emily)

Hard to Stay (Brad & Lexi)

Hard to Leave (Jack & Chloe)

THE PROTECTIVE SERIES

Whatever It Takes (Quinn & Charlotte)

Whatever You Need (Marco &Amelia)

Whatever You Want (Logan & Ava)

THE ATLANTA ARROWS SERIES

Fumbled Love (Maverick & Kinley)

Fumbled Beginning (JP & Rylee)

Fumbled Arrangement (Rhett and Natalie)

ABOUT THE AUTHOR

S. Jones is a contemporary romance author from Central New York. She has a strong passion for writing and reading stories that will rip your heart out before it's put back together again.

If she's not buried in her writing cave, she's usually reading or planning out her next vacation.

She loves to travel to new places and spends all her free with her husband, two adult children and her dog, Winnie.

When she's not holding a glass of wine in one hand and her kindle in the other, she loves to hear from her readers at:

authorsjoneswrites@gmail.com

www.ingramcontent.com/pod-product-compliance
Lightning Source LLC
Chambersburg PA
CBHW030609170726
48283CB00002B/529